EVAN AND ELLE

A cozy Welsh village mystery

RHYS BOWEN

Constable Evan Evans Book 4

JOFFE BOOKS

Revised edition 2022
Joffe Books, London
www.joffebooks.com

First published by St Martin's Minotaur Books in 2000

This paperback edition was first published
in Great Britain in 2022

Cover art by Nick Castle

ISBN: 978-1-80405-466-6

NOTE TO THE READER

Please note this book is set in the 1990s in Wales, a time before smartphones, and when social attitudes were very different.

CHAPTER 1

The Reverend Tomos Parry Davies, minister of Chapel Bethel in the village of Llanfair, sang loudly to himself as he drove up the pass from Caernarfon. Heaven had certainly smiled on him today! What a stroke of luck that he had spotted the advertisement for a government surplus auction. This van was the answer to his prayers — high mileage, of course, and painted a depressing institutional grey, but it seated fifteen and was perfect for his needs.

He had long been aware that his congregation was dwindling. There was little interest in religion these days, and no fear of the hellfire that he preached so eloquently. All over Wales chapels were being abandoned and turned into beauty parlours, garages, or even worse, New Age healing centres. Tomos Parry Davies shuddered.

Chapel Ebenezer, only a couple of miles down the pass from Llanfair, had been abandoned last year. Tomos feared for the souls of its former flock. If a way could be found to bring them up to Llanfair . . . but many older parishioners didn't drive and there were no buses on Sunday. That's when the idea of a van came to him. To put it in non-Christian terms — if Mohammed couldn't come to the mountain, then the mountain would come to Mohammed. He had said nothing to anyone except his wife, and Roberts-the-Pump at the petrol station, who always had an ear to the ground when it came to second-hand cars for sale — and he had watched, waited, and prayed. And now his prayers were answered!

He closed his eyes and pictured all those new worshipers pouring out of his van and into Chapel Bethel, while his rival, Rev. Powell-Jones of Chapel Beulah across the street, could only stare in disbelief. A satisfied smile spread across his plump, middle-aged face. And so cheap, too. A stroke of luck indeed — or rather the Lord's doing. The Lord knew which chapel He wanted to prosper!

And this was just the beginning, Rev. Parry Davies said to himself. A bigger congregation meant more money coming in. Then he could replace the oil stove in the corner with a real central heating system, and maybe update the sound system to reach out to the young people. He'd have slide shows and video presentations to enhance his sermons. He was going to bring religion back to Llanfair in a big way.

He drove through Llanberis, carefully negotiating the last holidaymakers of the season as they crossed the street to catch the mountain railway to the summit of Yr Wyddfa, which the English insisted on calling Mount Snowdon. Right after Llanberis the road began to climb. He put his foot down and heard a satisfying roar of power from the engine. He chose not to notice the black smoke that hung behind him in the clear mountain air.

The village of Nant Peris passed by in a blur. He knew he should have slowed to thirty, but he was so excited by the power of his new vehicle that he couldn't slow down. Besides, there was no policeman closer than Constable Evans up in Llanfair. Nobody here to give him a ticket.

He came to the last straggling buildings before the pass narrowed and climbed again to reach Llanfair. He turned to look at the abandoned chapel whose congregation he hoped to round up every Sunday. It had been a sad sight, with windows boarded up and door nailed shut. He had almost passed it when he realized that something was going on there. He braked and rammed the heavy gear into reverse with much grinding, followed by an ominous clank. A builder's lorry was parked outside and two men were carrying in a slab of marble.

Tomos's face grew hot with anger. What kind of dirty trick was the Lord playing on him? To reopen the chapel when he'd just spent his savings on the new van! Was his beautiful plan now doomed to failure?

Then he saw the sign over the arched doorway to one side:

CHEZ YVETTE. RESTAURANT FRANÇAIS.
HIGH QUALITY FRENCH CUISINE.

Over it a banner proclaimed, *Grand Opening Tomorrow!* Tomos felt his blood pressure rising to boiling point. The Lord's house — or what had been the Lord's house until recently — being turned into a restaurant! And not only a restaurant, but a French restaurant. Chez Yvette. Even the name sounded positively sinful.

Tomos Parry Davies put his foot down and roared on up the pass to spread the dreadful news.

CHAPTER 2

Constable Evan Evans of the North Wales Police came down the steep mountain track. It was a crisp autumn evening. Snowdon and her sister peaks were already black silhouettes against a clear pink sky. The last swallows swooped overhead, ready to fly south. Below him the village of Llanfair lay nestled in an autumnal haze. Evan paused and sniffed the smell of wood smoke with satisfaction — so different from the smell of the coal fires he remembered from the cottage of his early childhood. That had been an acrid smell that clung to the nostrils and sent him to bed with bronchitis every winter. Now most of the cottages had radiators and it had become a status symbol to have a wood-burning fireplace.

It had been another glorious day — the latest of a prolonged Indian summer that people were already calling a drought. Of course one week without rain counted as a drought in North Wales. Evan could feel the windburn on his face, the result of a long day's climbing on Glyder Fawr, the peak across the valley from Snowdon. His sore muscles were beginning to remind him that he was no longer in climbing condition. There never seemed to be time for weekend climbs these days. His job as community police officer in Llanfair couldn't exactly be described as strenuous, but he found it hard to say no to the constant stream of volunteer projects.

And then, of course, there was Bronwen. The young village schoolteacher shared his love of the outdoors and expected to share his weekends. Not that he objected to spending his free time with Bronwen, but it meant that he hadn't done any serious climbing in a while and he missed it.

His corduroy trouser legs swished through dying bracken as he continued down the mountain. To his right the dark square of a Norwegian Spruce plantation broke the smooth sweep of the pastures. Evan looked at it with distaste. Another ugly blot on the landscape, like the Everest Inn, Evan thought. Nobody asked the locals before they came in and planted their Christmas trees!

Lights were coming on in Llanfair. He'd better hurry if he wanted to get back before dark. Discreet floodlights already outlined the monstrous shape of the Everest Inn, perched, like an overgrown Swiss chalet, at the top of the pass. Like the rest of the villagers, he felt that it looked completely out of place on a Welsh mountainside.

The village itself was a poorly lit straggle of cottages except for the Red Dragon pub. Harry-the-Pub had invested in a floodlight this summer, now that more tourists were coming to Llanfair. Not everybody was in favour of a floodlit pub sign. The two ministers of Chapel Bethel and Chapel Beulah, usually deadly enemies, had teamed up for once to denounce this brazen advertisement of the demon alcohol — especially when lit on the Sabbath. Evans-the-Meat had gone one step further and lodged an official complaint, saying that the light was a public nuisance and shone directly into his bedroom. The joke around Llanfair was that Evans-the-Meat's system couldn't take the shock of seeing Mrs Evans-the-Meat in her face cream and curlers. But nobody else had complained. In fact some people felt that the extra light had long been needed on the dark village street.

Sheep scattered at Evan's approach and the sound of their bleating echoed across the valley. Now that the sun had gone down, a cold wind was blowing from the Atlantic. It sighed through the grass, rattled the dry bracken, and moaned through the crags. Suddenly Evan felt a tension invading the tranquil scene. With his fine-tuned senses, he was almost certain that he was being watched. He stopped and looked around.

He heard the splashing of the young stream close by and the distant drone of a car as it climbed the pass. The dark shape of a ruined sheep byre loomed to his right. He peered in that direction, imagining he saw a fleeting movement. His torch was in his pack but he didn't want to stop and retrieve it now — not when a pint of beer in the Red Dragon was calling. If anyone was sheltering up on the mountain, it was probably nothing more than a passing tramp or a courting couple from the village, which would explain the tension and watchfulness he sensed.

He had only gone a few more paces when he heard the tread of boots on the path close behind him. He spun around.

"*Noswaith dda*. Evening, Constable Evans," a deep voice called.

"Oh, it's you, Mr Owens," Evan breathed a sigh of relief as the farmer caught up with him. "You're out late. Anything wrong?"

"No, nothing wrong. I've just been to take a look at Rhodri's cottage — I wanted to make sure those English people closed the gate this time so that they can't accuse my sheep of eating their bloody flowers!"

"They've gone, then?" Evan asked, looking across to the low squat outline of the shepherd's cottage perched above the village.

"My wife saw them go this afternoon. And good riddance, I say." Evan looked at him in surprise. Mr Owens was usually the most mild-mannered of the villagers.

"Nothing but trouble they've been since they bought the place." He moved closer to Evan. "I don't blame old Rhodri for going to live with his daughter — he was getting on in years, poor old chap, but he had no right selling his cottage to foreigners, did he?"

"I hear they offered him a very good price," Evan said. "And nobody in the village was interested."

"Well, nobody in the village was daft enough to put all that money into an old shepherd's cottage, were they? You should see it now, Mr Evans. My wife goes up there to clean for them and she says they've got all mod cons, including an indoor bathroom with one of those French beedy things. Must have cost them a fortune, but then the English always did have more money than sense."

Evan grinned. "Still, it's good for business to have visitors, isn't it, Mr Owens?"

"It would be if they bought anything locally. My wife says they come with ice chests packed full of food every weekend. They probably think good Welsh produce would poison them." His wheezy laugh betrayed years of smoking and ended in a rattling cough. "I don't rightly know why they want to come here. They don't seem to like us very much."

"Lots of English people are buying cottages in Wales," Evan said. "They like to get away from the cities for the weekend, and I can't say I blame them. I couldn't wait to escape from Swansea like a shot when I lived there."

"I don't mind English people, look you, Mr Evans," the farmer said, leaning confidentially close. "Old Colonel Arbuthnot who used to stay with us was the salt of the earth, wasn't he? But then he was of the old school — he had manners. I just don't like it when they come here and act all toffee nosed, as if they're the landlords and we're the peasants."

"Do these people act like that?" Evan asked. "I can't say I've seen much of them, apart from their Jaguar driving past."

"Too bloody fast, I'll warrant," Mr Owens commented. "He nearly hit my dog the other day. She's not used to cars, is she? That Englishman came up the track, driving like a madman and at the same time my bitch decides to go after a sheep that's wandering off. He bloody near hit her, and then instead of apologizing, he had the nerve to tell me to keep her under control. That's the kind of people they are, Mr Evans. Acting like they own the place."

"Lucky they're only here on weekends then, eh, Mr Owens?" Evan said. "And I don't suppose we'll see much of them when the weather finally turns cold."

"My, but it's been a lovely long summer this year, hasn't it, Mr Evans?" Mr Owens spoke with pride in his voice, as if he was personally responsible for the weather. "I've got the hay all stacked and ready for winter, which is more than I can say most years." He looked at the rope hanging from Evan's pack. "You've been climbing today, I see."

"I have. Up on Glyder Fawr."

"There's some good climbing country up there — good challenging rocks."

"A little too challenging," Evan confessed. "At one point I thought I'd got myself stuck. I'm afraid I'm out of practice. I thought I'd have to call for the mountain rescue."

Farmer Owens slapped him on the shoulder. "What you need is a pint at the Dragon."

"That's just what I was thinking," Evan said with a smile. "A pint of Robinson's would go down a treat. Are you heading that way too?"

The farmer glanced at the lights of his farm, just above the houses of the village. "Mrs Owens is waiting for me, worst luck, and she doesn't like it when my dinner dries out in the oven." His face lit up. "But it's Sunday, isn't it? We usually have cold on Sundays! And she won't know exactly how long it took me to get up to the cottage and back, will she now?"

* * *

As the voices died away, a figure came out of the ruined sheep byre and stood watching. That was a close shave, having the local copper almost find him. One good thing — he now knew where the policeman was. He'd be safely in the pub until it was too late.

He could feel the blood pounding in his temples as the adrenaline raced through his body. He followed the track across the meadow to the cottage gate. A movement in the hedge to his left made him jump, until he saw an old sheep lumbering away into the darkness. Obviously hoping to get at those flowers again, he thought with a grin. Well, too late now. By the time he'd finished there wouldn't be any flowers.

The garden gate squeaked as he opened it. He walked up the newly flagged front path to the door. Then he paused and took the pack from his back. The can clanked loudly as it put it down on the front step and he felt his heart jump again. Calm down, he told himself. There's nobody for miles around. You have all the time in the world to do this.

He took the rags from his pack and put them down beside the path while he saturated them. Then, one by one, he dropped them through the letter box.

Then he went around to the back of the house. The windows were all locked but it was easy enough to break a pane and pour more petrol inside.

Then he used up the last of the can on the creeper growing up the front of the house and the bushes beneath the front window. It would take a bit to get a really good blaze going in an old stone cottage like this.

Lastly he took out a fuse. It was the kind they once used in the old slate mines — especially slow-burning, to give the men time to get back to the surface. By the time the fuse burned all the way down from the letter box to the rags on the floor, he'd be far away.

He secured the fuse through the open letter box, then, fingers trembling with excitement, he lit it. There was a gentle hiss, like exhaling breath, and the end of the fuse glowed red. He stuffed the empty can and any other telltale bits of rubbish into his pack and hurried back down the path. At the gate he paused and took a piece of paper from his pocket. The note was made up of words he'd cut from a newspaper. It said,

GO HOME. YOU'RE NOT WANTED HERE.

He found a nail protruding from the gate and he stuck the note on it. When he turned to look, the fuse was glowing like a red eye in the darkness. Then he fled down the mountain.

CHAPTER 3

The bar at the Red Dragon was crowded as Evan pushed open the heavy oak door and ducked under the beam to enter. A fire was burning in the big fireplace on the far wall. The air was heavy with cigarette smoke.

"Look you — there he is now!" A high voice rose over the murmur in the bar. Betsy the barmaid's face lit up as she spotted Evan. *"Noswaith dda,* Evan *bach!"*

Heads turned in their direction.

"We were wondering where you'd got to, Evan *bach,*" Charlie Hopkins called. "It's not like you to miss opening time. Betsy was all set to send out a search party . . ."

"I was not!" Betsy said, her cheeks flushing. Evan was startled to see that Betsy's hair was a dark, rich auburn colour this evening. Ever since she had almost been seduced by a famous opera singer who liked his women dark, she had been experimenting with hair colour. She was also wearing a leopard-print velour tank top with a low scooped neckline. The result was disconcerting, to say the least.

"I know very well that Evan Evans can take care of himself," Betsy went on, giving him a challenging smile. "I mean, he's built for it, isn't he?"

"Unless he managed to find himself trapped by you someday," Charlie Hopkins said, and his skinny body shook with soundless mirth, revealing missing front teeth. "I'd like to see him fight his way out of that!"

Betsy smoothed down her tank top, pulling the low neckline to an almost X-rated level. "When I manage to get Evan Evans alone, he won't want to fight his way out!" she announced to the assembled crowd. "And it won't be bird-watching that will keep us busy, either . . . unless I decide to go ahead with those tattoos I've been thinking about."

The low ceiling echoed back the laughter. Evan gave a good-natured grin and decided there was nothing he could say that Betsy wouldn't take as encouragement.

"So what will it be tonight, Evan *bach?* Your usual Guinness?"

"I think I'll join Mr Owens-the-Sheep and have a Robinson's tonight," Evan said. "I've worked up a powerful thirst."

Betsy's hands deftly drew two pints of Robinson's bitter with just the right amount of froth on top. "Here, get those down you, and then you can tell us where you've been."

"I told you he went out climbing today," Roberts-the-Pump said. "I saw him heading for Glyder Fawr."

There was nothing that escaped the Llanfair bush telegraph.

"I heard that Bronwen Price had a teachers' meeting at the university in Bangor," Evans-the-Milk said with a knowing wink.

"Bronwen-bloody-Price!" Betsy muttered and set down a pint glass none too gently. Evan loosened his collar. It really was warm in here tonight.

"Young Betsy was dying for you to come back, Evan," Charlie Hopkins said, "so that you could invite her to the new French restaurant."

Betsy gave Evan a challenging smile. "I wouldn't say no to an evening with Evan Evans, but I don't fancy a French restaurant, thank you. They eat snails and frogs' legs, don't they — and little birds with the heads still on them . . ."

There was a mixed expression of disgust and laughter from the crowd.

"They do," she insisted. "I saw a travel program once on the telly."

"Just a minute — what French restaurant are we talking about?" Evan interrupted.

"The new one that's opening in the old chapel above Nant Peris," Charlie Hopkins said. "Reverend Parry Davies spotted it this afternoon, didn't you, Reverend?"

"Indeed I did, Mr Hopkins. It made my blood boil to see a house of the Lord turned into a den of iniquity." The voice came from a table in a darkened corner. Unlike his counterpart at Chapel Beulah, Reverend Parry Davies was not above an occasional pint at the pub — so that my congregation knows I am human, was how he explained it. In fact he often took the back exit from the chapel and the back path to the Red Dragon with other male members of his congregation on Sunday nights.

"It's a restaurant, Reverend," Evans-the-Milk pointed out, "Not a brothel."

"How do you know, boyo?" Barry-the-Bucket, the young bulldozer driver, chuckled. "It might be a front. I think I'd better go and check it out for myself, anyway. Chez Yvette, I like the sound of that — I bet she's hot stuff. I bet she wears black lace corsets — Frenchwomen wear that sort of thing, you know."

"And how would you know that, Barry-the-Bucket?" Betsy's voice was scathing.

"I've been around."

"You've never been further south than Birmingham," Betsy said triumphantly.

"I wouldn't mind seeing you in a black corset, Betsy." Barry grinned at her.

"And I wouldn't mind winning the lottery. The chances of either happening are about equal, I'd say."

Evan laughed with the other men. He had always admired Betsy's quick wit.

"Well, I'm not going near any French restaurant," Evans-the-Meat said loudly. "There are too many foreigners here already. Planting stupid fir trees and wrecking the hillsides, buying up all our cottages . . . If I had my way—"

"You'd build a bloody great wall around Llanfair and make people show a Welsh passport before they were allowed in," Evans-the-Milk chuckled, getting a general laugh.

"I would indeed," Evans-the-Meat agreed. "Same again, Betsy love, if you don't mind."

Betsy refilled the pint glass. "Tell Evan Evans about your van, Reverend," she said. "He's bought himself a big van—"

"To bring in the people from down the valley," the minister said. "I've been worrying about those poor people who've had no chapel this past year and no way of getting up here on a Sunday when the buses don't run. The van was the answer to my prayers."

"You'd better ask Farmer Owens here to be your driver," Barry-the-Bucket said. "He's good at rounding up sheep. Maybe he'll lend you his dogs."

"Speaking of dogs, how is your bitch now, Mr Owens?" Roberts-the-Pump asked. "All right, is she?"

"Luckily," Mr Owens said.

"Why, what happened to her?" Betsy asked, leaning across the bar and stretching her neckline enough to make the patrons stop drinking again.

"She almost got run over by that Englishman, didn't she?" Roberts-the-Pump said. "And not even on the road either. Driving up the track to the cottage."

"And he had the nerve to shout at me and tell me to keep her under control," Mr Owens said. "On my own land, too!"

"I knew we were in for trouble when Rhodri sold his cottage to foreigners," Evans-the-Meat said angrily. "I told you, didn't I? No good can come of it, letting foreigners into the community. It's not as if they frequent the local shops, do they? Only once I think she's been into my shop, and then she had the nerve to ask me if I spoke English and she waved her arms around as if she was speaking to an idiot."

"Perhaps she thought you were Evans-the-Post's brother," the milkman chuckled. "Perhaps she thought daftness was in the family."

Evans-the-Meat put down his glass with a bang. "If anyone's related to that daftie, it's you!"

Evan had been standing at the bar, downing his drink, too tired and relaxed to feel like joining in the conversation. Now he stepped out between the two men, just as Evans-the-Meat raised his fists.

"Easy, Gareth *bach*. I'm an Evans, too, remember," he said lightly.

Evans-the-Meat lowered his fists. "I just wish I'd known Rhodri's cottage was for sale. I'd have bought it myself."

"And gone to live up on the mountain? Don't be daft, boyo."

"Anything to stop foreigners buying it!"

"Too late now, anyway," Farmer Owens said. "They've put a lot of money into that place. They're not going to leave in a hurry."

"Unless somebody makes them," Evans-the-Meat muttered.

"Well, they've gone now for a while," Farmer Owens added. "And they won't be coming back so often when the weather turns nasty. A few good rainstorms and that track will be a rushing stream. Let's see him get his Jaguar up there then!"

"I don't see what all the fuss is about," Betsy said. "They don't bother us. It's not like they've ever been in here."

"There you are, that's what I've been saying," Evans-the-Meat said triumphantly.

Everyone looked up as the door was suddenly flung open. A young man came in, his sandy hair windswept and his freckled cheeks glowing from the wind.

"Well, if it isn't young Bryn," Charlie Hopkins exclaimed. He turned to the other men. "You know my daughter's boy, don't you? He's just joined the fire brigade. I told him now we'll have to call him Bryn-the-Bell."

"Where's the fire then, boyo?" Barry-the-Bucket called, chuckling loudly.

"Don't just stand there. Come and have a pint," Charlie began, lifting his arm to slap his grandson on the back.

The young man shook him off. "Not now, *Taid.* I need a telephone. I've got to call the station right away. There's a fire on the mountain!"

CHAPTER 4

Instantly the pub emptied out, the occupants scrambling up the steep mountain track in their polished Sunday boots.

"It's Rhodri's cottage!" Evans-the-Meat shouted. "What's the betting those bloody English people left the gas on?"

Flames were already consuming the cottage, shooting out through shattered windows and the partially collapsed roof. Sparks shot into a clear night sky.

"What a sight. This is better than Bonfire Night!" Barry-the-Bucket exclaimed.

"The fire brigade better get here in a hurry or the whole mountain will go up." Farmer Owens glanced nervously at his meadows full of sheep.

"All right everybody, not too close," Evan yelled over the roar of the flames and the excited shouts of the men. "Keep well away from the track so that the fire engine can get up here. Come on. Move over, please." He ushered the spectators to one side.

"Shouldn't we see if we can start putting it out, Mr Evans?" Farmer Owens asked. "I've got spades at my place . . ."

Evan hesitated. There was a real danger of the whole hillside going up, but he didn't want to risk putting inexperienced people in harm's way.

"Let me get to it." Bryn pushed past Evan. "Don't worry. I'm trained to do this kind of thing, Constable Evans." He was halfway down the path when he called. "They've got a tap here with a hose on it, Constable Evans. Now let's just hope they haven't turned the water off."

A feeble stream of water came out of the hose. Evan didn't believe it could possibly do any good against the raging inferno a few yards away, but Bryn stood there, steadfastly wetting down the ground around the cottage until the sound of a siren echoed up the pass, then the fire engine lurched up the track. It was followed by a tanker whose powerful hoses rapidly extinguished the blaze.

"At least it didn't spread." A grey-haired fireman came over to Evan as the men dragged their hoses away from the ruined cottage. "Thanks for keeping the crowd back." He held out his hand. "Geraint Jones. I'm the head of this mob. You must be Constable Evans."

"That's right." Evan shook the offered hand. "We were lucky you got here in such a hurry. And we were lucky young Bryn happened to be up here visiting his grandmother. He stopped it from spreading until you got here."

Captain Jones nodded. "He's a good lad. A bit too keen, but then I expect I was too at his age." He tapped Evan on the arm. "I imagine you'll want to notify your chaps about this, won't you? Definitely a suspicious fire."

"You think it was deliberately set?"

The fireman sucked through his teeth. "When we arrived the whole place was already in flames, so I can't tell you where it started, but I do know from experience — it takes a lot to make one of these old cottages burn like that. Stone walls, stone floors. Fires don't spread without a little help, you know. I'd put in a report, just to cover your rear end."

"Thanks, I will," Evan said.

"And I'd keep people out of the place until your arson specialists have taken a look in daylight. You'd be amazed what people like to cart away as souvenirs."

"Thanks. I'll cordon it off tonight, then," Evan said. "I'd better call HQ and see if they want to send up someone to keep watch for the night."

"I'll be leaving a couple of my men up here for a while anyway," Captain Jones said. "They might need to wet down hot spots. We don't want the hillside catching fire if a wind gets up, do we?"

"I'll get these people back to their homes." Evan headed toward the crowd that was still watching, fascinated. "All right everybody. Show's over. Go home. And I don't want anybody near this place until we've finished up here."

He was slightly surprised at the power of his own voice and at the way they meekly began to leave.

"Come on, boys. The Red Dragon's still open," Charlie Hopkins called. "Where's young Bryn? I want to buy him that pint now."

Evan watched the old man make his way down the hillside with his arm around his grandson's shoulder.

As the crowd was dispersing a woman's scream rose above the murmured conversation. "He's not here! Oh my God — where is he?"

Evan pushed through the crowd to see a distraught woman looking around her in utter terror. He recognized her as the owner of the cottage next to Bronwen's school. Her name was Ellie Jenkins and she worked as a maid at the Everest Inn.

"What's the matter, Mrs Jenkins?" He grabbed her arm.

"My Terry. You haven't seen him, have you? He's missing." She could scarcely get the words out.

"Young Terry? No, I can't say I've seen him."

"He has to be up here." Her eyes darted around nervously as she spoke. "Where else could he be?"

Evan put a restraining hand on her arm. "It's going to be all right, Mrs Jenkins. Young boys are always getting into mischief, you know that. Now take a deep breath — when did you see him last?"

The breath came out as a shuddering sigh. "I thought he was in his bed, didn't I? Then I heard the fire engine go past and I was surprised he didn't get up to see what was going on. He's mad about fire engines. That's when I saw his bed was empty. So I was sure he must have come up here and . . ."

Evan tried to give her a reassuring smile. "I'm sure we'll find him, Mrs Jenkins. Don't worry. Come on. I'll help you look."

The crowd was now streaming down from the mountain. Evan stopped any young boys he met, asking them about Terry Jenkins but nobody seemed to have noticed him.

"I don't know what I'm going to do with him, Mr Evans," Mrs Jenkins sighed as they made their way up to the fire engines beside the smouldering ruin. "He's that wild since his father walked out on us. I can't make him see sense anymore. Anything dangerous — that's what he likes. Fires, explosions, bombs. All those action shows on the telly and people being blown up. I don't know what I'm going to do with him—"

"Just a second," Evan interrupted. He had overheard one of the firemen yelling, "Out of the way, son, or you might get hurt."

Evan caught sight of a small figure darting among the tall shapes carrying the hose.

"Terry?" he shouted.

The boy looked up.

"Terry Jenkins, get over here this minute!" His mother's voice drowned out every other sound.

Evan went over to the boy who was wearing a red anorak over his pyjamas. "Come on, Terry. Your mum's been looking for you."

Terry looked up at Evan and wiped a sooty hand across his face. "I'm in for it now, aren't I, Constable Evans?" He grinned. "But it was worth it. Did you see the way the water came out of that hose? It was brilliant. And those flames — they must have gone hundreds of feet up into the air! I want to be a fireman some day and put out fires like that."

"Terry Jenkins, you'll be the death of me." His mother stepped forward and yanked him by the arm. "What do you mean by sneaking out into the night like that? You might have been burned alive!"

"Aw, Mum." Terry looked embarrassed. "I had to go and take a look at the fire and I knew you wouldn't let me. You should have seen it — the roof fell in and the flames went whoosh! It was spectacular!"

"I don't know what I'm going to do with you," Mrs Jenkins went on. "If only your daddy was here . . ."

"Yes, well he's not, is he?" Terry said angrily. "He doesn't care what I do."

Then he broke free and ran ahead of her down the track. Evan watched her go, feeling sympathy for the woman. Terry was just getting to that difficult age and he wasn't an easy child to begin with. Evan had caught him a few weeks previously trying to extract chocolate bars from the machine at Roberts-the-Pump's petrol station. He hadn't seemed to think he was doing anything wrong — and that type made the worst kind of criminal.

Evan made sure the last of the stragglers came down with him from the mountain. He was on his way to the police station to call in his report when he saw Bronwen running down the village street, her long red cape flying out behind her like wings.

"Evan, are you all right?" she called. "I've just heard there was a fire."

"I'm fine," he said, smiling at her as she came up to him. "Old Rhodri's cottage went up in flames. Nobody was hurt. The fire brigade's just finishing up right now."

"I don't know about you," she said, standing so close that she was looking up into his face. "I can't leave you for one day without some great drama happening behind my back."

"Then you'd better not go away again, had you?" Evan teased. He reached out and stroked her cheek, even though he was aware that this action would undoubtedly be all around the village by morning. "You worry too much. And I've told you often enough that a policeman's job isn't all beer and skittles, haven't I?"

Bronwen nodded. "You're right. I'm a born worrier. I'm glad nobody was hurt. Do they know what started it?"

Evan shook his head. "The English people had gone hours before and the place was all locked up. We'll have to take a look in daylight."

Bronwen wrapped her arms around her as she stared up at the headlights of the fire engine on the mountainside. "I don't like it, Evan."

"Don't like what?"

"That it was that cottage which burned — the one recently bought by outsiders. I hope that kind of thing's not starting here."

CHAPTER 5

"So you're at it again," Sergeant Watkins called as he got out of his police car the next morning. "You're a bloody nuisance, you know that, don't you?"

"Hello, sarge." Evan smiled as he shook the sergeant's extended hand. "The fire brigade told me that they regarded the fire as suspicious, so I had to report it. I'm sorry you were the one who got dragged up here."

"So you should be," Watkins said, but he was half smiling. "I had a lovely relaxing weekend with the family. I get to work, raring to go on Monday morning and what does DI Hughes tell me? He says, 'Watkins, you're off the case.'"

"What case is that?" Evan asked.

"Only the juiciest thing to happen around here in a long while. You remember hearing about the yacht that was found off Abersoch with a bloody great hole in her side? Well, her ownership has been traced and it appears that she was one of a fleet used to import drugs from the continent, via Ireland. They'd been mainly coming in through Holyhead before, but the Anglesey division had put extra surveillance on there. So now it appears they're trying the mainland instead."

"Abersoch?" Evan mused. "That would be ideal, wouldn't it? Not many tourists on the Llŷn Peninsula at this time of year."

"Ideal, as you say. I might have been in on a really big international drug bust. And instead what happens? The DI says 'I'm sending you up to Llanfair, Watkins, because you're familiar with the territory up there.' So I get sent to look into a cottage that burned down last night, probably because the owner was frying chips and watching telly at the same time."

"The owners weren't there, sarge," Evan said. "The cottage was only recently sold to English people."

"Oh, is that a fact?" Watkins's face became serious. "Oh, I don't like the sound of that. I don't like the sound of that at all. Don't tell me it's all starting again?"

"But there hasn't been a holiday cottage burned up here for a long while, has there?" Evan asked. "Not since I've been here, anyway."

"No, there hasn't, but that's not to say it couldn't start up again. We've heard that there's a new group operating in the area. They call themselves Meibion Gwynedd — the Sons of Gwynedd — and they're pretty radical. They're not going to stop until they get complete Welsh independence."

"That's bloody daft," Evan exclaimed. "Welsh independence? Do they really think we could exist with no support from England?"

Watkins shook his head. "I don't suppose they've thought it through that far. What most extremists want is the best of both worlds, isn't it? Independence for Wales but full protection from Britain."

"So do we have any names?"

"We've got our hands on a couple of their newsletters and we know they've had meetings at a chapel in Bangor. I'd say they were pretty much the loony fringe — the kind of people who would burn down cottages to prove a point."

Evan was frowning. "Then someone up here must have told them about English people moving in recently . . ."

Watkins picked up on where this thought was going. "Which means someone up here is involved in the group in some way?"

Evan tried not to think of Evans-the-Meat, but he couldn't help it. He remembered the butcher muttering "Unless somebody makes them." He was so fiercely nationalistic, and hot-headed, too — just the type to be enticed into a radical fringe group like the Meibion Gwynedd. "It's certainly possible," he said.

"Maybe that's something you could look into on the quiet," Watkins said. "I know what it's like in a village. Everybody knows everybody else's business, don't they?"

Evan glanced across at the butcher's shop. "But you'd better come and take a look for yourself before we go jumping to conclusions. As you said, we might find that someone left a cigarette in the wastebasket and all this worry will have been for nothing." As he spoke a thought struck him. "Come to think of it, sarge, I came right past the cottage myself, not too long before."

"And? Did you see anybody?"

"Only Farmer Owens. He came from the cottage to join me."

"Farmer Owens, eh? Is he known for his radical tendencies?"

Evan laughed. "On the contrary. He's very much live and let live, although . . ." Although he had certainly made it plain what he felt about English people buying the cottage, Evan thought. And he admitted having been there . . . Evan recalled the sudden tension and watchfulness he himself had felt. He shook his head. "I don't think it could have been Farmer Owens, but I'll have a word with him, if you like. He might have seen something useful."

The two men set off up the hillside. Morning mist had draped the valley like sheep's wool but as they climbed they came to clear blue sky and the sound of larks.

"My, but I could get used to this weather," Watkins said with a sigh. "They do say the world climate's changing, don't they? Maybe Wales is going to be the next Riviera."

"Don't tell Evans-the-Meat that," Evan laughed, then his smile drained as he saw Watkins staring at him. "You don't think he was involved in this? Not this time, sarge — it's just not possible. He was in the pub with us when the alarm was sounded."

"There are ways of delaying a fire, you know. A good arsonist can be miles away by the time the thing goes up."

"I'm sure it wasn't him," Evan said. "He was being his usual self — loud, offensive but not at all nervous."

"Maybe he's a cool customer."

"You know he's not. Look how he went to pieces that time we hauled him in for questioning."

"But he could have been the tip-off man, you have to admit that."

"Yes, I do admit that," Evan said. "He's the kind of bloke who might well want to join the Meibion Gwynedd. He might know something. I'll try asking a few discreet questions."

They had reached the blackened remains of the cottage. Only the shell of four walls was still standing, the grey stone hidden under a layer of soot. Inside the walls they could make out the shape of a stove and a bathtub, but everything else was a blackened, soggy mess.

"Bloody 'ell," Watkins muttered. "They certainly did a good job, didn't they? There's not much left to go on." They picked their way carefully around the perimeter of the cottage. "But I'd pretty much bet it was arson. Look how the ground is blackened here. That had to be some kind of flammable liquid." He looked up at Evan. "Nobody thought of taking pictures, did they?"

"Pictures?"

"Yeah. Photos or videos. Either would do. It's a known fact that arsonists like to watch their handiwork, see? It would have been good to have a record of the crowd, just in case it happens again."

"I think I could tell you who was here," Evan said. "Nobody from outside the village, anyway."

"That's worth thinking about," Watkins said.

A scrap of white fluttering amid trampled bracken caught Evan's eye. He went to investigate and found it was a scrap of paper, charred at the edges.

"Hey, look at this, Sergeant," he called. "I think this probably confirms your theory." He came back holding the paper cautiously with two fingers and handed it to the sergeant. Watkins read it and looked up. 'You're not wanted here'?" He let out a big sigh. "You know what this means, don't you? It means we're in for Peter Potter and his wonder dog Champ."

"Come again, sarge?" Evan grinned.

"Oh, you won't be smiling when he gets here, boyo. He's our new arson expert — trained at Scotland Yard, no less."

"North Wales Police has imported an English arson expert?" Evan was impressed.

"Not exactly. His wife got a job up here with a posh hotel in Llandudno, so he asked for a transfer. It just happened that he was an arson expert complete with sniffing dog. It seems it was his own dog he was using and the dog came, too."

"Well, that's good news, isn't it?"

"If you happen to want people like Peter Potter around. He's a bloody know-it-all. I've only had one encounter with him so far but he almost patted me on the head and said, "Run along and play, sonny."

"He'll learn," Evan said.

Watkins peered in through one of the former windows. Shards of glass had twisted and melted onto the stone, running down like tears. "I think we'd better keep well away from doing any more here. I don't want to be accused of cocking up the evidence." He paused and stared thoughtfully. "We are sure there was nobody in here, are we?"

"They went home hours earlier," Evan said. "Besides, it's not a big place. Anyone could have got out and sounded the alarm before the fire took over."

"Unless the person was drugged, drunk, or in some way unconscious."

Evan peered in the other window. "But you'd see a body, wouldn't you?"

"Not if the fire was hot enough. What do you think crematoriums do? Ashes to ashes, dust to dust."

"And this fire was certainly hot."

"Have the owners been contacted yet?"

"Not by me. I filed a report last night and gave their names and addresses. Apart from that I'm only—"

"I know — a humble village bobby. I've heard that one before." Watkins turned away and started down the mountain. "But if you want my advice, that's the part you should play when you're dealing with Peter Potter and his wonder dog."

* * *

As soon as Sergeant Watkins had gone, Evan went up to find Farmer Owens. He caught him coming from an upper pasture on his motorbike, a dog on either side of him. He shook his head slowly. No, he couldn't remember having seen anything unusual the night before . . .

"Too bad I didn't have my dogs with me. They'd have spotted right away if anything was wrong. Sharper than humans they are, aren't you, girls?"

Two black-and-white heads looked up at him and tails wagged furiously. "Whoever wanted to burn Rhodri's cottage made a damned good job of it," he commented. "Not much left of their antiques or their French bathroom."

"Any idea who might have wanted to do a thing like that?" Evan asked cautiously.

"Someone with an axe to grind, obvious, isn't it? Spiteful thing to do, if you ask me."

Evan didn't point out that Farmer Owens himself had an axe to grind — the Englishman had almost killed his dog. But he just didn't think that the kindly farmer would go around setting buildings on fire.

His next visit should be to the butcher, although Evan wasn't looking forward to it. Evans-the-Meat was noted for his quick temper and his belligerence. Extra tact would be needed if Evan was going to get anything out of him.

"*Bore da*, Evans-the-Law," the butcher greeted him as he sliced a lamb's liver with a murderous-looking knife. "I take it this isn't just a social visit."

"No, it's not, Gareth. Look you, I know you've got strong feelings about foreigners so—"

"So you think I sprinted up the mountain and set fire to their cottage last night? Are you out of your bloody mind?"

"I wasn't suggesting you did, Gareth. You were in the pub when I got there, so you could hardly have been up on the mountain starting fires, could you now? But it's possible that you might know the kind of people who were involved . . ."

The butcher's face flushed red with anger. "And if I did, do you think I'd turn them in to you?"

"Not for a minute," Evan said. "But I wish you would, if you do know anything. One day these people may go too far. The next cottage they burn might have a baby sleeping inside. Think about that, eh?"

Evans-the-Meat went back to his liver slicing. "Well, thanks for the lecture, Evans-the-Law. If I come across any arsonists, I'll let you know, then, shall I?"

Evan walked toward the door, then turned back. "We've got an arson expert coming. If I were you, I'd keep my opinions to myself for a while."

"I can't pretend I'm sorry that their place burned down. Good riddance is what I say, Constable Evans," the butcher called after him.

All in all, it was a pretty unsuccessful interview. But then it's not up to me, Evan decided. I'm supposed to get along with the locals. I'll leave the interrogation to the CID.

He glanced at his watch and saw that it was almost two. Mrs Williams would have his lunch ready and be upset that it was spoiling. He went back to the station to check his messages, then hurried down the street to his landlady's house. It was one of two semi-detached houses, opposite the row of terraced cottages, and Mrs Williams therefore felt herself very superior. It even boasted a small front garden, complete with rosebush and, at this time of year, chrysanthemums.

"Is that you, Mr Evans?" The high voice greeted him as it always did as he let himself in.

"Yes, it's me, Mrs Williams. Sorry I'm late. I got held up."

"Oh well. It can't be helped. A policeman's life isn't easy, is it?" She bustled over to the stove as she spoke, opened the oven and produced an earthenware casserole with the same flourish as a conjurer bringing a rabbit out of a hat. "Luckily I made your favourite" — she hesitated for a second while Evan tried to guess which dish was supposed to be his favourite today — "lamb cawl."

She took the lid of a bubbling pot of the traditional Welsh lamb stew. Carrots, turnips, and big succulent chunks of lamb lay in a deep brown gravy that smelled of herbs. She reached into the oven again and produced an enormous baked potato.

"Get that inside you and you won't do too badly," she said, putting it on his plate.

Evan sat down, his mouth watering in anticipation.

"You make a beautiful lamb cawl, Mrs Williams," he said.

"I'm a fair enough cook, I'll grant you that, Mr Evans," she agreed modestly. "Plain food, though. Nothing fancy. That's why I'm thinking of taking this course."

"Course?"

"Yes, there was a letter come in the post today from that new French restaurant. It seems this Madame Yvette is going to be giving cooking lessons. Charlie Hopkins's wife wants me to take the course with her, so I said I would."

"You're going to take French cooking?" Evan looked up in astonishment.

Mrs Williams blushed pink. "I'd like to know how to make some fancy stuff. Our Sharon did that cooking course — remember I told you? And now she's a lovely little cook.

She'll make some man a wonderful wife someday." She looked at Evan wistfully. Unfortunately Evan had met her granddaughter — a large girl inclined to giggle.

"I'm sure she will, Mrs Williams," he said on hastily returning to his plate of stew.

He had only taken a couple of bites when there was a knock at the front door.

"Now who can that be?" Mrs Williams was completely reliable in her responses. "Don't move. I'll go."

Evan heard her opening the door. "I'm sorry, he's having his dinner, just," Evan heard her say in English.

"Well, tell him to stop having his dinner and get himself back to work," a voice barked. "I haven't got all day."

Evan put down his fork and went to the front door. The man outside was thirtyish, dark haired, with the kind of very short haircut favoured by football players. He was dressed in an oversize navy sweater and faded blue jeans. Evan took him to be a hiker or climber. "Hello. What can I do for you?"

"You can jump to it and take me to the cottage that burned down, laddie." The man barked out the words with a decidedly Home Counties whine.

"Oh, you must be Peter Potter," Evan said. He held out his hand to the newcomer.

"Sergeant Potter to you, son. I suppose you've got used to taking long lunch hours where there's nobody to keep an eye on you."

"Actually I didn't get off duty until ten minutes ago," Evan said, "and quite often I get no lunch hour at all, and no weekend off either if something important's going on."

"Important, up here?" Peter Potter chuckled. "Like car keys dropped in the grass, you mean?"

"We've had our share of crimes," Evan said, determined not to let this man annoy him, "and it looks like we've got another one now."

"Oh, so you're the arson expert, are you?"

"No, but I was the one who found the note that said 'Go home'." Evan pointed to the track. "It's up here."

Instead of following, the sergeant walked back to a parked car. He opened the back door and a large Alsatian dog jumped out.

"Oh, Champ the wonder dog!" Evan exclaimed. He held out his hand and the dog took a step forward, wagging its tail.

"His name's Rex," Sergeant Potter said coldly. "Get back here, you," he snarled at the dog. "You know better when you're on duty! And you'd no right to encourage him either." He glared at Evan. "Obviously discipline is lax up here."

"Sorry, but we don't get to work with dogs much," Evan said. "No need to really — not for a few lost car keys." He started up the track at a very fast pace. To his delight Sergeant Potter was red faced and puffing by the time he caught up with Evan at the ruin.

"Keep well away, Constable. Don't go mucking up my evidence," he said. "Here. You hold the bags for me and give them to me when I ask you, not before."

"Right, Sergeant," Evan said, resisting the desire to salute.

Sergeant Potter and his dog got as far as the front door opening and stopped. "Hello? It looks like the old rags-through-the-letter-box trick again," he said with satisfaction.

"How do you know that?" Evan was grudgingly impressed. Sergeant Potter gave him a patronizing smile. "When you've been doing it as long as I have, son — it's one of the preferred methods. If the fire started somewhere else the front door would likely be scorched but not completely consumed."

The dog was sniffing excitedly at the ground.

"See? Rex can smell traces of the flammable liquid used. He's got a great nose — he can sniff a thimbleful of accelerant in a place the size of Buckingham Palace."

They made their way around the cottage, with Rex sniffing, Sergeant Potter bending to take samples and then handing the plastic bags back to Evan. "He did a thorough job, I'll say that for him." He glanced back at Evan. "So have you got statements from potential witnesses yet?"

"No sir. I wasn't asked to," Evan said.

"Initiative, man! Use your bloody initiative!" Potter barked. "You want to be promoted someday, don't you? You don't want to spend the rest of your life in this godforsaken place."

Evan glanced wistfully at the mountain peaks above, clearly etched against a glass-blue autumn sky.

The mountains were one of the perks of this godforsaken place. He wished he was up there now. "Go and question all the locals. Someone must have seen something. They're always minding everybody's business in a small place like this. And find out who's been buying cans of petrol lately, too!"

"It would be easy enough to get up here without being seen," Evan said. "He wouldn't necessarily have started from the village."

"But he's carrying a bloody great can of petrol, man. How far can he lug that, eh? Unless he drove up here?"

"He didn't do that," Evan said. Potter looked up sharply. "I was on the mountain myself only a short while before. I'd have seen a vehicle."

"Well, ask your questions anyway." Potter snapped his fingers for the dog, and presumably also Evan, to follow him. "I'd do it myself but I haven't got the hang of the bloody lingo yet. They're making me take classes, if you've ever heard anything so ridiculous! Apparently it's required these days."

Evan smiled to himself as he imagined some poor person trying to teach Peter Potter Welsh.

"Ah well, I suppose you might need to communicate with the natives someday," Evan said. "Sign language doesn't always work, does it?"

"Too much bloody nationalism if you ask me," Potter said. "It only leads to trouble — like this stupid gesture." He pointed at the cottage. "With any luck some group will come forward and claim responsibility and we'll have our work done for us." He started down the track again. "Come on, don't just stand there," he called to Evan.

Evan was suddenly feeling more sympathy for the Welsh nationalists (as well as for Champ the wonder dog).

CHAPTER 6

Although he felt it would be a wasted effort, Evan dutifully did the rounds and got statements from the villagers. He also compiled a list of all the locals who were in the Red Dragon. Nobody had seen anything unusual before the fire. Nobody even remembered seeing a stranger in the village, nor a strange car. In addition, as Roberts-the-Pump pointed out, all the local farmers, plus at least half the young men owned motorbikes and were always buying cans of petrol. The other half had lawn mowers, weed whackers, or needed cans of paraffin for their oil stoves.

Evan was just preparing a report with which even Sergeant Potter couldn't find fault when the door of the police station burst open and yet another stranger came in.

Evan opened his mouth to say "Can I help you?" but before he could get the words out the man demanded, "Are you the officer on duty here? Where's the person in charge?"

"Yes, and you're looking at him," Evan said, attempting a friendly smile. "I'm the officer stationed here. This is only a subpolice station."

"See, I knew it would be bloody useless," the man said to a woman who had entered the room behind him. Evan recognized her. He had seen her in the village street on a couple of occasions.

"You're the couple from the cottage, aren't you?" Evan got to his feet. "I'm very sorry—"

"Yes, but have you caught the bastards yet?"

"It hasn't even been twenty-four hours, sir. We've launched an investigation."

"I bet you have." The remark was dripping with sarcasm. "I bet you're all doing your private little victory dance because you got us out of here. They warned me when I said I was buying a cottage in Wales. They won't make you welcome there — that's what they said. I told them I didn't give a damn whether I was welcome or not. But I never thought it would come to this!"

"Savages, that's what they are," the woman added. Venom distorted a perfectly made-up face. "Nothing more than hooligans and savages. Too bad they outlawed corporal punishment. A good caning with the birch — that's what they deserve."

"We've had an arson expert on the scene, madam . . ."

"And what are *you* doing about it, Constable? It doesn't look as if we're exactly high priority here." The woman glared at him. "Why aren't you out there looking for the criminals?"

"As a matter of fact, madam, I . . ." Evan began but the man thumped his fist on Evan's desk and leaned forward to glare into Evan's face. "I want action, Constable! Get off your backside and find them! That's what I pay my taxes for."

He headed for the door. "We'll be going to see your superiors to lodge an official complaint. Then maybe we'll see some action!"

They stormed out. Evan heard the Jaguar rev up and drive away. He sighed and ran his fingers through his hair. He'd had just about all he could take for one day. He locked the station and walked up the village street. Children were running past with satchels bouncing up and down on their backs. One of the boys called out to him, "Hello, Constable

Evans? *Sut wyt ti?* Have we got rugby practice tomorrow night?"

Evan answered and watched them run past, carefree now that school was over for today. He just wished adult life could be that simple.

The realization that school was out made him quicken his pace up the hill. The village school was the last building before the two chapels. As he approached he noticed that Rev. Powell-Jones was busy putting a new text on the bill-board outside Chapel Beulah. It read, "Many are called but few are chosen." Evan grinned and looked expectantly at the rival billboard across the street. Rev. Parry Davies had chosen for his weekly text, "Go out into the highways and by-ways and bring the people in, that my house may be filled."

Obviously Rev. Powell-Jones had found out about the van!

The schoolhouse was divided into classroom and teacher's living quarters. Smoke was coming from Bronwen's chimney. The last hollyhocks were still in bloom outside its windows and it looked cosy and inviting. But before he was halfway across the playground, the door opened and Bronwen came out. She stopped short when she saw Evan.

"Hello, were you on your way to see me? Is something wrong?"

"Not anymore." Evan stood there looking at her, enjoying the way the wind blew wisps of sun-streaked hair across her face and how her eyes crinkled when she smiled. "I've had a rotten day so far. I needed a sanity break, Bron."

Her face fell. "Well, actually I was on my way out. I was going to catch the four o'clock bus down to Caernarfon. I'm signing up for the French cooking class and my kitchen is woefully lacking implements."

"You're doing the French cooking class, too?" Evan grinned. "So's Mrs Williams."

"And half the village by the sound of it," Bronwen said. "It's a once in a lifetime opportunity to take lessons from someone who trained at the Cordon Bleu school in Paris — and so cheap, too."

"I wonder what made her come here, if she's as highly qualified as she says?"

Bronwen shrugged. "I suppose you could definitely say that our restaurants need upgrading — there's no French restaurant that I know of closer than Manchester. In fact there's only the Gegin Fawr café between here and Llanberis — and their area of expertise doesn't go much higher than beans on toast. I think Madame Yvette could do well here."

"Have you seen her yet?" Evan asked.

Bronwen smiled. "No, but according to Terry Jenkins she's 'ever so sexy'. We had a big discussion this morning about the French and their strange habits, like eating snails. Very creative geography lesson!"

"Terry Jenkins? How did he manage to see her?"

"He rode his bike down there on purpose to scout her out." She shook her head with a despairing smile. "There's not much that gets past young Terry."

"How is he apart from that? A bit of a handful?"

"You could say that again. But I like him. He's got spunk."

"His mother is about to give up on him. He's running her ragged since his father left. I caught him trying to help the firemen with their hose at the fire."

"Sounds typical. But it could be worse. At least he's acting out his anger."

"Maybe I should do that," Evan said. "I've had to put up with the most obnoxious people today and just stand there being polite. I'd have felt much better if I'd been allowed to act out my anger a little . . ."

"Better, but probably in jail." She smiled up at him. "Look, if it's important I won't go into Caernarfon. It can wait."

"Don't be silly," Evan said. "I wouldn't want to hinder your cooking lessons. Besides, I'm feeling better already. Come on, I'll walk you to the bus stop."

"Problems with the cottage that burned?" Bronwen asked as they crossed the playground and Evan opened the gate for her.

Evan nodded. "I've had the owners here yelling at me because I haven't found the perpetrator yet, and our new arson specialist is treating me as if I was the village idiot." He shrugged. "It's all part of being a public servant, I suppose. Nothing that a pint at the Dragon won't cure."

"I might join you there later when I get back from Caernarfon. I might even show you my new egg whisk, if you're good." Her eyes held his.

"I can't wait." Evan grinned. "Maybe we should try out this new French place for ourselves this weekend?"

"That would be lovely." Bronwen's face lit up. "Then you can tell me what dishes you liked, and I'll learn to cook them."

"That's what I like to hear — a woman cooking to please her man." He dodged, laughing, as she swung her shopping basket at him.

The bus roared toward them, belching black smoke. Bronwen stepped forward and stuck out her hand to hail it. It came to a halt with a squeal of brakes. She leaped nimbly on board and the bus roared away again. As Evan watched it go Bronwen's face appeared at a window. She waved and blew him a kiss. He waved back, then walked down the hill. Suddenly everything was right with the world again.

* * *

The next day Sergeant Watkins called to say that tests had confirmed the residue to be from petrol. Also there were fingerprints on the note, which they were going to try and match to known extremists. He thought they'd have the case sewn up before long, which was good because the English owners had been raising bloody hell at headquarters.

Evan sighed with relief. It seemed that it was now out of his province and he could go back to his usual duties. The first of these was a call from Mrs Powell-Jones, the minister's wife, complaining that a large grey van was parked on the street, creating a traffic hazard. Evan suspected it wouldn't be the last he'd hear on the matter of the van.

He'd just returned from smoothing out that situation when there was a light tap on his door and a woman came in.

"Zis ees zee police station, *oui*?" she asked, her eyes darting around nervously.

Evan got up. "That's right. What can I do for you?"

She spread her hands in a very continental gesture. "I'm not sure. Maybe it's just a joke, but I don't know . . ."

She reached into a large black patent handbag and produced an envelope.

Evan pulled out a chair. "Please. Take a seat. I'm Constable Evans."

"Yvette Bouchard," she said, giving him a little half smile as she sat.

Evan had guessed this might be the famous Madame Yvette. "You've opened the restaurant. How's it going so far?"

"We shall 'ave to see, won't we?" She had a deep, throaty voice and she looked exactly the way Evan expected a French restaurant owner to look. She was probably in her late thirties, with a somewhat beaky nose and full, voluptuous lips. Her deep-set, dark eyes were made even darker by the addition of liner around them, and her thick, dark hair was piled high on her head in an old-fashioned bun. She wore a black, high-necked blouse with a scarf wound around her neck and a wide black belt that nipped in a tiny waist and emphasized a generous bust. When she sat, she crossed her legs and revealed black stockings.

Terry Jenkins had been right in his first impression, Evan thought.

"So how can I help you, Madame Yvette?" he asked.

"Zis." She handed him the envelope. "I received it zis morning."

Evan carefully removed the letter. It was printed with a thick red marker pen in capital letters:

GO HOME. YOU'RE NOT WANTED HERE. GET OUT BEFORE IT'S TOO LATE.

Evan examined the envelope. "Interesting. No stamp on it."

"I found it on zee mat with zee rest of zee post," she said. "I didn't know what to sink. Eez zis a joke or no?"

"Maybe not," Evan said. "There is some anti-foreign feeling around, I'm afraid. We had a cottage burn down earlier this week. So we must take this seriously."

"But who would not want good food to be brought to zair town?" Yvette demanded. "Before me zere ees nothing. No restaurant at all. Zat ees why I come 'ere. No competition."

Evan nodded. "I'm all for it, but don't worry. It's only a few loonies on the fringe who feel like this. The local women are all excited about taking your cooking courses."

Yvette beamed. Her whole face became animated when she smiled, making her look a lot younger — not much older than himself, Evan decided. "I know all about zee good PR, as you say. I wish to make friends with zee local people. I will show zem that good French cooking ees not all exotic things — no escargots. When zay get a chance to taste lamb and fish zee way I prepare zem, zay will never want to go back. And zay will all bring zair 'usbands to eat at my restaurant."

"Good idea," Evan agreed. "I've made plans to come there myself on Saturday."

She eyed him appraisingly. "You will bring your wife?"

"No, I'm not married."

Before he could clarify this and mention the word *girlfriend*, Madame Yvette's eyes lit up. "Ah, zen zee local ladies zay all fight over you still, eh?"

"Not really, they . . ." Evan couldn't complete the sentence. He felt himself blushing and cursed his fair Celtic skin.

"Don't be bashful. You are a 'andsome man. You should be proud zat women admire you."

Evan cleared his throat. "Yes, well. About this letter, Madame Yvette. I think I should show it to the criminal investigation division. They'll want to compare it to other notes that have been found. And in the meantime, keep your eyes open and call me if there's anything suspicious . . ."

The dark eyes opened wider. "What sort of sing?"

"A stranger hanging around. Any more threats. Anyone who's rude to you. A hostile neighbour, for example."

"*Mon dieu!* You don't really think I'm in danger, do you?" She put her hand to her breast in a dramatic gesture.

"No, I don't, but you shouldn't take any chances until the detectives have checked out the note. As I say, I'm not far away. Give me a call if you're worried."

"Sank you. You are *très gentil*, as we say," she said. "You speak French, maybe?"

"I took it in school, but I've not had much call to use it since. I can probably still conjugate a few verbs."

"Ah . . ." She gave him a long, slow smile. "You never know when you might need to conjugate . . . verbs. I 'ave to go now. I look forward wiz pleasure to serving you at Chez Yvette. *Au revoir*, Monsieur Evans."

Evan escorted her to the door. Phew, he thought. A woman like that is going to make some waves around here.

* * *

On Saturday evening Evan escorted Bronwen to his old bone-shaker.

"I'm not sure that I should introduce you to Madame Yvette," Bronwen said. "She's very — French."

"I know. I already met her."

"You did? when?"

"She came into the station. Someone had sent her a threatening letter telling her to go home."

Bronwen frowned. "Like the one at the cottage?"

"Similar."

"How awful. I hope that sort of thing isn't going to spread."

"I think it's a few extremists, maybe just one bloke, but probably not. There are fingerprints on both the notes. Unfortunately not the same prints, and not the same method either. One was words cut from a newspaper, the other was printed in capital letters."

"So it looks as if a group is involved?"

"Possibly. People who write threatening notes usually like to stick to the same method. Which suggests it wasn't the same person."

"Unless he couldn't find all the words he needed in the newspaper this time," Bronwen suggested.

Evan opened the car door for her and she climbed in. "So what did you think of Madame Yvette?" she asked.

Evan got in beside her. "I agree with Terry. Very sexy. In fact, I think I should sign up for those classes myself, just so I can watch her bending over a hot stove. Ow!" he added as Bronwen hit him.

"We had our first lesson today," she said. "It was fascinating. I'm going to try out the recipe she taught us and if it's anything like the original, I'll cook it for you. Actually it mightn't be a bad idea if you did take cooking classes. You've got to learn to live alone someday."

"I don't see why," he said. "I always thought that's what women were for — no, don't hit me when I'm driving!"

He was backing into the parking area outside Chapel Beulah so that he could turn around. Suddenly he swore under his breath and jammed on the brakes. "Bloody young idiot," he shouted as he stopped the car and flung open his door.

"What is it?" Bronwen asked.

Evan was already half out of the car. "Young Terry. I almost backed into him." He was already yelling. "What were you thinking, riding that close to me, Terry? You could see I was backing up."

"I was coming to find you," Terry shouted. His voice was high and shrill. "There's another fire!"

"Where?"

"Up there — the Everest Inn."

"Another fire, Bron," Evan yelled as Bronwen emerged from the car. "Go and call 999, will you?"

A flickering glow outlined the giant chalet as Evan started to run up the hill. As he passed Charlie Hopkins's cottage young Bryn emerged ahead of his grandfather.

"Another fire, Mr Evans!" he shouted. "My grandma's calling the brigade. Don't worry. We'll soon have it out!"

* * *

The next morning Sergeant Watkins joined Evan at the Everest Inn car park.

"I'm surprised that Peter Potter let you come before he's been over the scene himself," Evan said.

"His day off, isn't it?" Watkins chuckled. "We've put in a call but he's not at home. Probably gone back to England for the weekend. I bet you're glad to see me instead of him, aren't you?"

"You can say that again," Evan muttered.

"Gave you a hard time, did he? Don't worry, he's not winning any popularity contests with the rest of us either, but I gather he's the cat's whiskers when it comes to arson."

They walked across the car park together.

"It doesn't look as if much harm was done this time," Watkins said.

"Luckily it was only a storage shed at the back that went up. It could have been worse."

"Any sign of a note this time?" Watkins asked.

"Not that we've found so far."

"So it could be accidental," Watkins commented, stepping carefully over the rubble. "Phew," he added, pointing at a pile of scorched cans. "Paraffin. Lucky they put the fire out before that lot went up."

Evan was staring thoughtfully at the giant Swiss chalet shape of the Everest Inn. "You know what I keep asking myself, sarge — why this?"

"Because the inn's full of rich foreigners?"

"In that case why not go the whole hog and try to burn it down?" Evan asked. "Why bother with a piddling little outbuilding that does no real damage?"

"Maybe they got cold feet about burning something as large as the inn," Watkins said, scowling at it, "or maybe they knew that flammables were stored in here and they expected the whole lot to explode and spew burning liquid on all these nice cars."

"It doesn't make sense to me," Evan said. "Why not torch some of the cars, if that's the aim? Nobody has come forward to claim responsibility yet. There's not much point in burning down buildings if nobody knows who's doing it."

Watkins nodded. "You've got a point there. We're busy trying to match up fingerprints but no luck so far. I hope we get them before there's much more of this."

"So you think it is arson again, then?"

Watkins bent and retrieved something with his handkerchief. "This looks like the same type of fuse that was used at the cottage. I reckon it was the same bloke all right."

* * *

As Evan and Watkins came down the street from the inn, the Reverend Parry Davies was standing in the pulpit addressing his newly acquired flock.

"My dear friends," his voice boomed out through open windows, "a great evil has come among us, an evil that mocks one of the Ten Commandments — a heathen foreigner who thinks she can besmirch the Lord's day. I am referring to that new house of iniquity down the pass — the French restaurant. As I drove up with a vanload of new worshipers today, what do you think I saw? I saw that the restaurant was open — open today on the Sabbath!

"My dear friends, I, your pastor, warn you to stay away from that house of sin. Any place that does commerce on the Sabbath day is a house of the devil and anyone who frequents it is asking for an eternity of hellfire and damnation."

Across the street the Reverend Powell-Jones couldn't help overhearing. "Vanity!" he boomed at his own congregation. "Vanity is a tool of the devil! There are those among us who seek to better themselves, who seek to better their own position in life — who waste money on costly vans to swell their congregations. And why? Not for the salvation of more souls, but to swell the amount of money in the collection plate!"

As soon as his service was over he rushed out to his billboard and pasted a new text: "Before you criticize the speck of dust in your neighbour's eye, remove the beam from your own eye!"

"And very apt too, Edward," Mrs Powell-Jones commented, glaring at the van parked across the street. "If it's not nipped in the bud, that Parry Davies woman will be using that van to get members for her women's prayer group and then there will be no stopping her!"

CHAPTER 7

On Monday morning Evan received a brief visit from Sergeant Potter on his way back from his inspection of the crime scene.

"It looks like we've got ourselves a serial arsonist here all right," he said. "Same modus operandi — same accelerant dropped in through a broken window, same type of fuse."

"But no note found this time," Evan pointed out.

"Not yet. It could have been burned by mistake." He stood staring out of the open doorway, then suddenly turned to Evan. "So who is it, then?" the sergeant demanded. "Come on, man, you must have some idea. It's a village. Everyone knows everything about everyone else, don't they?"

"Are you saying that someone from the village has to be responsible?" Evan asked.

"Stands to reason, doesn't it?" Potter barked. "Two fires in a week, both around Llanfair. Which makes me ask, why here? It's not exactly a tourist mecca, is it? I mean, who cares if Llanfair burns down? So it has to be a local. And the fuses — I understand that all the men around here used to work in the slate quarry before it shut down. They'd all have had access to fuses like that, wouldn't they? Start putting the screws on, Constable. Find out who might have kept a fuse or two around the house. Get a statement from everyone in the village and see who has an alibi for the half hour before the building went up. I want this bloke nabbed before he does any more damage."

He didn't wait to hear Evan's answer as he stalked out again.

Evan did as he was ordered and made the rounds of the village once more, but with no obvious success. Nobody admitted to having old fuses around the house. There had been a European League game between Real Madrid and Manchester United on the telly that kept a lot of men home from the pub. Evans-the-Meat remained sullen and unhelpful. And he had a cast-iron alibi for the night of the second fire. He said he was down at a darts club meeting in Caernarfon. Evan noted the name and address of the club; that might prove worth looking into.

Evan arrived at Mrs Williams's house for lunch with a good appetite and great expectations. They'd had leg of lamb yesterday, which should mean shepherd's pie today, and Mrs W. made a top-rate shepherd's pie.

Mrs Williams's face looked flushed and nervous as she opened the oven. "Here," she said. "I hope you like it!"

Then she put a plate in front of him. It contained three round dabs of food, each about the size of old half crowns.

"Uh — what is it?" Evan asked cautiously.

"It's French cooking, that's what it is," she said with a hint of pride in her voice. "What we learned in our class. That's a lamb noisette" — she pointed at the brown morsel — "that's puréed leek, and that's whipped potato made with garlic."

"Mmmm — very nice, I'm sure," Evan said. It *was* very nice, too, but it only took six mouthfuls to finish his plate.

"There — wasn't very much, was there?" he said as he put his knife and fork together.

"That's the French way," Mrs Williams said. "Just enough to excite the taste buds, that's what Madame Yvette said. If you want to fill up, you eat bread in France . . . and of course she said we had to have red wine, but I'm not going that far."

Evan sighed and reached for the bread.

On his next visit to the Red Dragon he discovered he wasn't the only one who was now on a starvation diet.

Betsy had put a new blackboard on the wall above the bar. Underneath heading Red Dragon Bistro there was written Tonight's special: Leek and Gruyère Soufflé.

"What the devil is a soufflé?" an old farmer demanded. He pronounced it to rhyme with *shuffle*.

"It's soo-flay," Betsy said, "and I learned to make it at our cooking class."

"Bloody cooking class," one of the men growled. "You should see what my wife served me last night. Bloody mashed-up muck with garlic, that's what it was. I told her any more of this and I send her back to her mother."

"Don't worry, this Madame Yvette won't last long," Evans-the-Meat said.

"Oh, why not?" Evan's ears pricked up.

Evans-the-Meat looked flustered. "Stands to reason, doesn't it? Nobody wants that kind of food around here. And have you heard what she's charging? You can get a whole serving of fish and chips for what she charges for a bit of lettuce and a couple of spring onions. No, she'll be out of here by Christmas, you mark my words."

"You wouldn't be thinking about helping her to make up her mind, would you, Gareth?" Evan asked quietly.

"Meaning what?"

"Someone sent her a threatening note."

"Well, it wasn't me. More likely to be Mr Parry Davies, if you ask me. I gather his sermon about her was a real scorcher. He called her a Jezebel and worse."

Evan decided it might not be a bad idea to get a sample of printing from the minister in the morning — and one from the butcher as well.

* * *

The next day Evan collected samples of printing from most of the villagers. Evans-the-Meat gave his, complaining all the time about duress and the police barking up the wrong tree as usual. Rev. Parry Davies sighed and gave a good impression of a Christian martyr. His wife complained more vocally than either her husband or the butcher, and Mrs Powell-Jones flatly refused, threatening to contact her MP and the commissioner about defamation of character.

Evan duly sent the samples down to headquarters. He waited expectantly but heard nothing more. It wasn't until the next morning that Sergeant Watkins appeared as he was making himself a cup of tea.

"Slacking off again? Sergeant Potter wouldn't like that." Watkins put his head around the station door.

"Oh, morning sarge. How's the inquiry going?"

Watkins sighed. "Going nowhere, if you ask me." He came into Evan's office and pulled out a chair. "I can't say it's their number-one priority at HQ right now. All DI Hughes can talk about is this Operation Armada, as he calls it."

"Operation Armada?"

Watkins made a face. "The drug sting. Sinking all the boats. Rule Britannia, you know . . ."

Evan grinned. "So it's just you and Peter Potter working on this case. I'd help if I was allowed to."

"I wish you bloody would." Watkins sank onto the chair. "Tell me honestly, Evans, have you really got no clue about these fires? I mean, you're normally the one who gets the hunch that puts us on the right lines. We've done everything we can — we've fingerprinted any known Welsh extremist — anyone who has written a nationalistic letter to the newspaper, anyone who belongs to a club like your butcher up here. But we can't match the prints to either note."

He sighed and leaned against the door of his car. "I tell you one thing — I've had it up to here with Peter-bloody-Potter. He's been breathing down our necks, calling us incompetent provincials and worse. Apparently he normally has this kind of thing wrapped up in a day or so. He says the method used was the same for both fires, in both cases quite efficient and professional. This was someone who knew a thing or two about starting fires. But the prints don't match to anyone who's known for burning down cottages. So this is a new bloke and I'm damned if I know how to find him. I'm thinking we may have to plant a spy in this extremist group — these Sons of Gwynedd. I was wondering . . ."

"Don't look at me, sarge," Evan said quickly.

"No, not you. Of course everyone knows who you are. I was thinking of your butcher. He'd be a useful man, if you could persuade him to do his part for law and justice."

Evan chuckled. "The police dragged him into jail kicking and screaming not too long ago — do you really think he'd want to help?"

"You get on with all the locals. We thought that maybe you could persuade him."

"I don't think I've got a hope in hell," Evan said. "In fact I suspect that he knows more than he's letting on. But I'll make the suggestion if you want me to."

"What I'd really like you to do is solve this bloody case for us, so I can get back to Operation Armada and see a little action for once."

"They haven't caught anyone yet?"

"Nah — they've been lying low, probably waiting for us to lose interest, or pull off our men. But it's only a matter of time. We think they'll be using several small boats and running them into different harbours at the same time — on the theory that the police can't be everywhere at once."

"They're right about that," Evan agreed.

"Criminals are getting too bloody smart these days," Watkins growled. "Do what you can, won't you, boyo? Or I might have to suggest to HQ that you'd be great as Potter's full-time assistant."

When he'd gone Evan locked up and walked slowly up the street, deep in thought. Watkins wanted the impossible. There was no way he'd get Evans-the-Meat to cooperate with the police to nab Welsh extremists. And he had no bright ideas himself. Madame Yvette hadn't called him again with any more trouble. And being stuck on duty in a village hardly gave him the scope to track down terrorists . . . He felt annoyed and powerless. What he needed now was luck. If a serial arsonist was at work, then it was only a matter of time before he struck again, and maybe the third time might be lucky. Eventually the arsonist would make a mistake or leave a traceable clue.

That night Evan was getting ready for bed when there was a tap on his bedroom door.

"Mr Evans? Are you in there?" Mrs Williams asked, although she had seen him go up the stairs half an hour earlier. "Telephone for you — she says it's an emergency."

Evan reached for his dressing gown and ran down the stairs.

"Ees zat Constable Evans?" The voice was tight and breathless. "I am so sorry to disturb you but anozzer note has come . . . just a few minutes ago I see it. I am worried zat zee man ees still outside my 'ouse."

"Keep the door locked and watch out for me," Evan said. "I'll be down there in a few minutes."

He scrambled back into his clothes, grabbed his torch and drove as fast as he dared down the pass, his headlights cutting crazy curves through the darkness as he negotiated the bends. He parked and switched on the torch. It felt heavy in his hand and comforting in the absence of a weapon as he got out of the car.

He had just completed a tour of the outside of the building when he sensed someone standing behind him. He turned to see Madame Yvette standing at her door, wearing a white satin dressing gown with feathery trim at the neck and matching slippers.

"Oh, you 'ave come. Sank you so much. I am so afraid when I sink zis man might still be zere, watching me."

"Don't worry. I've checked all around the place. If anyone was here, he's gone now." He followed her into the restaurant. What had once been a chapel now contained six tables covered in red-and-white checked cloths. There were curtains at the windows and Impressionist prints on the walls. Evan nodded with approval.

"You say you just got the note?"

"I found it when I went to check zat zee doors were locked for zee night and I call you right away. It was not zere when zee restaurant was open or my customers would have seen it."

Evan looked around at the tables laid with polished silver and white linen napkins, unsure where to sit. It was as if Madame Yvette read his mind.

"I start small," she said. "Only six tables. That way I can do wizout 'elp until it gets going. And I live 'ere — upstairs, where zee old balcony used to be. It ees small but how you say" — she spread her hands in a very French gesture — "cosy enough for one person, *non?*"

She crossed the restaurant and pushed open a swing door into a kitchen. Gleaming pots and pans hung above a big stove. Strings of garlic, onions, and bunches of herbs hung over a central wooden table. "Zis way, please," she said. She turned to her left. There was a back door on the far wall and beside it a wooden staircase climbed the side wall. She went up without turning around, her slippers flapping on the bare boards. Evan got a tantalizing glimpse of bare leg as she hitched up her robe.

The upstairs living area was one good-size room, like a loft, above the kitchen. There was a small sofa, armchair, and coffee table at the near end, with a TV on a cabinet in the corner. On the far wall was an unmade bed with various pieces of clothing, including a black lace bra, thrown across it.

"Please. Sit down. Anywhere you like."

Evan perched hastily at the end of the sofa closest to the stairs, with his back to the black lace. "Now about the note, Madame," he began.

"Would you like a glass of wine perhaps?" Madame Yvette crossed the room.

"Not while I'm on duty, thanks."

"Not even a cognac?" She opened the corner cupboard beneath the TV. "I sink I will have one, if you don't mind. To steady zee nerves."

She poured amber liquid into a brandy glass and came to sit on the other arm of the sofa. She took a sip, sighed and put the glass down on the coffee table in front of her before reaching for a packet of Gauloises. "Cigarette?"

"No thanks, I don't."

"Very wise. Feelthy habit. I should quit, but I don't seem to be able to."

She lit the cigarette and inhaled deeply. Evan wasn't sure, but he thought she deliberately blew the smoke in his direction.

"Show me the note you got," Evan said. "Is it the same as the last one?"

She pulled it from her dressing gown pocket. "'ere it ees."

Evan unfolded it. It was also written in bold letters in black marker. It just said, GO HOME OR ELSE.

"Short and to the point." Evan looked up to see her watching him. "It will be interesting to see if the prints on it match."

"Prints?"

"Fingerprints. There were some clear fingerprints on the last note. I presume this came from the same person."

She shrugged. "Who knows? Maybe everybody wants me to go away. I thought it would be a good place. My friend takes zee 'oliday and says Yvette, zere are no French restaurants up in North Wales. Why don't you open one up zere? But now I'm not so sure. I nevair expect zis kind of thing."

"It's only a few extremists," Evan said. "And the Welsh take their time to accept newcomers — especially anyone foreign. But we like to eat. If you serve good food you'll win people over."

"Zat ees what I hoped," she said. "I needed to buy a place where property was not so expensive."

"Did you come here straight from France? Did you have a restaurant over there?"

"No, I once had a restaurant wiz my husband on zee coast in Sussex, but we had nozzink but bad luck. My husband died and I was in zee hospital for a while. I didn't have zee 'eart to start again down there."

Evan nodded in sympathy. "I'm sorry," he said. "You must miss your husband."

"My 'usband? Pah! He was 'ow you say — zee bastard! Zee monster!" she said with great venom. "It was the 'appiest day in my life when I escape from 'im." She paused, reached for the brandy glass and took a gulp. "I mean, when he die." She slid down to the sofa beside him. "So now I'm all alone," she said. "It ees not easy for a woman alone."

"No, I'd imagine not." He was beginning to feel uncomfortable. The sofa was rather snug for two people.

"Maybe I expect too much," she went on, her brandy glass poised just below her lips. "I sink I will make zee success because I know how to cook. And everysing starts so well too — zee newspaper come to interview me and take my picture. Zee Taste of Wales people come and eat 'ere last weekend. You know about zee Taste of Wales?"

"They give out awards for good cooking, right?"

"Zay say zay might nominate me for Best New Restaurant — *pas mal, non?* I cook for zem zee Welsh foods, you see. My rack of lamb wiz rosemary and my purée of leeks. Zay were impressed, I could see . . ." Her eyes had been alight as she spoke, but then her face fell again. "But now zis! What good ees to win zee award if people don't want me 'ere?"

"I'm sure most people want you here," Evan said.

"You sink so?" She put down the glass but the cigarette still rested between the fingers of her left hand. "I'm 'appy someone want me 'ere."

He felt the silk of her dressing gown brush against his hand and made to get up. "I suppose I'd better be going. There's not much more we can do before the morning."

"You sink not?"

Evan cleared his throat and went on. "I imagine Sergeant Watkins or one of the detectives will want to talk to you about the note tomorrow and then we'll try and match the prints."

She put out her hand and rested it lightly on his arm. "Don't go," she said quietly. "I don't want to be alone tonight."

Evan had an idea of what she was hinting at, but just in case he said, with great professional detachment, "I can understand you'd feel a bit nervous after what happened. I could telephone HQ and see if they could send up a female officer to be with you if you like."

There was amusement in her dark eyes. "You Englishmen — *toujours le* 'gentleman', *n'est-ce pas*? It ees not zee woman PC zat I want to keep me company . . ."

"I'm not an Englishman. I'm a Cymro — a Welshman," Evan said, "and we're even more reserved, I'm afraid."

"But the same fire burns underneath, I sink?" She crossed her legs and the tip of one bare toe touched his leg.

"I really should go," he said. He was finding the room uncomfortably warm.

He tried to stand up, but her hand put pressure on his arm. "Why do you deny that you would like to stay 'ere wiz me tonight? I can see in your eyes zat you desire me — and what is wrong with zat? You are a healthy young man and I — I am a woman of experience. And we are both alone and unattached. It would be very good, I assure you."

"I'm sure it would . . ." Evan managed to extricate himself from her grip. "But I'm really not the kind of bloke who . . . I don't go in for casual . . . I mean I'm sort of dating a girl."

She laughed at his embarrassment — a deep throaty laugh. As she leaned back on the sofa Evan was pretty sure she wasn't wearing anything under the robe. Get out of here now — he could hear the warning voice echoing through his head.

"You are engaged to zis girl?"

"No — it hasn't got that far yet."

"In France it is considered *de rigueur* that a man has a wife and a mistress, and maybe a girlfriend as well. Besides — who ees to know if you stay 'ere tonight?"

Evan laughed shakily. "Everybody. You don't know North Wales yet. Everyone will already know that I was called down here. They'll all know the exact time that I get back."

"So zat ees what worries you?" She got up, too, and moved closer to him. "Your fine, upstanding reputation wiz zee citizens? Then it doesn't have to be the whole night, if zat's what you want. In fact I'm sure we could be very quick if you wanted to, and no one would ever know . . ."

"I'd know," Evan said. "And it really wouldn't be fair to the girl I'm seeing, would it?"

"She's a lucky girl, zen." Madame Yvette put her hands on his shoulders. "I hope she keeps you satisfied?" Without warning she moved her hands to his face, pulled him toward her and planted her lips firmly on his. Then she released him again. "If you ever change your mind, you know where you can find me. And I'll show you the difference between a girl and a woman."

She gave his cheek a playful pat. He had no recollection of how he got down the stairs and out to his waiting car.

CHAPTER 8

By the end of the week the investigation was apparently no further along. At least if it was, nobody had bothered to tell Evan, who felt his isolation, stuck in the Llanfair substation with nothing more to do than warn Rev. Parry Davies that Mrs Powell-Jones had complained about his van blocking the street again. Evan could only presume that none of the prints had been identified and that no more fires had taken place. However, he reminded himself that the last two had happened at weekends. This weekend he was going to be on the alert.

* * *

On Saturday morning the women of Llanfair assembled again in Madame Yvette's kitchen. Yvette looked around at the group.

"I see zere are not so many ladies zis time. Zay are perhaps busy?"

"Their husbands won't let them come," Betsy said bluntly.

Yvette was instantly alert. "Zay do not like it zat I am here? Zat I am zee foreigner?"

"No, it's nothing to do with that," Betsy said. "They didn't like the French food."

"Not like zee food?" Yvette put her hand to her breast. "Zat is zee same leek purée I serve to zee Taste of Wales judges and zay say it was *magnifique*."

"It wasn't what they were used to, I think," Bronwen said gently.

"And it wasn't enough," Mair Hopkins added. "My Charlie had to make himself a couple of cheese and pickle sandwiches when he'd finished what I'd cooked for him."

"Ah. It ees not enough? *Je comprends.* Nevair mind. Today we make zee classic boeuf bourguignon and zen zee éclairs — I guarantee zay will satisfy all 'usbands."

They began chopping vegetables and cutting beef into cubes.

"It's just like a lamb cawl, but with beef," Mrs Williams muttered to Mair Hopkins. "I don't see what all the fuss is about, personally."

"Zen we take zee red wine," Madame Yvette said, lifting the bottle. "A Bordeaux would be preferable, but any red wine you have around zee house will do."

Mrs Williams looked horrified. "We're chapel! We don't have wine around the house!"

Madame Yvette smiled to herself. "Maybe zee 'usbands would not complain if zay 'ave a glass of wine wiz zair food." Then her smile faded and she looked up thoughtfully. "When you say zee 'usbands forbid, I sink maybe zat one of zee husbands write me zee note."

The women looked up from their cutting.

"You hear, I suppose, zat someone write me zee notes, telling me to go 'ome."

"No! My, but that's a nasty thing to do," Mrs Williams exclaimed. "It better not be anyone from Llanfair who's doing it or he'll get a piece of my mind!"

"Who'd do a thing like that?" Mair Hopkins asked.

"There are people around here who'd want to get rid of her because she's foreign," Betsy said. "I could name some."

"I think Constable Evans is already looking into it, Betsy," Bronwen said quickly.

"Well, you'd know, wouldn't you," Betsy retorted. "I've no doubt he updates you on his cases when you're . . . birdwatching."

Yvette smiled to herself as she chopped. "Zis Constable Evans, 'e has been most helpful to me. So kind . . ."

"That's Evan the boy scout," Bronwen muttered.

"And 'e ees a 'andsome man, *n'est-ce pas?* What 'e needs ees a woman to make 'im 'appy."

"That's what I keep telling him," Mrs Williams said. "'Time for you to think about settling down,' I say. My granddaughter Sharon is a lovely little cook and housekeeper and a beautiful dancer, too. She's that light on her feet . . ."

"I think Evan can make up his own mind when the time's right, Mrs Williams," Bronwen said smoothly.

"He'll come to his senses one day," Betsy said. "He'll wake up and realize what he's been missing."

"Oh, you think he's missing something?" The knife flew up and down in Bronwen's hand and carrot slices went flying.

"It's obvious, isn't it? I mean birdwatching is all right, when you're a boy scout . . ."

"Not everybody wants to spend their nights at raves, Betsy. People do grow up," Bronwen said. More carrot slices flew.

Yvette chuckled deep in her throat. "You English — excuse me, Welsh. You are so afraid to talk about sex. A man and a woman desire each ozzer. What could be more natural? Why pretend zat it doesn't exist? Your Constable Evans was so funny when 'e was wiz me zee ozzer night . . ."

"What?" Bronwen and Betsy stopped chopping simultaneously.

Yvette went on coating chunks of beef in flour. "'E was 'ere zee ozzer night — you did not 'ear? 'E say zat people will talk about us. We have a good time togezzer. How you Welsh would say politely . . . zee nice little chat, *n'est-ce pas?*" She gave her throaty laugh. "Now I sink 'e know zee difference between zee girl and zee woman."

"Evan would never . . ." Bronwen began.

"I 'ad to trow 'im out at one o'clock." Yvette said. She threw chunks of beef into a hot pan. "Zis ees zee secret of zis dish. Start by making it 'ot enough to sizzle."

"He wasn't home when I fell asleep about midnight," Mrs Williams muttered to Mair Hopkins. Bronwen went on cutting as if she hadn't heard, but her cheeks were flushed.

* * *

That afternoon Evan strolled up the village street to visit Bronwen. He smiled to himself in anticipation — a free weekend and good weather. Maybe they'd take a hike tomorrow, or a picnic on the hill above the village . . .

Bronwen opened her front door. "Oh, it's you, Evan." She didn't immediately invite him in, but stood with her hand across the doorway.

"Hello, Bron. We didn't make any plans for the weekend yet."

"Didn't we?"

There was something wrong but he wasn't sure what. "I still haven't taken you to dinner at the French restaurant, I know. Don't think I've forgotten. But I think I should stick around here tonight and tomorrow. The other fires happened at weekends. This time I'm going to be on the lookout. But I thought that maybe you'd like to demonstrate what you learned at cooking class?"

"What I learned?" She was looking at him steadily. Then she tossed back her hair. "I'm sorry, Evan, but I'm busy this weekend. I've already arranged to get together with some people I met at last week's conference."

"Tonight?" Evan's face fell.

"We thought we'd have dinner together and do something tomorrow too. They were very amusing and it's time I mixed more socially. I've been burying myself, shut away in this village."

"Oh. I thought you liked it here."

"Oh, I do like the teaching. Socially it doesn't have much to offer, does it? Now if you'll excuse me — I need to get changed . . ."

She turned away and went to shut the door.

"Bronwen, have I done something wrong?" he asked.

"You'd know that better than I, wouldn't you?"

"What are you talking about?" he demanded.

"I really have to get ready. I have friends waiting for me."

She closed the door, leaving him standing outside. Evan shook his head as he walked away. What was all that about? He would never understand women if he lived a million years. He was clearly out of favour for some reason and now it was up to him to find out why. It crossed his mind that the sex-with-no-strings-attached approach offered by Madame Yvette might not be such a bad idea after all.

* * *

The weekend didn't improve much after that. Mrs Williams served him a few chunks of beef and a couple of pearl onions in gravy that tasted of nothing because she refused to buy wine. Evan hung around outside the pub, keeping an eye on the street, but there was no fire. Worst of all, Bronwen was gone all weekend. Evan began to wonder if the other teachers she had met were all women.

On Monday Evan timed his afternoon patrol through the village to coincide with the end of the school day. Bronwen was standing at the gate, chatting to one of the mothers as he approached. She glanced up, noticed him, frowned and went back to her conversation. Evan lingered around until the woman led her child away by the hand.

"So how was your weekend?" he asked.

"Very nice, thank you. We're thinking of doing it more often," Bronwen said. "It makes a change to be with stimulating company."

"I was thinking we never set a date to go to that French restaurant, did we?" Evan persisted.

"Funny, but I've gone off French food," Bronwen said. "Now, if you'll excuse me . . ." She hurried over to break up a fight.

Evan went home even more despondent and confused.

That evening in the pub Evans-the-Meat was waving a copy of Monday's *Daily Post* featuring a half-page write-up of Chez Yvette with a photo of Yvette standing at her stove, managing to look sultry and sexy as she stirred something in a large pot. At the bottom of the article was an added note that Chez Yvette had received a nomination for Best New Restaurant from the Taste of Wales committee.

"Would you look at that?" Evans-the-Meat threw down the newspaper as he came into the pub that night. "Nominated for Taste of Wales! How can a bloody French restaurant be called a Taste of Wales — that's what I'd like to know?"

"She's using classic Welsh ingredients, so she says," Betsy commented, pulling the butcher a pint of Robinson's without being asked. "Get that inside you and you'll feel better."

Barry-the-Bucket peered over the butcher's shoulder. "See, what did I tell you? She's a sexy bit of stuff, isn't she? Good pair of knockers on her—"

"Do you mind?" Betsy demanded. "This is a respectable establishment. We'll have none of that talk here." She thumped a glass down none too gently so that froth spattered onto the bar top. "In fact I don't think I'm interested in hearing any more about that woman and how sexy she is. Nothing but trouble, if you ask me."

Evan had been drinking his pint, too caught up in his private depression to be interested in the conversation. Now he looked at Betsy with interest. Betsy was not one to fly off the handle like that. She usually liked to trade risqué banter with the customers. Something about Madame Yvette had upset her. He heard an echo of Bronwen's unusually sharp retort, "I've gone off French food."

Madame Yvette — that had to be the reason for Bronwen's strange behaviour. The local grapevine must have been at work again and reported that he had visited Yvette late at night. He was stupid. He should have told Bronwen himself before the gossipmongers started.

He put down his glass and slipped out of the pub.

"Where's Evans-the-Law off to in such a hurry?" he heard someone call after him. "Don't tell me there's another fire."

"More likely a craving for a little Taste of Wales," Betsy retorted.

A strong wind blew in Evan's face as he ran up the street.

* * *

Bronwen came to her door in her flannel dressing gown and slipper socks. "What is it?" she asked, her eyes darting nervously. "An emergency?"

"It is an emergency when you're angry with me and I don't know what I've done."

She shrugged. "If you don't know what you've done, then I can't help you."

"Bronwen — is this something to do with going to Madame Yvette's late at night last week?"

A spasm of hurt crossed her face, but then she tossed her head defiantly. "What you do with your spare time is no concern of mine."

"Bronwen" — his voice rose — "I was called out. She got a threatening note and she was upset."

"Called out at eleven, I understand, and didn't get home until she kicked you out at one?"

"Kicked me out? Who told you that?"

"She did."

Evan could feel the heat rising to his uniform collar. "The nerve of it! Kicked me out? She asked me to stay because she was scared and upset."

"And so you, being the good boy scout as always, stayed to comfort her?"

"Yes, I did . . . until I found out what she really wanted from me. Then I made a polite but hurried exit."

"Oh." Bronwen stared hard at him as if she was trying to see inside his skull. "That's not how it was related to me."

"And you believe a lot of old gossips?"

"It was Madame herself. She told me that she showed you the difference between a woman and a girl."

Evan actually laughed. "Come on, Bron. Do you really believe that I'm the kind of bloke who winds up in bed with strange Frenchwomen?"

"How do I know?" Her voice was edgy again. "I've no idea what makes men tick. I thought maybe it was too good an offer to refuse."

"Well, I refused it."

They stood in the light of her doorway, staring at each other.

"I'm sorry," she said. "I've no right to get upset about what you do or don't do."

"You've no right to get upset with me without checking with me first," he said.

"I know. I'm sorry. I'm so stupidly insecure. I thought she had something to offer you that I don't have."

Evan smiled at her. "She does. A black lace bra."

"She showed you her bra?"

"It wasn't on her at the time."

"That's even worse," Bronwen said, but she was smiling now.

"Bronwen," Evan said quietly, "it's cold out here. Aren't you going to invite me in?"

CHAPTER 9

The following Saturday night Evan and Bronwen finally went to dinner at Chez Yvette.

"I'm not sure I want to do this," Bronwen said as Evan parked the car.

"Don't be silly. We agreed, didn't we? I want her to see us together."

"I want you to taste all my food first," Bronwen said as they walked up the flagstone path to the front door. "She might have poisoned it."

"So you'd rather *I* died. That sounds like true love." He opened the door for her. Bronwen grinned.

The restaurant looked different, lit only with candles in glass globes. No longer was it an austere former chapel. The flickering candlelight created little pools of intimacy at each of the six tables. The vaulted ceiling above and the far corners were lost in darkness. Madame Yvette was serving at the one occupied table as they came in. She looked up and the delight registered on her face as she saw Evan. "Ah, Monsieur le Policeman. You come back! *Magnifique*."

"I've brought my girlfriend for dinner, Madame," Evan said. "She's been taking your cooking classes and raving about your food, so I've come to try it." Evan's hand was on Bronwen's shoulder as he steered her across the parquet floor.

Madame Yvette nodded graciously. If she was at all put out, she wasn't showing it. "Please — take a seat. Here — my best table, in the corner. So romantic, *non?* I bring you a menu and the wine list."

They studied the wine list and Bronwen suggested a Merlot.

"Any suggestions on food?" Evan muttered to Bronwen. "I don't know one French dish from another."

"Why don't we let her choose the menu?" Bronwen suggested. "That way we'll get her favourite dishes."

Madame Yvette seemed delighted. "'Ow very kind. I make you zee superb meal. We start, I sink, wiz zee scallops in white wine and ginger, zen my famous selle d'agneau — zat is zee local lamb — very good and tender, and a salad of baby greens. And zen, for dessert, zee *specialité de la maison*." She left them with a mysterious smile.

The first two courses were exquisite, the scallops delicate, melt-in-the-mouth, floating in a light creamy sauce, accompanied by crisp lattice wafers of potato. The lamb was rich brown on the outside, pink and succulent in the middle with just a hint of garlic and herbs.

"If she has any animosity, she's not showing it," Bronwen whispered.

"I think she's happy to show off her cooking expertise," Evan said. "She certainly knows how to cook."

"And it's lucky we came early," Bronwen said. The door opened, sending in a cold breeze that ruffled napkins and flickered candle flames. A noisy party of four people, English by the sound of them, came in, and almost immediately a lone man followed, choosing the small table on the opposite wall.

Madame Yvette bustled from table to table, beaming.

"You liked your Welsh lamb zee way I cook it?" she asked as she came to remove their plates.

"It was wonderful," Evan said as Bronwen nodded agreement. "The best meal I've had in years."

"Ah, you wait for zee dessert!" Her eyes sparkled like those of a naughty child keeping a secret. "I will take zee orders from zese people, zen I return."

She disappeared, then came back with a bottle of wine for the lone man and a bottle of champagne for the noisy party of four. Then she wheeled a trolley up to Evan and Bronwen's table.

"I make for you my special crêpes Suzette," she said. There was a small spirit stove on the trolley. "I bring zee Cointreau," she said, and crossed the room to the bar. The man at the far table beckoned her. She bent to him, had a brief conversation, then came back to Evan's table, stopped, stared into space and then said, with an embarrassed laugh, "Ah, zee Cointreau. I forget my head next!" and crossed the room again.

Evan watched her as she came back and fumbled with the bottle top.

"Here, let me," Evan said.

"Sank you. I don't know why I can't . . ." Her voice was shaking.

Evan glanced back at the man in the alcove, but he was calmly sipping a glass of red wine.

She folded a crêpe and placed it in the pan. She tipped up the bottle and liqueur came splashing out onto the tablecloth and floor. "I am sorry," she said. "So clumsy of me."

"Is something wrong?" Bronwen asked.

"No. No, nozzink at all." She shook her head. "Now we make zee flame . . ." She lit a match. Flames shot high from the pan, licking out so that Evan could feel the heat. Bronwen stared at him in alarm. Madame Yvette stepped back with a muttered *"ooh-la-la!?"* Evan reached for his water glass but almost immediately the flame died down again.

"Voilà!" Madame Yvette tipped the first crêpe onto a plate and put it in front of Bronwen. She completed the rest of the crêpes with no more conflagrations.

"What was that about?" Bronwen whispered as Madame Yvette made a hurried retreat with the trolley. "She was upset about something, wasn't she?"

Evan nodded. "Maybe someone complained about her cooking. They're supposed to be temperamental, these famous chefs."

They lingered over coffee, so wrapped up in their conversation that Evan was quite surprised when Bronwen whispered, "I suppose we should go. She might be waiting to close up."

Evan looked around and saw that they were the only patrons left. They paid the bill, exchanged pleasantries, and went.

"Brilliant meal," Bronwen said. "I can see now why she was nominated for the award."

"She certainly can cook," Evan agreed.

He felt relieved and content as he finally let himself in to Mrs Williams's house just before midnight. The evening had gone smoothly. Bronwen had forgiven him, Madame Yvette seemed to have accepted the fact that he had a girlfriend, and the food had been outstanding — even if his pay cheque. wouldn't stretch to that kind of meal again for a while.

He was halfway up the stairs, tiptoeing with his shoes in his hand so that he didn't disturb Mrs Williams, when the phone rang. Evan ran down again and caught it on the second ring.

"Constable Evans? This is the dispatcher at HQ. We've just had a 999 call about another fire. The chief thought you should be there, since it's not too far from the other arson fires we're investigating. He's calling in Sergeant Watkins, too, and Sergeant Potter."

"Right," Evan said, slipping his foot back into a shoe as he spoke. "Where is it?"

"Just down the hill from you, I gather. The old chapel that's now a restaurant."

* * *

A few minutes later Evan was back outside Chez Yvette. Flames were shooting up at the rear of the building, silhouetting the arched roof and illuminating the tall arched windows. The fire brigade had obviously arrived just ahead of him and men were rushing to hook up hoses.

Evan pushed his way to the nearest fireman through the small crowd that had gathered. "Where's Madame Yvette?" Evan shouted above the roar and crackle of the inferno. "Do we know if the building was empty?"

The fireman glanced up, recognized him and went on dragging out lengths of hose. "She got out all right. She had to — apparently she called from a neighbour's house to give the alarm."

"Where is she now?"

"Haven't seen her." The young man sounded tense.

"And there was no one else inside?"

Captain Jones overheard as he ran past. Rivulets of sweat were running down his soot-smudged face. "Oh, Constable Evans — you got here pretty quick. There was no one in the restaurant. The front door was locked. I had to break it down and the place was empty. I couldn't get into the kitchen, though. That was already completely involved. They said she didn't have any kitchen staff working back there?"

"No, she did everything herself."

"That's good." He turned back the men who were dragging the hose. "We'll go straight in from the top, boys. The roof's already gone at the back."

Evan stepped out of the way to let the firemen work. He scanned the crowd but couldn't see Madame Yvette. "Do you know what happened to the French lady who owned the place?" he asked a couple of local youths. "Did she get taken to hospital?"

"No, my mam took her down to the pub — the Vaynol Arms down the road. She was really upset."

"So she was okay? Not burned at all?"

"Just crying a lot, as far as I know," the boy said.

"You're sure she was all right?" a man in a cloth cap asked. "This is a terrible thing to happen. I can't say we wanted her here, but I wouldn't have wished this on my worst enemy."

"And you are?" Evan asked.

"Owen Gruffudd. I own the Gegin Fawr. The café down the hill. We're neighbours."

Evan looked at him with interest. Neighbours and rivals, he thought. But Mr Gruffudd looked truly distressed. Evan would keep the name in mind for future reference, just in case.

Before he could head down to the pub, two cars drew up almost simultaneously. Sergeant Watkins got out of one and Peter Potter out of the other. They looked at each other with obvious distaste.

"No need for you to have been called out, Watkins," Potter snapped in his flat southern voice. "I can handle this. You can bugger off."

"My DCI. told me to come, and if he says jump, I jump." Watkins walked past him to Evan. "I see they got you out of your bed, too. What news?"

Evan shook his head. "Not much. The restaurant was already shut when the fire started. The owner must have got out through the back door, gone to a neighbour's house and called the fire brigade. I was on my way to get a statement from her."

"I'll come with you," Watkins said. "We'll let wonder boy get on with his job." He glanced at Peter Potter, who was already prowling around the building. "With any luck a wall will fall on him."

The Vaynol Arms was a long, whitewashed stone building about a quarter of a mile down the road. Madame Yvette was sitting on a bench close to the fire with a glass of brandy in her hand. She wore a black raincoat over her satin robe, pulled up high around her neck as if she was cold. Her face was hollow and tear-stained but her hair was still elegantly piled on her head. She held out a hand imploringly to Evan. "Zay want to get rid of me and now zay succeed." Her voice cracked. "Who would do such a wicked sing, Mr Evans, eh?"

"You have reason to think it was set deliberately, Madame?" Watkins asked.

Yvette gave an expansive shrug. "Why should my restaurant burn down? Zay send me zee warning notes, *non*?"

"Did you see anything suspicious at all tonight? Did anything unusual happen?" Watkins asked.

Yvette shook her head. "Nossing. It was a good evening. Almost full, *n'est-ce pas?* Constable Evans can tell you. He was zere."

Watkins grinned. "Moving up in the world, eh, Evans? French restaurants now, is it?"

"This was the first time, sarge," Evan said. "We were the last customers to leave, just before ten."

"So tell me when you discovered the fire, Madame."

Yvette shrugged again. "All was well when I close up for zee night and I finish cleaning zee kitchen. Zen I am watching zee television and I must have fallen asleep in my chair. I wake to smell zee smoke and see zee flames at zee bottom of my stairs. I put my coat over my 'ead and run down zee stairs to zee back door. I am lucky to get out alive!"

Evan cleared his throat. "You say you fell asleep watching the telly. Is there any chance you were smoking and a cigarette could have dropped out of your hand?"

"Then 'ow could the flames be downstairs and not upstairs wiz me?" she demanded. "And anyway, I am trying to quit. I tell you, someone wants me to go."

"But you had no warning?" Evan asked. "No threatening phone call tonight? No note?"

"Nossing!" Tears started rolling down her cheeks again. "Whoever did zis is a monster. He ruins my life. He takes all I have worked and slaved for."

Watkins put a hand on her shoulder. "You get a good night's sleep. I'd imagine they've got rooms here, haven't they, Evans?"

"Oh yes, sarge. I don't suppose they're fully booked at this time of year. I'll go and find out."

"There you are, then," Watkins said, patting Madame Yvette on the shoulder. "Constable Evans is going to arrange for you to stay here tonight. We won't disturb you anymore. We'll come back in the morning." He motioned for Evan to follow him.

The fire had died down to a dull glow as they walked back together. Their footsteps echoed in the clear night air.

"If it was as she suspects," Evan began, "then they've gone one step further."

"What do you mean?"

"I mean they've always been careful to target empty buildings before."

"Either that, or we're not dealing with the same perpetrators," Watkins suggested. "This might be some kind of private vendetta. What do you know about this Madame Yvette?"

"Almost nothing," Evan said. "She just arrived here about a month ago. I know she was married and her husband died, and they once had a restaurant in the South of England. And I know she went to the Cordon Bleu school in Paris. That's about it."

"Where have you two been?" Potter demanded as they approached the smouldering remains.

"Interviewing the owner of the building," Watkins said. "Needed help, did you?"

"There's not much I can do until I can get inside and take samples," Potter said. "But from what I can see, I'm inclined to suspect we're not dealing with the same serial arsonist. It wasn't the same method, for one thing. This fire started at the back of the building. The front door was almost untouched."

"The kitchen was at the back," Evan pointed out.

"Which makes me wonder if it wasn't just a simple accident," Potter said. "Maybe she went to bed and left the gas on. Maybe tea towels were drying over the fire and one of them fell down. It happens all the time."

"Only this was a very modern kitchen," Evan said. "I didn't see any kind of open fire."

"So — there are plenty of other ways. She could have left a pan of fat cooking. She could have been smoking a cigarette. Anyway, we'll know for sure in daylight. In the meantime, Constable, I want you to get a list of everyone who was in the crowd tonight. Compare it to the two previous crowds. If anyone was in all three, I want them fingerprinted. Got it?"

"Yes, sarge," Evan said.

"Oh, and Constable. I want you to remain on duty here until I can get a bloke sent up from HQ to stand guard tonight. We don't want to find trespassers have been mucking it up."

"Right you are, sarge."

"Bloody little Hitler," Watkins muttered as Potter went back to his car. "Who does he think he is?"

Evan grinned. "God?" he suggested.

Watkins clapped him on the shoulder. "See you in the morning then, boyo. I'll get on the phone and make sure you're not stuck up here too long."

"Thanks." Evan smiled grimly. "I suppose I better get started on those statements, then." He pulled out his notebook and approached the nearest members of the crowd. The fire was now more or less out but a thick, cloying smoke hung in the air. People were already moving away to their homes. Evan yelled for everyone to stay put. He started with Mr Gruffudd from the Gegin Fawr. The man still looked quite shaken. He'd been drinking in the bar at the Vaynol when someone had come in to say the restaurant was on fire. Several men from the village had been there with him all evening — Evan got their names.

As he worked his way around the crowd he almost bumped into a bicycle.

"Terry?" Evan grabbed at the handlebars. The young boy looked alarmed, then managed a grin. "Hello, Mr Evans. I got here too late this time. Pity they already put it out. Was it a big blaze like the others?"

"Pretty big," Evan told him, "but what are you doing out in the middle of the night? Does your mother know?"

A look of scorn crossed his face. "Of course not. I always sneak out down the drainpipe. I heard the fire engine, see, so I came to take a look. Have you found out who did it yet?"

"Not yet and don't go anywhere," Evan said firmly. "I've just got to get some names and addresses then I'm driving you home as soon as my replacement gets here."

CHAPTER 10

Next morning, when Evan's alarm woke him just before seven, he wondered why he felt so terrible — until he remembered that he didn't function well on less than five hours' sleep. It had been almost two when he'd left the burned restaurant and then he'd had to drop off young Terry. He'd also allowed Terry to climb back up the drainpipe so that his mother would never suspect his absence. Evan could remember a few forbidden things he'd done at the same age.

When he was in his room, he found himself too wound up to sleep so he started studying the lists of people he'd noted at each of the fires. The comparison of the lists had been disappointing. As far as he could tell, no spectators had shown up at all three fires, except young Terry, who was hardly likely to be able to get his hands on cans of petrol, or to carry them on his bike. So either they were looking at two different arsonists or this latest blaze was indeed an accident with unfortunate timing.

Evan put on his uniform and went downstairs. Nobody was stirring, which was unusual. Mrs Williams was always up at the crack of dawn. So he drove down the hill without the fortification of a cup of tea. It was another beautiful day, crisp and autumnal but so clear that the sky looked like an arc of blue glass and the colours of the landscape glowed.

The front of the former chapel was still in good shape, but the back was a ruin. The top floor and the roof had fallen in. Charred timbers and large roof beams lay haphazardly. Evan looked around for a note, but had found nothing when Sergeant Watkins arrived. Watkins looked as washed out as Evan himself was feeling.

"Solved the crime yet?" he asked, as he approached Evan.

"I haven't a clue this time. I've compared lists of people and nobody was at all three fires."

"I'm more inclined to think this was an accident in the kitchen," Watkins said. "I mean, if someone was outside, surely she'd have heard him. She says she was just dozing. She'd have heard a door being forced or a window breaking, wouldn't she?"

Evan stared, deep in thought. "Something's just struck me, sarge," he said. "She said the smell of smoke woke her. Why not the smoke alarm? This restaurant was brand new. It must have had a fire inspection before it got its licence to operate. So why didn't the alarms go off?"

"Good question," Watkins said. "Come on, let's have a little snoop before wonder boy gets here."

He started to pick his way through the rubble to the back of the building.

"Not much left back here," he commented.

Evan nodded. "This part used to be two stories. She had her living quarters in the old organ loft above the kitchen."

"That's why it burned so well." Watkins bent to retrieve a twisted cooking pot. "She had all those furnishings up there to fuel it."

"And the wooden floor and stairs, too." Evan stared down at the jumble of charred beams. There was nothing now to indicate that Madame Yvette's upstairs room had ever existed — no sofa or bed in the corner. Nothing but blackened ashes.

Something caught his eye beneath a half-consumed roof beam. He moved closer and looked again, then he nudged Sergeant Watkins. "Is that what I think it is?"

They were looking at a charred hand.

"Oh God," Watkins muttered. "Here, help me lift this beam."

The two men were struggling to move it when they heard a shout behind them.

"'Ere. What do you two think you're doing?" Peter Potter leaped from his car and stalked toward them. "I thought I told you to touch nothing until I'd had a look in the morning!"

"Yes, well, things have shifted a bit," Watkins said dryly. "It's moved from your territory to mine."

"Meaning what?"

"Meaning that it looks as if we've got a body under here."

Potter came closer. "Christ. You're right. Come on. Let's get these away."

The body lay sprawled amid the ash and mud. If it had been wearing clothes they had now melted into the charred flesh. It was hard to tell if it had been a man or a woman, impossible to believe that it had been a living person until recently. It reminded Evan of the Egyptian mummies he had seen on a long-ago visit to the British Museum.

"I thought she said she'd checked the place and shut up for the night?" Potter demanded.

"She was wrong, wasn't she?" Watkins pulled out his cell phone. "Don't touch the body, please, until Dr Owens has had a chance to take a look at it." He moved aside and Evans heard him requesting the Home Office pathologist.

While they waited, Evan was studying the way the body was lying amid the beams. "It looks to me as if he might have been upstairs," he suggested. "See how that one beam is under him."

"Not necessarily," Potter said. "If he'd been trying to get out when the top floor collapsed, a beam could have crashed in front of him and then he could have been struck or felled by smoke."

Evan nodded, appreciating this possibility.

"You weren't wrong in what you said last night." Watkins came back to join them. "This certainly is one step further, all right. Whoever it is has just moved from arson to manslaughter."

"If it is the same person," Potter said. "I've got the dog in the car, and I'll bring him out to take a sniff around, but I don't see any immediate evidence of the area being doused with petrol this time."

"Is it possible that this was the bloke who set the fire and then got trapped in his own blaze?" Watkins asked.

"It's happened before," Potter said, "but I'd have thought in this case it would have been simple enough to get out. There was a back door here, wasn't there?"

"Madame Yvette managed to get down the stairs and out of the back door after the fire started," Evan pointed out.

"And you thought that the bloke might have been upstairs, too?" Potter looked at him with sudden interest. "You're suggesting that she was in bed with someone and she got out and he didn't?"

"But then why wouldn't she have told the firemen right away that someone was possibly trapped up there?"

Potter shrugged. "Didn't want to ruin her reputation?"

Evan had to laugh. "She isn't that kind of woman. I don't know her well, but I can't imagine she'd be the type who would just leave someone to burn."

"The first thing is to find out who he was," Watkins said.

"You're sure it was a he?"

"Pretty big bones," Watkins said. "And look down here, where the beam was lying across his feet — that definitely looks like the remains of a man's shoe, doesn't it?"

Potter knelt beside the body. "If the beam was covering his foot there's a good chance the inside of the shoe might be intact. No oxygen will have reached it to go on burning."

Watkins took out a clean handkerchief and cautiously eased off the shoe. The inside leather at the heel was still brown, and in one spot, shiny. Watkins held it up so that Evans and Potter could both examine it.

"I think it says *Made in Spain*." Watkins's disappointment showed in his voice. "That doesn't tell us anything. All shoes come from somewhere else these days."

"If we take it to the lab, they could possibly identify the model of the shoe and where it was sold. But as you say, people buy their shoes all over the place these days. The wife stocked up in Italy last year."

"It says forty-six here, I think." Evan pointed at the numbers. "That's continental sizing, isn't it? That probably means it wasn't made for the English market."

"The boy's quick, isn't he?" Potter was half-mocking.

"Yes, he is," Watkins agreed. "So you're suggesting that the bloke was a foreigner?"

"Or, as Sergeant Potter says, he buys his shoes abroad," Evan added "Although I'd imagine you can buy imported shoes easily enough here."

"Not much to go on." Watkins sighed. "I suppose the next thing is to find out if anyone was reported missing this morning. If he was a local and he didn't show up last night, we'd have heard by now."

He pulled out the phone again. "Wonderful invention, these things, aren't they? Too wonderful sometimes. The wife knows where to find me when she realizes we're out of potatoes, or to check on why I'm late."

Potter brought out his dog and they moved around the ruin, examining burn patterns and taking samples. Evan waited for the medical examiner to arrive, glancing every now and then at the sprawled figure and trying not to feel pity. He'd been on the force long enough now. Why was he still so disturbed by death?

About half an hour later the white incident van pulled up beside Evan's car. The first person out was DI Hughes, Sergeant Watkins's boss and Evan's least favourite detective inspector. He didn't wait for the doctor to emerge from the other door, but strode toward the waiting group of men.

"So we've got a body this time, have we?" he called in his high, clipped voice. "I hope you and your wretched dog haven't disturbed anything, Potter."

"No sir." Potter's face was sullen. "Nobody's disturbed anything, except for taking the beams away to get to him."

"Ah, so he was covered in debris, was he?" Hughes peered down at the body.

"Yes sir. There were three big beams over him," Watkins said. "And some slates where the roof caved in."

"Ah, quite." He stared at the body for a long moment. "Poor devil," he said. "Not a pleasant way to die, I'd imagine. Look how he's grimacing. Any idea who he was?"

"No sir," Watkins answered. "I put in a call to HQ to see if anyone's been reported missing. Evans and I interviewed the restaurant owner last night. She gave no indication that anyone else might have been inside. She says she locked up for the night. The next thing she knew, she woke up to smell smoke."

"I suppose it's possible he was a customer trapped in the gent's loo," Hughes observed dryly.

Potter sniggered.

"It's not that unbelievable, Potter," the DI said. "If you'd grown up here like these gentlemen, you could attest to the fact that bathrooms tend to be on the primitive side and doors have a habit of jamming on you."

"But not in this case, sir," Evan said. DI Hughes's look implied that mere village policemen, like Victorian children, should be seen and not heard.

"Oh — so you've visited the bathroom in question, have you, Evans?" DI Hughes managed the ghost of a smile.

"No sir, but the whole place had been remodelled, and I was a customer there last night. My girlfriend and I were the last to leave."

Hughes began to look interested. "How long was this before the fire?"

"About an hour, hour and a half maybe."

"And you saw nothing out of the ordinary? No strange cars parked nearby when you left? Nobody hanging around?"

"No sir."

"Nothing else that struck you as any way unusual?"

"I don't think Evans goes to French restaurants often enough to know what's unusual," Watkins chuckled.

"There was one thing, sir," Evan said. "A man came in alone and after she spoke to him she was upset."

"Ah — now that's interesting," Hughes said. "That's definitely something to go on."

He broke off as Dr Owens approached, followed by two young PCs, one with a camera slung over his shoulder.

"Do you want me to start taking pictures, sir?" he asked, giving a friendly nod to Evan and Watkins.

"Yes, go ahead, Dawson. Try to get where he was lying in relation to the known plan of the building."

Dr Owens knelt beside the body. "Luckily the blaze wasn't too consuming," he said. "We still might learn something from this chap."

Evan shot him a look of admiration. "You can still do a post-mortem on a body like this?"

"Oh yes. I think we'll find that the internal organs are pretty much intact — nicely browned on the outside perhaps, but pink in the middle, like good meat."

A painful recollection of the lamb he had eaten last night sprang into Evan's mind. He wondered how pathologists could make jokes about their work.

"So you'll be able to get DNA samples?" Watkins asked.

"Yes, if we have anything to match them to. If the chap's not on anybody's file anywhere, we're none the wiser. I'd say we've more chance of identifying him through his teeth. He's got a couple of gold fillings. We haven't used those in Britain since the National Health came in."

"So you think a foreigner?" Hughes asked.

"That would be an initial guess." He turned to the young police constable. "Now if you'd bring the stretcher from the van, Thomas, we'll let Constable Dawson finish taking his pictures and then we'll get the body back to the lab."

As Evan helped PC Thomas slide the stretcher under the body, he caught the glint of metal below the hip. "Hold on a second. We might have something here," he called and dug out a coin. It was bent out of shape but the words *République Fra* were still legible.

"A French coin," Hughes said, taking it from Evan. "And right where his trouser pocket would have been, too. This confirms that he was recently over there at least. A Frenchman comes to visit a Frenchwoman and she fails to mention it? Either he slipped in without her knowing, or she's in this up to her neck. Get the body back to the van and then I'll go and talk to her myself." He handed the coin to Watkins, who dropped it into a plastic bag, then he brushed his hands clean. "All right boys, if Dr Owens has finished, you can take him away now."

"I can't do any more until I get him back to the lab," Dr Owens said. "Cover him up, Thomas, and get him to the van."

Evan helped the other constable carry the body. It felt surprisingly light as they carried it back to the van.

"I'll give you my report as soon as I can," Dr Owens said.

"And you get me your analysis as soon as you can, too, Potter," DI Hughes said, wiping his hands on a spotless handkerchief as he picked his way back through the debris. "Watkins, you might want to check local hotels to see if any guests didn't show up last night." He reached the van and opened the passenger door. "Frankly, I don't think it should be too hard to find out who he was. He must have got here somehow. Check for parked cars nearby and ask local taxi drivers."

"Right you are, sir," Watkins said.

Evan said nothing. He was used to being dismissed, sent back to his beat.

"I'll be getting back to Llanfair, then, sir," he said.

"Hold on a minute, Evans," DI Hughes said. "On second thought I'll go and talk to Madame Yvette myself right now. I'd like to see her reaction before she has time to hear the news from anyone else. Watkins, you can ride back in the van with the others and I'll take your car. Evans, you can show me the way."

"Yes sir." Evan tried to hide his pleasure. "It's just down here at the pub."

"Now Evans," Hughes began as they walked away, "tell me about this lone man last night. Could he have been our victim?"

"It's possible, sir. He came in at the same time as a party of four other people. He sat alone on the far wall. It was pretty dark in there so I didn't get a good look at him, but I'd say he was around forty, maybe, good-looking in a sort of outdoor way — with dark curly hair, greyish at the sides. He was wearing a leather jacket with a dark turtleneck under it."

"Foreign, do you think?"

Evan shrugged. "It's hard to tell where someone comes from these days. Everyone looks pretty much the same, don't they, sir?"

"And how did Madame Yvette react to him? Do you think she knew him?"

Evan considered this. "I don't think so, sir. She was at our table when he came in and she didn't react at all that I could see. She went over and took his order and brought him a bottle of wine. It was only later that he called her over and then she seemed upset. It might have been nothing at all. Maybe he complained about the food. Anyway, he left quite a while before we did and I don't think she even spoke to him again."

"As you say, it might have been nothing at all," Hughes said. "You've met her a couple of times. What's your impression of her?"

"Well, she'd had those two threatening notes," Evan reminded him. "She was very upset about them. My impression is that she's very proud of her cooking and she wanted to make a success of her restaurant."

"That's one ambition that's gone up in smoke now," Hughes said as they neared the long white building. "I'd imagine it would take her quite a while to start up again after this. If nationalist extremists are really responsible, I'm going to nail them good and proper this time. I don't like anyone burning down holiday cottages, but when it comes to destroying someone's livelihood . . ."

"And maybe killing into the bargain," Evan ventured.

"You've got a point there, Constable. They're looking at manslaughter at the very least this time." He went ahead and pushed open the studded oak door. "Oh, and Constable," he murmured as they stepped into the flagged hallway, "don't mention the body unless I bring it up."

Evan nodded then rapidly ducked his head as he stepped under a beam.

* * *

Madame Yvette was sitting in a dark oak booth, sipping dubiously at a cup of pale frothy liquid. She looked hollow around the eyes but her hair was still well groomed in her usual top-of-the-head style, and she had brightened her pale cheeks with rouge. She was wearing a garish red-and-purple Fair Isle jumper with a knitted brown scarf wrapped around her throat, which didn't enhance her appearance. She looked up with resignation as the publican's wife ushered them in.

"Good morning, Madame," Evan said. "I've brought Detective Inspector Hughes to have a word with you."

She looked up with hope in her eyes. "You have caught zee man who did zis terrible crime?'

"Not yet, Madame. What makes you sure it's a man?"

"What woman would do such a terrible thing? I sink it must be zee same man who write zee notes? You 'ave not caught him either?"

"We're still working on it," Inspector Hughes said. Evan noted his voice was even tighter and more clipped than usual. He obviously hadn't expected to be attacked. "And we're not at all sure that the notes were written by the same person. Our handwriting expert isn't convinced. And Forensics says it wasn't the same pen that was used."

"Zat ees interesting." Madame Yvette nodded, then took a sip of coffee and made a face. "Zay 'ave no idea how to make coffee." She put the cup down. "And you must excuse my appearance. Zay are very kind and lend me clothes, but . . ." She motioned helplessly at her Fair Isle arm. "I 'ave nozzing," she said simply. "All is gone, *n'est-ce pas?*"

"Have you been to take a look for yourself?" Hughes asked.

"I 'ave not yet been outside. Zay give me a pill to make me sleep. It ees very powerful, I sink. But I watch the fire from zee window 'ere last night. I sink not much is left after zat blaze."

"No, there's not much left, I'm afraid," Evan said.

"Now if we can just ask you a few questions," Hughes began. "You say the restaurant was closed and you locked up for the night."

"Zat is correct."

"Did you check the whole place? The men's toilet, for example?"

Dismay showed on her face. "I sink so. Now I am not sure. You are saying zat maybe someone — zee person who burn down my restaurant — was hiding in there?"

"It's a possibility," Hughes said. "He had to have got in somehow and if you'd already locked the doors . . ."

"Maybe he didn't come in," she said. "When zee cottage ees burned down, zay tell me zat zee fire ees started through zee letter box, no?"

"But your letter box was at the front door. That part of the building was least badly burned." Hughes paused. "You say you woke to smell smoke?"

She nodded. "I have my usual nightcap in front of zee TV. I must 'ave fallen asleep. Suddenly I am coughing. I hear zee crackling from downstairs. I look — *mon dieu*, zee kitchen ees on fire. Flames going up to zee ceiling. Zere ees no way I can put it out. I grab my coat. I put it over my 'ead and I rush down zee stairs. Luckily zee back door ees beside zee stairs, ozzerwise I would not have escaped."

"Excuse me, Madame," Evan interrupted. "Why didn't the smoke alarm wake you? I know this is a new business so you must have had a fire inspection?"

She looked flustered and embarrassed. "Ah, you see . . . I turn off zee smoke alarm." She looked from Evan to Hughes. "I know, it ees very foolish of me. But zay put it in zee wrong place. Every time I try and cook, zee smoke alarm go off. It drive me crazy so I turn it off. I call zee man to come and put it where it will not drive me crazy." She gave a very French shrug of resignation.

"So you smelled smoke and got out just in time," Hughes repeated. "And, as far as you know, you were the only person in the building at the time?"

"*Mais oui.*"

"You're sure about that?"

Her eyes darted suspiciously. "Of course. I tell you. Why do you ask zis?"

"No real reason." DI Hughes paused, drumming his fingers on the oak table for a moment. Then he looked up suddenly. "There was a man who came to your restaurant last night, Madame. He sat alone, according to Constable Evans. Was he someone you knew?"

She shrugged. "Zee customer? I never see 'im before in my life."

"But he said something to upset you?"

Her eyes darted to Evan for a second. Then she smiled and shrugged again. "It was nozzing really. 'E asked for lobster and I 'ad none. 'E said 'e was disappointed. 'E had heard how well I prepared lobster. So naturally I was upset. I am still trying to build up my reputation, Inspector. I have to give zee customers what zay want."

DI Hughes nodded and stared down at the table again. It was an old surface, much scratched, and decorated with graffiti like a school desk.

"Was he a Frenchman?"

Again the briefest wary look and another shrug. "We speak to each ozzer in English. It ees possible 'e 'ave an accent. I really can't remember everysing zat happen wiz every customer who come 'ere."

"Have you notified your insurance company yet?" Hughes asked.

"I will do it today, I suppose," she said. She gave a long sigh. "I do not look forward to zee days ahead. It ees not easy to begin again when you are a woman alone in zee world."

"You don't have a husband or family?"

"Neither, monsieur. My husband died five years ago. I ran our restaurant alone and zen I was very sick in zee hospital and zen I was recovering for about a year."

"Where was this restaurant?"

"On zee south coast, near Eastbourne. Do you know it?"

"I might have been there once. Sort of genteel place like Bournemouth where old rich people go to retire?"

She nodded. "Old rich people. You are right. My 'usband sink zat people 'ave time and money to eat at good restaurants."

"And did they?"

"Not enough of zem. And we were outside of town. Old people do not drive at night."

"So why come here?" Hughes asked.

She gave a tired smile. "I come where I can afford to buy property. And where zay do not yet 'ave too many French restaurants. After zis — I 'ave no idea where I go next."

Hughes got up. "I think that will be all for now, Madame. But please don't go anywhere for the time being. We'll need to talk to you again and I'm sure you want this whole thing cleared up as quickly as we do."

"But of course. Please do your very best for me, Inspector. I am counting on you." She held out her hand to him. For a second Evan thought that Hughes was going to kiss it, but he changed his mind and gave it a brief shake.

"You didn't tell her about the body, sir," Evan mentioned as they came out into the bright sunshine.

"No." Hughes smiled. "I thought I'd wait awhile after all. If she knows nothing about it, then no harm's done. If she does, then it might do her good to stew for a while." He squinted as he stared up at the green slopes. "She's a cool customer, Evans. She had an answer for everything, didn't she?"

"Either that, or she was telling the truth, sir."

"As you say. Oh well, time will tell, I'd imagine." He strode out briskly toward Watkins's police car.

CHAPTER 11

Llanfair was still quiet and deserted when Evan returned. No sign of Evans-the-Milk delivering or Evans-the-Post reading postcards or children running to school. He looked about him in bewilderment, wondering what could have happened, until he realized that it was Sunday morning. As he opened the car door he heard the sound of a distant church bell, mingling with the bleating of sheep on the hillside. Smells of Sunday morning fry-ups wafted from windows. Harry-the-Pub came out with a bucket and started washing down picnic tables and putting up umbrellas in the hope of catching late-season tourists.

It always surprised Evan that life could go on its normal peaceful way right next door to tragedy and violence.

Evan glanced at his watch — only nine o'clock. He felt as if he'd already done a day's work and by his reckoning it should be lunchtime. Then he remembered that he'd gone out without breakfast. No wonder his stomach was complaining. He expected he might be needed again on duty later in the day, so he'd better nip home while he could. With any luck Mrs Williams would have his normal Sunday breakfast waiting . . .

"Oh there you are, Mr Evans," his landlady greeted him as he put his key in the front door. "Treadful just, isn't it?"

"What is, Mrs Williams?" Evan asked. *Dreadful* was one of the few English words Mrs Williams often used, only she pronounced it with a *t*.

"They say there was a body in that chapel!" She spoke in a hushed whisper, even though they were alone.

Again Evan had to admire the efficiency of the Llanfair grapevine.

Evan saw no point in denying it. "How did you hear about it, then?"

"I saw Mair Hopkins when I went to get the newspaper." Mrs Williams leaned closer. "And she said that Charlie had been driving past to make an early delivery and saw the van and Dr Owens. He knew what that usually meant so he pulled up and watched and sure enough, they carried something out on a stretcher. Poor devil. Do they know who it was?"

"Not yet," Evan said. "They're still checking out missing persons, vehicles left parked overnight, hotel guests who didn't show up last night . . ."

Mrs Williams put her hand to her mouth. "*Oh esgob annwyl!* Deary me!"

"What is it?"

"Mair told me that Elen Prys was worried because her husband, Glyndaff, hadn't come home last night."

"Glyndaff Prys?"

"You know Prys-the-Farm down beside Llyn Gwynant on the way to Beddgelert? You know the white building you can see from the road?"

"Oh, right." Evan paused, thinking. "Maybe I should go down and talk to her. This Glyndaff Prys — is he the sort of bloke who often stays out all night?"

"Oh no. I don't think so. He's a good family man by all accounts. They've got five grown children, all fine young people. And they go to chapel . . ."

"Thanks, Mrs Williams," Evan said. "I'll go down right away." He looked longingly in the direction of the kitchen.

"But you never had your breakfast." Evan could have hugged her. "Can't you stop for a bite to eat first? I've got the kettle on the boil and Evans-the-Meat made some lovely sausages this week . . ."

"I wouldn't say no to a cup of tea," Evan said.

"And have your breakfast, too," Mrs Williams insisted. "Ten minutes won't matter, will it? And it is supposed to be your day off."

Evan succumbed. "I suppose you're right. Ten minutes won't make much difference."

Fifteen minutes later Evan was on the road, feeling full and content. Amazing what some rashers of good bacon and sausages could do for the soul!

Ty'r Craig was a square, solid farmhouse, well maintained with newly whitewashed walls and a good slate roof. It was nestled on a narrow strip of land at the bottom of a narrow valley. Rocky cliffs rose sheer on both sides, blocking the sunlight this early in the day. Two black-and-white border collies rushed out barking as Evan got out to open the gate.

"Meg, Gel, come here at once," a shrill voice called and the dogs obeyed, throwing suspicious looks at Evan as they slunk back to the farmhouse.

Mrs Prys was a round, middle-aged woman with the brown, leathered face of a farmer's wife. She wiped her hands on her apron as she greeted Evan.

"I know you. You're the policeman from up in Llanfair," she said. "You've come about my husband, have you? It's not bad news, is it?"

She went on wiping her hands, twisting the apron nervously as she spoke.

"No, it's not bad news. Have you reported him missing yet, Mrs Prys?"

"Not officially like. I've told a few friends and the word gets around, doesn't it? But I didn't like to call up the police and maybe make a fool of myself."

"Has he ever done this sort of thing before — stay out all night?"

"When he was younger, once or twice like when Wales beat England in the rugby at Cardiff Arms Park. But he's not the type. And he was only going to his club meeting."

"Club? What kind of club?"

"He belongs to a men's social club in Porthmadog. They meet once a month to play darts, dominoes, that kind of thing. They're mostly older farmers like Glyn."

"Have you called any other members of the club?"

She looked down at her feet. "I don't rightly know any names. Glyn never talked much about what he did and I didn't like to ask him. He's a very private person, Constable Evans."

"Do you know where this club meets?"

"Oh yes, I know that right enough. They meet at a pub called the Old Ship right by the harbour."

"I know it," Evan said. "I'll get on the phone to HQ and they'll send someone out right away, Mrs Prys. Don't worry. He'll turn up."

"I hope so." She choked back tears and started fiddling with her apron again. "I'm sorry. I'm that upset, I didn't even offer you a cup of tea. Why don't you come inside — the kettle's on."

"Thanks, but I just had my breakfast, and I'd like to get on this as soon as possible. We'll find him for you."

The dogs escorted him back to the gate and sat there, tongues lolling in silent laughter as he drove away. He was tempted to drive straight down to Porthmadog and take a look for himself, but he reminded himself sternly that he had no right to go poking his nose into other officers' territory.

When he got back to Llanfair, the village had more or less come to life. Men and women in their Sunday best were walking up the street to the two chapels. Evan spotted Evans-the-Meat, hair slicked down and wearing his dark Sunday suit, escorting his wife to Chapel Beulah.

"Hold on a second, Gareth," he called, running to catch up with him. "I need to ask you something."

The butcher looked annoyed, then gave his wife a gentle push. "You go on, Siân *fach*. Save me a seat. Constable Evans needs to have a word with me."

His wife opened her mouth to protest, then thought better of it. "*O'r gore.* All right," she said and hurried to join a group of women ahead.

The butcher turned to Evan. "You had another fire last night, so I hear," he said. "Haven't you found out who's starting all these fires yet"

"Not yet. But we will." Evan moved closer to the butcher. "Gareth, what do you know about a man called Glyndaff Prys?"

"The farmer, you mean?" The butcher looked surprised.

"Yes, do you know him?"

"I've met him a couple of times. I can't say I know him well. I've bought lambs from him. Why? You don't think he's anything to do with this?"

"You don't think he'd be a likely candidate to go around burning down foreigners' property?"

Evans-the-Meat laughed again. "Old Glyndaff? I don't think he'd hurt a fly."

"So he's not known for his nationalist sentiments then?"

The butcher stared up at the distant peak of Mount Snowdon. "Well, he's proud of being Welsh all right. But then so are a lot of us. That doesn't mean that we go around burning buildings."

"And what about a men's social club that meets at the Old Ship pub down in Porthmadog?"

"What about it?" Evans-the-Meat's voice was suddenly sharp.

"I'm just wondering if more might go on there than the occasional darts game?"

"I wouldn't know. I'm not a member personally." He started to walk on. "Sorry I can't help more."

Evan crossed the street with the feeling that possibly he was onto something. Evans-the-Meat was prone to ranting and raving and waving his cleaver around. This sullen dismissal might mean that he knew more than he was letting on.

Was it possible that a farmer from Nant Gwynant — a man with a round, red-faced wife and two laughing sheep-dogs — was also a terrorist who had somehow been caught in his own conflagration? It didn't make sense. Evan had been a policeman long enough to know that people who committed crimes didn't necessarily look like criminals. Anyway, it was out of his hands now. He'd pass on the information to Sergeant Watkins, who could act on it if he wanted to.

He was about to let himself into the police station when a large grey van roared past, belching smoke. Evan watched with interest as it came to a halt outside Chapel Bethel. Rev. Parry Davies leaped out of the driver's seat then opened the side door, assisting several large and elderly ladies out of the van and escorting them proudly into chapel.

Evan went into the station and pressed the HQ autodial button.

"Sorry, Sergeant Watkins isn't here," the young dispatcher said in an indifferent voice. "Can one of the detective constables help you?"

Evan hesitated. He wasn't exactly on the best of terms with the detective constables, who felt that he had no right to go poking his nose into murder cases. Then he reminded himself that Mrs Prys was down at Ty'r Craig farm, wiping her hands on her apron while she waited for news of her man. The sooner he was found, the better.

"All right, put one of the constables on, then," he said. "I need to speak to someone."

He had a frustrating conversation with DC Perkins, who couldn't have sounded less interested. It finished with a "Thanks Evans. We'll look into it and get back to you then."

Evan waited around at the station, reading the Sunday paper, then went home to a late lunch and still the phone didn't ring. He hoped it wasn't Sergeant Watkins's day off. He was sure the detective constables wouldn't call him.

By mid-afternoon he was feeling restless and unable to concentrate. A whole Sunday wasted when he could have been out hiking with Bronwen or even climbing again. Time for a stroll around the village to blow away the cobwebs. The clear morning had turned into a blustery afternoon with large woolly clouds racing in from the west. The wind was chilly, too, more seasonal for this time of year. It might even rain later and then things really would be back to normal.

Evan strode up the village street, past the row of shops and cottages. He gazed at the overgrown-chalet shape of the Everest Inn and wondered whether they'd come any closer to solving the fire there. It could easily have been a disgruntled employee, he thought. Major Anderson was a former royal marine. Evan didn't imagine he'd be too soft on his employees.

But then Potter had said that the method used for starting that fire was identical to the one at the cottage. Evan wondered if Potter had come to any conclusions about the restaurant fire yet. He probably wouldn't bother to pass them on to a village bobby. He didn't know why he felt so frustrated about this particular case. Usually he was content to leave the headaches to the detectives.

"Penny for your thoughts?" a soft voice asked as a light hand was placed on his arm. Evan jumped. "Oh Bronwen, sorry, I didn't see you."

She was smiling at him. "No, I could tell you were miles away. I was working in my garden and you walked right past me. So I decided you must have something pretty heavy on your mind. The latest fire, I suppose."

"I was just thinking about . . ." Evan hesitated. "Bronwen, do you think that a village constable is an acceptable job for—"

"For someone with your ability?" she finished for him.

He nodded, grateful that she understood.

"Usually it doesn't worry me when I'm left out but this time — I don't know why — I'm itching to be in on this investigation."

"Maybe because you fancy Madame Yvette?" A quick, teasing smile crossed her face. "Sorry. It's not funny, is it? I feel so terrible for that poor woman. I can understand that you'd like to get the case solved."

"What really bothered me was that I came up with a good lead and I had to turn it over to Detective Constable bloody Perkins — useless young clod. I had to repeat the information three times before he got it. So now I'm going through it all again, asking myself if I made the right choice coming here."

"I'm the wrong person to ask that question," Bronwen said. "When I got a place at university I was sure I was going on to get my PhD. and then I'd write brilliant papers proving that King Richard didn't really kill the princess in the Tower. Instead I wound up here."

"What happened to change your mind?"

She paused and tossed her heavy braid of hair over her shoulder. "I fell in love during my final year and we decided to get married. He was going on to postgraduate studies. Someone had to earn the bread and butter. The plan was that I'd support us while he got his doctorate and then he'd support me when he became a high-powered scientist."

"Only it didn't work out that way."

"As you say, it didn't work out." She looked away, wisps of hair blowing across her face as she stared up at the peaks. Then she shrugged. "I'd taken a job in a nursery. I found that I loved it so much that I took my teaching certificate and came straight here, back to where I'd spent happy childhood summers."

Evan laughed. "It's funny, we've never talked about this before."

She looked up at him now. "I think that's because we both have things in our pasts that are better forgotten."

"We both came back to a place that made sense to us."

She nodded. "So why leave a good thing?"

Evan put his arm around her shoulders. "You're right. I should be content with my humble station in life and not want to—"

The last part of his sentence was drowned out by the roar of an approaching bulldozer. Barry-the-Bucket was coming through the village. Evan and Bronwen stepped up onto the grass verge as the huge vehicle rumbled past. As it drew level, however, Barry brought it to a halt.

"I was looking for you, Evans-the-Law," he yelled down. "Someone told me that you'd got your eye out for cars that might have been left overnight. Well, there's a maroon Toyota Camry in the car park outside the Vaynol Arms. It hasn't been moved since yesterday afternoon. I just thought I'd mention it because usually overnight guests go somewhere during the day, don't they? And it's a rental car, too."

"How do you know that?" Evan asked.

"Maybe because it's got a Hertz decal in the window," Barry said dryly. "It might be nothing, but I just thought I'd mention it."

"*Diolch yn fawr*, thanks a lot, man." Evan waved as the bulldozer continued with much grinding and clanking. He turned back to Bronwen with a delighted grin on his face. "How about that? And the DI walked right past it this morning! That would be a turn-up for the books if the car we're looking for has been sitting there all the time!" He squeezed Bronwen's shoulder. "Sorry, *cariad*, but I have to rush back and phone headquarters."

"Who was just saying he was content with his humble station in life?" Bronwen called after him.

CHAPTER 12

Later that Sunday evening Evan was watching the TV news when he saw Sergeant Watkins's car draw up. He hurried outside.

"Been doing some nifty pieces of detective work again, have you, boyo?" Watkins asked as he got out of the car.

"I just passed on information given to me," Evan said. "Was any of it any use?"

"Quite possibly," Watkins said. "Oh, we've found your missing man, by the way. Your farmer."

"You have? Where?"

Watkins grinned. "Asleep at someone's house in Porthmadog. He was too drunk to drive home last night so a fellow club member took pity on him and let him sleep on his sofa. He didn't wake until midday."

Evan let out a sigh of relief. "Well, that's good. I didn't really think that the body we found could have been him. For one thing if he was a farmer, he'd be too smart to get caught in his own blaze. I bet his wife was pleased to see him."

"You wouldn't think so by the way she yelled and shoved him into the house."

"And what about the car?"

"I'm coming to it." Watkins paused and leaned against his open car door. "That could prove to be what we're looking for. I've been on the phone to Hertz and it was rented at Dover by a Philippe du Bois. We've got his name, address, and credit card number. I looked up the town on the map and it's just across the Channel, about twenty miles from Calais. It should be easy enough to locate his dental records and make a positive identification."

"Philippe du Bois," Evan said thoughtfully. "I wonder if she knew him."

"She'd have to, wouldn't she? If a Frenchman dies in a Frenchwoman's restaurant in a remote part of Wales, it would be an amazing coincidence if they didn't know each other."

"Unless he was a customer who got himself trapped somehow, or he was up to no good in there."

"Came to torch the place and couldn't get out?" Watkins shook his head. "Nah. She has to be in on it. She knows something she's not telling us."

"Are you going to ask her?"

"I'm going to wait until we've got more details about him. It's a small town. It shouldn't be too hard to find out exactly who he was. Someone might even know what he was doing here. I've got young PC Davies in our new computer centre working on it right now — have you met her yet? She's a right little stunner, only don't tell her I said that. She's also the type who'd probably report me for sexual harassment if I mentioned that she's got great legs." He grinned.

"So she's going to contact France for us, is she?"

"She's looking up the address on the internet, so she tells me. Thank heaven it gets me out of phoning France. You know how the French always pretend that they can't understand you? At least that's how it seemed the only time I went over there. Have you ever been there yourself?"

"A couple of times. Once on a school trip to Paris and then once with a touring rugby side."

Watkins had his hand on the open car door. "I'm going to drop in at HQ on my way home and see if PC Davies has got anywhere yet."

Evan nodded. "Well, thanks for stopping by, sarge. It was good of you."

"What's the matter with you tonight?" Watkins asked. "You're very subdued. Woman trouble?"

Evan smiled. "No, nothing like that. I'm feeling frustrated that I'm sitting up here and the investigation's going on without me, if you really want to know."

"I told you to apply for plainclothes training, didn't I?" Watkins said. "You've only got yourself to blame, boyo. I knew all this peace and quiet would get to you in the end. It's not healthy."

Evan managed a smile.

Watkins started to get into the car, looked at Evan, then seemed to change his mind. "All right. Get in." He nodded toward his car. "You can come down to the station with me and see what our Glynis has turned up, if you're curious."

"Won't they think I'm poking my nose in where it's not wanted?"

"Of course not. You're keeping up with the future, that's what you're doing. We're all going to be computerized one day soon, if the DCI. gets his way. We won't need to talk to each other at all. We'll just sit in our offices and e-mail back and forth." He chuckled as Evan climbed in beside him. "I'd like to see them trying to teach me to use a computer. Our Tiffany tried and she said I was hopeless and that I'd never get it because I was too old."

Watkins manoeuvred the car through the zigzag bends until they passed the burned-out shell of the restaurant. "I wonder what Madame will do now? Rebuild, do you think?" he asked Evan.

"I suppose that all depends on what we find out, and what her insurance coverage was like," Evan said. "I can't help feeling sorry for her — a woman all alone, in a strange country. I'd imagine her life's been a struggle since her husband died, and now this."

"You always were too soft where women are concerned. What if we find out that she's a serial killer who lures men to their death and then torches their bodies?"

"I don't want to believe that she killed anybody," Evan said, "but I imagine we'll know more when we find out who Philippe du Bois was and what he was doing here."

* * *

"Thank God it's Sunday and we don't have to fight the traffic," Watkins commented as they negotiated the roundabout before the police station. Evan smiled. A traffic jam in Caernarfon meant five cars at the traffic light. Watkins drove into the police station car park and parked in an Officer on Duty space.

The grandly named computer centre was a smallish windowless room with two computers in it. It had, in fact, been a holding cell until quite recently. A young PC looked up and gave Watkins and Evan a dazzling smile. Evan had to agree with Watkins's assessment of her. She was startlingly attractive with an elfin face, long, copper-coloured hair and large brown eyes.

"I just paged you, Sergeant," she said in cultured English with barely a trace of Welsh accent. Most business was done in English at the Caernarfon Police Station, where not everyone came from Welsh-speaking Snowdonia. "I think I've located your Frenchman for you."

"Already? Glynis, you're brilliant."

Her fair skin flushed red. "Oh, it's quite simple, really. They have a website that pinpoints any address on a map," she said. "Do you want to see it?"

She punched several keys and zoomed in on a succession of maps until a street map appeared. "I think you're going to find this interesting," she said. The final screen was a detailed street map of a small town. "This is it, isn't it?

Abbeville, Seine et Oise? And there's the street number you want," she said, pointing at it.

Watkins leaned closer and stared at the screen. "*Hôpital?* Does that mean the same thing as hospital in English?"

"I'm sure it does. That's why I thought you'd be interested."

"The address Philippe du Bois put on his Hertz rental agreement's a hospital," Watkins said turning to Evan. "Oh, this is Constable Evan Evans by the way. I don't know if you two have met. WPC Glynis Davies, Evans."

PC Davies flashed him another dazzling smile. "I've heard about you, of course," she said.

"Nothing good if it was from the sergeant here," Evan quipped to hide his embarrassment. He didn't think he'd ever learn to handle praise or admiration.

"They say you're a whiz at solving tough cases," she went on. "Have you got this one figured out yet?"

"We don't even know if we're dealing with a crime," Evan said. "It could turn out to be a tragic accident — an innocent person trapped in an accidental fire."

"But you don't really think so?" She turned her large brown eyes on him.

"The restaurant owner swears she was the only person in the place and she cleaned up before she went to bed. She does smoke, so it's possible she left a cigarette burning somewhere, but—"

"But you don't think so?"

"I'd just like to know what the body was doing in the building."

"So how are we going to find out why Mr du Bois gave his address as a hospital?" Watkins asked.

"He could work there," Evan suggested. "Maybe he's a resident doctor."

"Why don't you just pick up the phone and call them?" Glynis Davies suggested. "I can find you the number easily."

"Call France?" Watkins looked horrified. "Just like that? I don't speak the lingo. I wouldn't know what to say."

PC Davies sighed. "All right. I'll do it for you, if you like. Hold on while I find the number . . ."

"You speak French, too?" Watkins asked.

"Yes. Pretty well, actually. I did French A level and I spent a summer in France on an exchange. It was a lot of fun. I was in a little village in the Alps and then in Paris . . ."

"There's no end to the girl's talents," Watkins muttered to Evan with admiration in his voice. "How come you're wasting all this in a police station?"

She blushed again. "I've always been interested in police work. I'd like to be a detective someday. It must be very exciting."

"Most of the time it's just plain boring," Watkins said, "but it does have its moments."

"Like this drug stakeout they're doing at the moment?" She saw the horror on his face. "Oh, don't worry. I only know about it because DI Hughes asked me to check on some internet addresses for him." She looked at the screen and smiled. "Ah, here we are. Phone number for the Hôpital Bernard. Do you want me to dial it?"

She didn't wait for Watkins's answer but started punching numbers on the phone. After what seemed like a long wait Evan could hear a muffled *"Allô?"* on the other end of the line.

"Bon soir. Ici le gendarmerie du pays de Galles. North Wales Police, yes. *Je cherche un homme qui s'appelle Philippe du Bois,"* Glynis said in correct, if Anglo-sounding French.

Evan watched her nod as a torrent of French escaped from the other end of the line. *"C'est vrai?"* She covered the mouthpiece and turned to Watkins. "He's a patient in the hospital."

"He's there? Right now? Ask if we can speak to him."

"Puis-je parler avec lui?"

They waited while the voice at the other end of the line babbled and her expression changed from excited to puzzled. Then she said, *"Ah, oui? Je comprends. Merci bien, mademoiselle. Au revoir,"* and put down the phone.

"Well?" Watkins demanded. "Was he there or not?"

"Oh yes. He's there, all right." She sounded shocked. "It's a mental hospital. He's been a patient there for ten years and he doesn't communicate with anyone."

* * *

"Back to square one," Watkins said. He lifted the heavy china mug and took a long gulp of tea.

He and Evan were sitting together in the station cafeteria, almost deserted at six o'clock, at a time when shifts changed and the day staff had gone home.

"Not exactly square one," Evan said.

"We still have no idea who our body is. I suppose it's safe to assume he's the same person who rented the car, but where do we go from here? We know he rented the car under a false name, and he had a credit card in that same false name — which must indicate he was going to considerable lengths not to be identified."

Evan poured a generous amount of sugar into his own tea. Somehow it helped to dilute the industrial strength of the police brew. "Also that he knew that the real Philippe du Bois was safely locked away in a mental institution."

Watkins nodded. "Good point. So it must have been someone who knew the real Philippe well — either a relative or a close friend . . ."

"Or someone who had worked in the hospital."

"Either way, we should be able to track him down. I'm going to see if our little language and computer whiz can get back in touch with the hospital in . . . whatever that French place is called. They should be able to come up with a list of relatives, visitors, and hospital workers who have left within the past couple of years."

"Of course, we've no way of knowing how long he's been carrying on this scam," Evan pointed out. "It might have been working beautifully for years."

"But why? If you're disguising your true identity you're on the run. Usually blokes on the run eventually slip up and get caught. My guess is he took the identity to come over here and . . ." Watkins paused, searching for inspiration. "Do whatever he had to do."

He drained the mug of tea. "Filthy stuff," he said. "If a policeman ever dies of food poisoning, that tea urn should be the first thing tested."

They were just leaving the cafeteria when DI Hughes emerged from his office. "Ah, Watkins." His voice echoed down the vinyl hallway. "I was just about to send somebody to find you. Come into the briefing room. I've got Dr Owens here. He's completed his findings." He noticed Evan for the first time and his eyes registered surprise. "What are you doing here, Evans?"

"Constable Evans located the car we've been looking for, sir," Watkins said. "We were just checking out details of its owner at the computer centre."

"Were you? Good man. Find out anything?"

"Only that he rented the car under a false name — the name of a mental patient in a hospital in France."

"Most interesting. You can brief us on it after we've heard what Dr Owens has to say." His gaze skimmed over Evan again. "You'd better come along, too, Evans, since you're looking into this car business and you're the one most familiar with the scenario."

He strode down the hall with Watkins and Evans in tow. Dr Owens was standing at the front of the briefing room. The two detective constables were sitting with notebooks at the ready. They glanced at Evan with a certain amount of surprise as he followed the other officers into the room. Watkins sat near the back of the room. Evan perched on a chair behind him.

"Sorry to keep you, Doctor. Please go ahead." DI Hughes pulled out a chair beside the doctor, facing the other officers.

Dr Owens cleared his throat. "I have completed a post-mortem on an unidentified man whose partially burned remains were discovered early this morning in the ashes of a fire at the Chez Yvette restaurant, Llanberis Pass. Probable age of the victim between thirty and forty, based on bone density and tooth condition. I was not able to determine ethnicity because skin and hair were burned too badly. Height about five feet eleven to six foot.

"The internal organs were as I suspected — in fairly good condition, considering what they'd been subjected to. He hadn't eaten in a while, by the way, which probably indicates he wasn't a restaurant patron. A good amount of alcohol in the system, though. Also my examination of the lungs showed no evidence of smoke inhalation."

He paused at a gasp from someone in the audience. "I take it you all appreciate the significance of this. This man was dead before the fire started."

"Any idea how he died?" Hughes asked.

"I couldn't find any traces of toxic substances in the body. I examined the heart to see if he had, in fact, died of natural causes. The exterior of the heart was — um — pretty well cooked, but contained less blood than I would have expected. On closer examination of the wall of the heart, it appeared to have been punctured."

"Due to the heat of the fire?" Watkins asked.

"No. In my estimation, I'd say he was stabbed in the chest with a rather large knife."

Evan felt his own stomach lurch.

DI Hughes rose to his feet. "You realize the importance of these findings, don't you? We're not dealing with a victim caught in a tragic fire anymore. We're dealing with a murder and a fire most probably set deliberately to cover it up."

CHAPTER 13

"You see, I told you that bloody Frenchwoman had her answers down too pat," Inspector Hughes said. The meeting had just concluded but the DI had held Watkins and Evan back as the room cleared. "I thought she was a cool customer." He perched on the edge of the nearest desk. "I'd always wondered what would make a Frenchwoman — and an outstandingly good cook, so we understand — come to a place like this. Now we know. She had something to hide." He wagged his finger at Evan. "And the chappy you saw had obviously tracked her down. He looked up inquiringly at Evan. "She said her husband was dead didn't she? Maybe this man had come to blackmail her, maybe to threaten her. In either case she was desperate. She grabbed a knife and killed him to shut him up. Then she panicked and set fire to the place. Only the fire didn't do its job."

"If she wanted the fire to burn up the body, why did she sound the alarm so soon?" Evan asked. "Why not slip out and wait until someone else called the fire brigade? One of the village boys told me that she had run to his mother and given the alarm."

Hughes nodded. "Of course, I'm just presenting one scenario. I'm not saying that she's guilty. But we have to go with the most likely suspect first, don't we? She claims she was the only person in a locked building." He paused, then sighed as he struck his fist against the palm of his hand. "Damn and blast. The last thing I need on my plate is a murder investigation right now. I'm supposed to be deploying maximum manpower for Operation Armada — a directive from the commissioner himself. He thinks it will be a feather in our cap if we manage to shut down a major point of entry in the drug trade, and I have to say I agree with him. But how can I stake out every possible landing point in our territory when we've got a murder to solve? I just don't have the manpower." He slid off the desk and brushed off his hands. "You'll have to do the spadework, Watkins. Find out who the man was and what connection he had to Madame Whatshername."

"Very good, sir," Watkins said.

"Get Evans here to give you a full description of the man he saw in the restaurant," Hughes went on.

"Excuse me, sir, but didn't Dr Owens say that the man probably wasn't a restaurant patron?" Watkins interrupted.

"I didn't notice him eating anything" Evan said thoughtfully, "only drinking red wine."

Hughes nodded. "It's still worth pursuing. Get his description, and the dental charts that Dr Owens has compiled for us, over to the French police ASAP. We may well find that he's wanted over there. It's not completely inconceivable that this is somehow tied in with the drug traffic. Who knows, maybe they selected her restaurant as a drop-off point."

"Maybe she set up shop there for that very reason, sir," Watkins suggested.

DI Hughes's face lit up. "Now, that's worth pursuing. Find out everything you can about her, Watkins. See if the French police have anything on her. And let's see what she's got to say for herself now."

"Do you want her brought in, sir?" Watkins asked.

"No, I think we'll wait awhile. We can't hold her on what we've got, and I don't want her getting the wind up and rushing back to France. Let's see if we turn up any more concrete evidence first. I'm sending up a lab team right away to go through the rubble and bring in anything that could be a possible murder weapon. I don't think we've got much hope of fingerprints after a fire like that, but you never know."

"Excuse me, sir," Evan said cautiously, "but if she was the chef, wouldn't her fingerprints be on all the knives?"

"Precisely," Hughes said. He looked delighted that he had scored a point on Evan, whom he had never quite forgiven for solving a couple of murders. "We'd expect to find her prints there. It would be other prints that would be of interest to us. Our legal system does assume a person innocent until proven guilty, you know, Evans."

"Yes sir," Evan said, suitably squashed.

The inspector headed out of the door, with Watkins and Evan following at his heels, like young doctors in the wake of a famous surgeon.

He paused outside his office door. "You know, I've just changed my mind. I think I'll go and talk to her right now. Evans, you can come with me. It's your territory up there. We won't charge her with anything yet, but we'll fingerprint her. Let's see if we can rattle that composure when she finds what we know about the body. Watkins, get onto France. Come along, Evans. It's just possible we're onto something really big here."

He swept out like a ship in full sail. Evan had to break into a trot to keep up with him.

* * *

"It's treadful, just, Mr Evans," said Mrs Williams when Evan came home, weary and emotionally drained, shortly after eight o'clock.

Evan looked at her warily. Surely it wasn't possible that even Mrs Williams and her spy network had managed to hear about the pathologist's findings and the evidence of murder that had been given in a closed room.

"What is, Mrs Williams?" he asked, taking off his cap and hanging it on the hook in the hall.

"The way they make you miss your dinner all the time. There's Sunday joint in the oven for you and now it's spoiled. I've never heard of such a thing — making you work on the Sabbath like this and keeping you from your leg of lamb, too. I'm going to have a word with the chief inspector down in Caernarfon and tell him that he's working you too hard."

"I really don't mind, Mrs Williams." Evan felt himself becoming hot around the collar as he visualized Mrs Williams lecturing the DCI. He could imagine the old man's remarks only too clearly. "It's all part of the job, you know. If something comes up, then I have to be on duty."

"I suppose you're still looking into that poor man burned in the fire. Do they know who he was yet?"

"Not yet," Evan said.

"But I heard that Barry-the-Bucket found his car for you. A rental car, they say it was, not a local at all. *Diolch am hynny.* I mean, you expect foreigners to go around killing people, don't you?"

"Not usually," Evan muttered as he followed her into the kitchen. An appetizing smell of roast lamb and onions was coming from the oven. A less appetizing smell of overcooked cabbage wafted from the stovetop.

Evan sat and let Mrs Williams put a heaped plate in front of him, but for once he didn't have much appetite. The DI's interview with Madame Yvette had left him upset and confused. He knew that everything pointed to her guilt, or at least to her involvement, but he didn't want to believe that she was capable of a crime. Would a woman who was contemplating a major crime actually invite intimacy with a policeman, he wondered. What if he'd taken her up on her offer and they'd become romantically involved?

Then another, more chilling, thought came into his head. It was possible that the entire seduction was deliberate. Maybe she was just testing the local police presence to see what she was up against and what chance she had of getting away with murder.

Mrs Williams tut-tutted a lot as she took away his half-eaten meal. "I know it was overdone tonight, Mr Evans, but I tried my best. Is there something else I could get you instead?"

"No, nothing, thank you, Mrs Williams. It wasn't your food, I promise you. I've just got too much on my mind."

"Is there nothing else you fancy, then? A boiled egg or two? Some Welsh rarebit? A slice of my bara brith?"

Evan smiled at her. "I'm not about to starve to death, Mrs Williams."

But she was still shaking her head. "That's what comes of working you too hard. Look at you, so exhausted you can't even lift good food to your mouth. It's not right, that it isn't."

At that moment the phone rang.

"Dear me now, there it goes again. Not a moment's peace." She bustled down the hall to the telephone.

"Yes, he's here, but he's already had a long day and he needs his rest," Evan heard her saying before he managed to politely wrest the phone away from her.

"Evans here."

He heard a familiar chuckle on the other end of the line. "I'm glad to see you're being well taken care of, boyo," Watkins said. "Got you tucked up with a hot water bottle and a nice cup of cocoa, has she?"

"Give over, sarge," Evan began but Watkins went on. "You wait until you're married, boyo. I pity the poor girl that gets you. Spoiled rotten, that's what you are."

"Did you call just to tell me that, or have you got something important to say?"

"First I wanted to hear how the DI's interview went. Did he manage to make her break down and confess, then?"

"He didn't manage to get anywhere with her," Evan said. "She stuck to the same story. She swears that she was alone in the place and she woke to smell smoke. She's no idea who the man could have been. She also swears she never saw him before that night."

"It could all be true, of course," Watkins said. "If this is in some way connected to the importation of drugs, then she could have been instructed to open a restaurant and the bloke who got himself cremated could have been a contact whom she'd never seen before."

"And he could have run afoul of a rival gang," Evan suggested, he realized he was still trying to create scenarios in which Yvette was innocent of murder.

"You've got her prints and all her particulars now, haven't you? Well, that's a start. Bring them down first thing in the morning, will you? Our little computer whiz is going to scan them and send them across to the French police. They'll do a match-up on their computer and by the end of tomorrow, we'll know if she has a record."

"You'll probably find tomorrow is a public holiday in France," Evan commented dryly. "They seem to have at least one a week."

Watkins chuckled. "Lucky we discovered young Glynis speaks French. I thought I was going to have to use you."

"My French isn't so bad," Evan said. "I seem to remember I made myself understood all right with the barmaids in the French pubs."

"Oh well, you would, wouldn't you — I've noticed you and the ladies! The Don Juan of Snowdonia — that's what they call you."

"Cut it out, sarge. You know very well I do nothing to encourage them."

"Then it must be that innocent boyish face — it makes them feel motherly." He chuckled again. "I'll see you down here in the morning then. I hope the French police are going to be helpful on this, although I'm not counting on it."

* * *

First thing on Monday morning Evan delivered his information and fingerprints to PC Glynis Davies at the computer centre. Her face lit up when she saw him.

"This is so exciting. This is my first murder investigation!" She scanned the fingerprints, then took the sheet of paper and began typing the information into the computer. "You're not officially in the plainclothes branch, are you?" she asked, looking up shyly at Evan. "But I hear you're an absolute genius at solving murders."

"I've just been lucky. I've been in the right place at the right time." Evan felt himself flushing.

"It's more than that. You've obviously got a flair for it. Not everyone has. You should apply for a transfer to the CID. I've just applied for one myself."

"You have?"

"Yes, I know I've only just started, but I want to show them I'm keen to get on. Wouldn't it be fun if we did the training course together?"

Evan was imagining Bronwen's reaction to his taking a course with the gorgeous and gifted PC Davies.

"I think I'm quite happy where I am at the moment," he said.

Glynis sighed. "And I don't think the DCI. will approve my transfer either. I'm the only person who knows anything about computers so I suppose I'll be stuck here until I can train someone to replace me." She glanced at the screen. "Ah, good. At least we've got an acknowledgement from the French police. They will do their best to be of assistance to their English brothers. How nice." She looked up at Evan again, this time with an angry frown on her face. "I just wish everyone didn't think that Wales was part of England."

"Are you from around here?" Evan asked. He hadn't taken her for someone with strong Welsh sentiments.

"Oh yes. I was born in Llandudno. My father's still a doctor there."

"You don't sound very Welsh."

She grinned. "That's because I was sent to boarding school in England. My Welsh is rather rusty, but I can still *siarad Cymraeg tipyn bach*. What I need is practice."

He got her hint but pretended he didn't. "Any news yet from the mental hospital?"

"No, and I don't expect any for a while. It will take time to look through old visitors' books and trace relatives, won't it? And I'd imagine they're all overworked at a place like that. I think our best hope is the police. If either person has a record, then at least we'll know where to go from here." She got up. Evan noticed she was tall, with long slender legs in sheer black stockings. Her uniform skirt must have been a centimetre or two above regulation. "I haven't had any breakfast yet. I'm going for a cup of coffee."

"In the cafeteria? You're a brave woman."

She wrinkled her nose. "Good heavens, no. There's a little coffee shop within walking distance. They do a good cappuccino. Do you feel like joining me?"

A good cappuccino with Glynis was sorely tempting but Evan forced himself to say, "I'd like to, but I should be back in the village as soon as possible. I'm the only officer on duty up there."

"Some other time, then," Glynis said.

Evan nodded. He felt strangely unsettled as he drove back to Llanfair. Why should there be any harm in going for a cup of coffee with a pleasant colleague, he asked himself. Of course he knew the answer. He found her attractive. Did that indicate that he wasn't ready to be tied to one woman yet?

Back in his office, he pushed Glynis Davies firmly from his mind and got down to work. The day dragged on. The only phone call was from Mrs Powell-Jones complaining that the diesel fumes from the Parry Davies's new van were polluting the atmosphere and would be detrimental to the rare Snowdon lily. She intended to report this to the National Trust immediately.

Evan found himself wishing he was down at the computer centre, right on the spot when the news came through. He had no idea what was going on, stuck up here. For all he knew they could have identified Madame Yvette and the dead man by now. He was just locking up for the night when the phone rang. He hesitated, then unlocked the door again and picked up the phone on the fifth ring.

"I wondered where you'd got to," Watkins said.

"You almost missed me. I was knocking off for the day. It's five o'clock."

"It's all right for some who can keep civil service hours," Watkins said.

Evan ignored the barb. "Any news from France?"

"Yes and no. Typical bloody French, about as unhelpful as they can be. Listen to this. They can't find a prints match, but they point out that most departments aren't online yet. If she'd committed a minor crime or been fingerprinted outside of a big city, only the local police would have a record of it, so we'd have to search district by district. They suggest we call the local police in the relevant department."

"So much for international cooperation," Evan said. "And what about the mental hospital?"

"They're working on it. Which probably means it's at the bottom of a huge pile in somebody's in-tray."

"At least we know that she's not a major international criminal on the run."

"Or she's just too smart to have been caught yet," Watkins pointed out.

"So what do you do next? Have PC Davies call every police HQ in France?"

"I can't just sit here and twiddle my thumbs," Watkins said. This could take weeks. We've told Madame Yvette not to go anywhere. If she really is innocent we shouldn't put her life on hold like this. Of course, if she'd been a little more helpful . . . You know what I've decided? I'm driving down to the south coast to check for myself. If she had a restaurant down there, someone will know something about her."

"Good idea," Evan said. "Watson, wait. It just struck me that her last restaurant was on the south coast, in a very convenient position for the English Channel. And now this new restaurant is in a great location to receive drug shipments coming in from local ports. So maybe there *is* a drug connection after all."

"That's what I was thinking."

Evan chuckled. "Your sense of direction isn't too wonderful. Do you reckon you can find your way all the way down to the south coast by yourself?"

"No. Do you want to come with me?"

"Oh, right. I'm sure the DI would approve of that!"

"No, seriously. He told me to do what I have to. I think I have to find out for myself what happened to her last restaurant and why she moved here . . . and everyone knows I have the world's worst sense of direction. Which is why I need a driver."

"I'd come along like a shot, but they wouldn't let me leave this place unmanned for a couple of days."

"I'll talk to dispatch. They can cover for you if I think it's really important. You were the one person to have seen the mystery man at the restaurant and you've had the most dealings with Madame Yvette. I'll tell them I'll wind up in Carlisle if I drive myself."

"In that case," Evan said, feeling a surge of excitement, "when do we leave?"

CHAPTER 14

After he had hung up the phone, Evan sat at his desk, trying to collect his thoughts while his mind raced ahead, planning the trip and wondering about what they might discover. Adrenaline raced through his body. He was being allowed to play detective and he found it exciting — which must indicate that he should seriously rethink his future. Maybe the village had served its purpose in getting him over a very bad time. Perhaps now he had outgrown Llanfair and it was time to move on. When this case was over he'd give serious thought to applying for training so that he could work officially with Sergeant Watkins, as a fellow detective.

He came out of the police station to find the sun setting and the valley bathed in warm, rosy light. Snowdon and its sister peaks were etched in black, and small clouds that clung around them were tinged pink, like escaped candy floss. From high on the mountainside came the bleating of sheep and the barking of dogs as they rounded up their charges. The smell of wood smoke hung in the air and mingled with the smell of dinners cooking. From the field behind the village hall came the shouts of boys playing football.

Evan smiled to himself. It was in moments like this that he knew why he had come here. Instead of heading to his landlady's house, he turned left and walked up the village street. People coming home from work called out to him as he passed. Evans-the-Meat waved as he lowered the blind on his shop.

"See you in the Dragon, then?" Charlie Hopkins called as he drove past.

"You might," Evan yelled back.

He continued his walk. A motorbike roared past. When the driver stopped and took off his helmet, Evan saw that it was young Bryn, Charlie's grandson, who disappeared into his grandparents' cottage. It was nice the way he visited the old folks, Evan decided. This led him to thoughts of his own future. He tried to picture himself with kids and grandchildren someday, but when it came to concrete pictures of the future, his brain somehow switched off.

When he reached the school playground, he saw smoke curling from Bronwen's chimney. He decided he should pop in to tell Bronwen that he was making this trip. The news would soon be all around the village, and it wouldn't be right for her to hear from someone else.

Evan tapped on Bronwen's front door. Bronwen appeared wearing an apron and with flour on her hands. There was even a smudge of flour on her nose, which Evan found very appealing.

"Oh hello," she said. "You've just caught me in the middle of trying my hand at Madame Yvette's soufflé recipe. You wouldn't like to be a guinea pig, would you? I should warn you I've never made a soufflé before."

"All right." He stepped inside, hesitantly, as if somehow Bronwen must know of his encounters with Glynis. "Although I don't think I'm a soufflé kind of bloke."

"Real men don't eat quiche, eh?" She gave him a teasing glance. "Don't worry. I won't let it get around the village and ruin your reputation."

"Everything gets around this village," Evan said. He pulled out a stool at her pine kitchen table and sat.

"Oh, before I forget," she said. "There's a concert at the university in Bangor this Friday night. I'd like to go. I wondered if I could drag you along. It's harp music, and I know you're not madly keen on that kind of thing, but . . ." She looked at him, her blue eyes silently appealing.

"I'm sorry love, but I'm not sure if I'll be here. I've got to go to Eastbourne with Sergeant Watkins."

"Eastbourne? You mean the Eastbourne in Sussex?"

Evan nodded. "Madame Yvette's last restaurant was in that area. We're not getting anywhere with this investigation and she's not being overhelpful, so Sergeant Watkins decided to look into her background. And he's taking me along as his driver."

Bronwen grinned. "His driver! He's taking you along because you're better at solving crimes than any of their bloody detectives and they all know it."

"No, I'm not. I've had a couple of lucky breaks, that's all. Watkins is a good man. He's just a lousy navigator. He reckons he'd wind up in Carlisle if he went alone."

"I see." She was still smiling. "So what do you hope to turn up in Eastbourne, or is it all hush-hush?"

Evan shrugged. "We've no idea really. But you've heard that there was a body in the restaurant, I suppose?"

"My kids could talk about nothing else," Bronwen said. "Young Terry was absolutely thrilled, as you can imagine. He was full of theories about crooks and mafia and shootings. He said he saw a foreign man with a gun that night and he just knew he was going to blow up the restaurant." She shook her head as she scraped the last of the batter into a tall dish.

"A foreign man with a gun? He might have seen the same man we did, but I don't know where he got the idea that he saw a gun."

"His imagination, I suspect. That child lives for violence. I've recommended that his mother take him to a psychiatrist. It's verging on the unhealthy."

"I don't think it's too unhealthy," Evan said. "He's angry at his dad for walking out on them and this is his way of handling his feelings. But I agree he's a handful. I caught him out on his bike after the fire — and that must have been close to midnight."

"I know. He told me you drove him home. He was very proud of it. You're one of his current heroes, by the way. You and Charlie's grandson. When he grows up he's going to be a fireman and a policeman, so he says."

Evan smiled. Bronwen bustled around, clearing away cooking utensils and laying the table.

"Is there something I can do?" he asked.

She handed him the mixing bowl. "You can put that in the sink, and find us a bottle of wine."

"White or red?" Evan asked. "I'm never sure of what's proper."

"White with a soufflé, I'd assume," she said. "I think I've got an unopened Chardonnay in the fridge."

"All right." Evan found the bottle and set about uncorking it.

"So what do they know about the body? Have they identified it yet?" Bronwen asked.

"No. In fact it's quite a little puzzle for us."

"No identity, you mean?"

Evan nodded. "The only lead we have so far is an abandoned rental car, rented by a Frenchman under a false name."

He saw Bronwen react to this. "Evan, do you think it could have been that man who came into the restaurant while we were eating? He looked French, didn't he?"

"My thoughts exactly," Evan agreed. "But we've no way of proving it."

"There were some strange vibes going on between him and Madame Yvette at one point, don't you think? She nearly set fire to our crêpes Suzette." Then she paused and shook her head. "But he left before we did. We were the last ones there before she closed up, weren't we?"

"We were. But there was something going on between her and that man at one point. At least, the man said something that upset her, but she claimed it was just that he wanted lobster and she didn't have any."

"I suppose it could have been something as simple as that," Bronwen said. "What exactly do you know so far?"

Evan poured the wine and handed her a glass. "It's hard to know where to begin," he said. "The body was burned too badly for fingerprints. We've got a dental chart but you need to know where a person comes from before you can match up his teeth."

"Poor Madame Yvette," Bronwen said. "I've been thinking about her. It must be awful. She's lost everything and now there's a strange man dead in her restaurant. It must be like a nightmare."

Evan said nothing. He didn't think that he should let on that the body had been stabbed and that Madame Yvette had to be considered a prime suspect at this time. Nor did he want to suggest any kind of drug connection.

"So what will she do? Where will she stay?" Bronwen asked.

"She's staying at the Vaynol Arms at the moment," Evan said. "She can't go anywhere until this business is sorted out."

"But how miserable staying at a pub, with no clothes, no nothing," Bronwen said. "I'll look in my wardrobe and see if I've got anything that she could wear, and I'll ask the village women, too. I'd have her to dinner here, only I wouldn't dare cook anything for her . . ."

"You're a kind person, Bronwen," Evan said.

"Yes, I do have some good points, I suppose," she said, making him wonder yet again if the Llanfair spies were so good that she had already heard about Glynis.

"I wish you were coming down to Eastbourne with me. It would be fun."

"I don't think the police would fund naughty weekends." Bronwen tossed him a challenging look. "And three is definitely a crowd. You've got Sergeant Watkins to keep you company. Besides, I have to keep thirty kids in line and stop young Terry from blowing anything up—"

She stopped, open-mouthed. "Evan, you don't think . . . ?" she asked.

He picked up her thought instantly. "That he started the fires?"

She nodded.

"He was at all of them," Evan said thoughtfully. "It did cross my mind, especially since he seems so obsessed with violence at the moment." Then he shook his head. "I just don't see how it's possible. A little kid like him — where would he get a can of petrol? How would he lug it up the hill without being seen? And someone would surely have noticed him at the Everest Inn . . ."

"But you have to admit it's just possible," Bronwen said.

"Yes, it is possible." Evan took a meditative sip of wine.

"So what do we do?"

"I'm leaving with Sergeant Watkins in the morning," Evan said. "I think I'll have a little talk with Terry tonight before I go, just to be on the safe side — let him know what I'm thinking. That should act as a deterrent for a while. And when I get back, we'll pursue it further. If you could get me one of his school papers we can check his fingerprints against the note that we found."

He shook his head again. "I could believe he'd go around starting fires, but writing the note? That's the kind of thing that adults do, not kids."

Bronwen went over to the dresser. "I've got some papers I brought home to mark. Here — Terry's geography test. Nearly all right. He's a bright boy. He just needs direction right now — a good positive male influence." She looked at Evan.

"You're suggesting that I take him under my wing?"

"He could do worse," Bronwen said.

"You're always saying that I'm too ready to volunteer for things and we never have enough time together," Evan pointed out.

Bronwen shrugged. "I'd do a lot to make sure my kids turn out well."

Evan came around the table and slipped his arms around her waist, drawing her to him. "Did I ever tell you you're very sweet? Especially when you've got flour on your nose."

He kissed her nose gently, then his lips moved down to her mouth, not so gently.

"Evan," she protested after a long minute, "don't distract me now. The soufflé will burn!"

She laughed as she bent to open the oven. "Not bad for a first attempt," she said, bringing out a crusty brown mountain of soufflé. "Exactly like Madame Yvette's looked, in fact."

"I'm impressed," Evan said.

"I'm rather impressed myself." Bronwen's face was pink. Then, before she could cut into it, the soufflé began to sink.

"Oh," Bronwen said, her voice as flat as the soufflé had become. "I think I still have some practising to do."

Evan went over to her and wrapped her in his arms. "I'll bet it still tastes good," he said. "Let me pour you another glass of wine."

She managed a weak smile. "All right. I might as well drown my failures."

"You're streets ahead of me," he said. "I still can't boil an egg."

He picked up the bottle of wine, then stood with it poised in his hand, staring into space.

"Are you having a vision or something?" Bronwen asked.

"Something just struck me," Evan said. "I'm no wine expert, but even I know that you don't serve red wine with lobster. If that French bloke in the restaurant was planning to have lobster, he'd never have ordered a bottle of red wine."

"Who knows, maybe he intended to drink the whole bottle before the main course came," Bronwen suggested, then shook her head. "No, that would spoil his palette, wouldn't it?"

"Which meant that we've caught Madame Yvette lying about one thing . . ."

"She might have been flustered and said the first stupid thing that came into her head," Bronwen said. "I'm sure we've all done that in our lives."

"You? You've never said a stupid thing in your life."

Bronwen came over to him and snuggled against him. "You're rather nice, too, did you know that? I wish I could come with you to Eastbourne tomorrow. Take care of yourself and don't talk to any strange women, will you?"

Evan didn't linger over his meal and went in search of Terry Jenkins before it was completely dark. He made for the field where he had heard the boys playing earlier. The football game had ended and the boys were coming from the field, laughing and talking noisily. Evan looked for Terry among them, but he wasn't there.

"Have you boys seen Terry Jenkins?" he asked.

"Off on his bike somewhere, poking his nose into something, I suppose," one of the boys said.

"So he wasn't playing football with you boys?"

"He didn't want to be on our team," a second boy agreed. "Off on his own, like Gwillum said."

Evan came out to the street again and continued up the hill to the Jenkins cottage. He was about to go in, when he noticed a fleeting movement out of the corner of his eye. He sprinted across the street and found Terry crouching behind a garden wall.

"What are you doing, Terry?"

"Nothing, Constable Evans. I wasn't doing nothin'," Terry said, but his eyes darted nervously.

"You're in someone else's front garden, Terry. That's called trespassing, so don't tell me you weren't doing anything. This is Mr Hopkins's cottage, Terry, isn't it?"

Terry nodded. "I didn't mean any harm, honest, I didn't. It's just that . . . Bryn's here right now. You know, Bryn the fireman? I was just taking a look at his motorbike."

"Then why try to hide? There's nothing wrong with looking at a motorbike. So what were you really doing?"

His eyes darted nervously. "I was . . . just trying it out . . . that's all. I was sitting on the saddle, seeing what it felt like. I'm going to get a motorbike when I'm old enough."

Evan put his arm around the boy's shoulder. "Terry, you know you're asking for trouble, don't you? I know you, but if another policeman saw you getting on a motorbike, you know what he'd think, don't you?"

Terry nodded. "He'd think I was trying to steal it."

"Right."

Terry glanced back at the Hopkinses' cottage. "It's just that Bryn—" He broke off, unable to find the words. "It's pretty cool being a fireman, isn't it, Mr Evans?"

"Not very cool, I'd say," Evan said. "Pretty hot most of the time."

Terry grinned. "You know what I mean. Exciting — all those flames and walls crashing down and windows exploding . . ."

Evan steered the boy out of the Hopkinses' garden and across the street. "Terry," he said quietly. "I'm going to be away for a few days, working on a case. I want you to keep your eyes open for me, and make sure there are no fires while I'm away. You're pretty observant, so I'm counting on you, okay?"

Terry nodded solemnly. "Okay, Mr Evans. I'll do what I can." His face lit up. "Tell me about the body, eh, Mr Evans. Did you see it? What was it like — all frizzled up and cooked and gross-looking?"

Evan had to smile. "Pretty gross-looking, Terry."

"I bet I know who did it," Terry said.

"Did what?"

Terry's face was still alight. "Killed him and then set the place on fire to hide the body."

Evan wondered whether this was just a clever guess or the result of watching too many gangster films. Surely even the Llanfair grapevine couldn't have heard the pathologist's findings?

"That's what they do all the time in movies," Terry went on. "I saw him, Mr Evans. He was all foreign looking and he was carrying a gun in his car. I saw it on the seat beside him, Mr Evans. He was driving a red car, wasn't he? He stopped me and asked me where the restaurant was. He spoke funny — foreign like."

"What did he look like?"

"I dunno." Terry frowned. "Foreign looking. He was wearing a leather jacket, I remember that. And dark curly hair. And he looked really creepy. I bet he was a mafia hit man."

Evan wasn't sure how much of this was Terry's imagination. It was a pretty accurate description of the man in the restaurant, the probable victim. And the car had been maroon. It was quite possible that Terry had indeed spoken to him, but had added the gun and the sinister appearance for effect. No gun had been found in the car or on the body.

"Thanks for the tip, Terry," Evan said. He didn't like to tell the boy that the man he had seen was now almost certainly dead.

"Right, Mr Evans. I'll keep my eyes open while you're away," Terry said. "In case he comes around again."

"Just one thing," Evan said. "I don't want you roaming around while I'm away. I want you to stay inside after dark. One of these days you might be hit by a car, so be a good boy and don't give your mother any grief while I'm not here, all right?"

"All right, Mr Evans." Terry grinned. Then he demanded, "Are you going to marry Miss Price, then?" He went on grinning. "I saw you kissing her."

"You are too inquisitive by half, young man," Evan said, forcibly shepherding the boy to his own front door. "One of these days you're going to find yourself in big trouble if you're not careful."

"I'm just practising to be a detective," Terry said. He opened his front door. "You should marry Miss Price. She's very pretty."

He darted inside, leaving Evan standing alone in the cool darkness.

CHAPTER 15

"We're here," Evan said. He had been driving since they switched positions when they joined the M25 and had made good time while Sergeant Watkins dozed.

Watkins roused himself from the passenger seat. They were driving along a wide boulevard beside a serene blue sea. Beds of late flowers separated the road from the broad promenade, along which elderly couples strolled arm in arm, and proud fathers were pushing prams. A military band was playing in the bandstand while pensioners relaxed in deck chairs. There were even a few brave children paddling at the edge of the waves or building castles in tiny patches of sand between the pebbles. Watkins blinked in the late afternoon sunlight.

"Are you sure you didn't overshoot and land us on the Riviera? This can't be England. I've been on holiday in England enough times. It always rains."

"That's because you always go in the summertime. You know August is the monsoon month." Evan looked around with approval. "It looks nice, doesn't it? Maybe we can stretch this investigation out to a couple of weeks. I rather fancy lying there in a deck chair and reading a good book, or staying at one of these posh hotels and having tea in the conservatory."

"We're on an NWP expense account. You're lucky they didn't provide us with a tent."

Evan chuckled. "So the first thing to do is find a place to stay and then a meal. I don't know about you, but I'm starving."

Watkins nodded. "My thoughts exactly. We're too late to do any business today, anyway. We'll get an early start in the morning."

"Do you think we should make a courtesy call on the local police before we start poking around on their turf?"

"Yeah, I suppose we'll have to do that, but I'd rather get my facts straight first. I want to get all the details on this restaurant, so that it looks as if we know what we're talking about."

"The town hall will have the records of business licences, won't they? Maybe we should start there."

"Good idea. We'll see what they've got and go on from there." Watkins sucked air through his teeth. "I wish I knew what we were looking for."

"We're checking out Madame Yvette's past, aren't we? We're trying to find out why a man with a false identity should choose her restaurant to be murdered in."

"I just hope we can come up with something substantial." Watkins sighed. "If we come back with facts we could have got over the phone, we'll never hear the last of it."

"There has to be something here, sarge." Evan pulled up at a zebra crossing and waited patiently while an elderly couple shuffled across the broad esplanade. It seemed to take forever. "People don't suddenly show up in a remote part of North Wales for no reason. Yvette must have had a good reason for opening her restaurant there. And I bet our victim had a good reason for seeking out her restaurant. Something more than wanting a lobster dinner. Once we've established a connection, it will all fall into place."

"You and your connections," Watkins said dryly. "So you're saying it was something more than educating the Welsh peasants in the culinary delights of French cooking that made her choose that site?"

The crosswalk cleared and Evan drove on, past elegant hotels with pillared porches and glassed-in lounges. The sort of places that would be serving tea on silver trays at this very moment, Evan thought wistfully. He wrenched his thoughts back to the matter at hand. "If you were French and you had to close one restaurant, you'd open up another one nearby or go back to France, wouldn't you? Why would anyone choose Wales without any Welsh connections?"

Watkins nodded. "I think you're right. Just say your prayers that we stumble across the answer down here. It's about time we got a lucky break."

* * *

Half an hour later, they checked into the Seaview Hotel.

It was an old-fashioned establishment on a back street, half a mile from the seafront. "We could report them for violating the trades description act," Watkins muttered as they went up the front steps. "You certainly can't see the sea from here!"

"And it's not really a hotel," Evan added. "When I was a kid we called a place like this a boarding house."

The woman who opened the door reminded Evan instantly of the old landladies he had encountered at those boarding houses during childhood holidays.

"No noise after ten o'clock," she informed them, eying them as if she suspected they might be all-night ravers, "and the front door is locked at eleven sharp. There's no reason to be out after that in Eastbourne. We're a quiet, refined establishment." She took a key from the rack and led them up a flight of carpeted stairs. "The bathroom rules are posted on the inside of the door," she went on, puffing a little from the exertion. "Basically it's no baths after ten o'clock at night.

The geyser makes a noise, you see, and people like to sleep." She reached the landing and put a key in one of the doors. "You're here on a late holiday, are you?"

"No, actually we're police officers," Watkins said.

"Police?" She looked horrified. "There's nothing underhand going on here, I can assure you. We're a respectable establishment."

"I'm sure you are, madam," Watkins said. "We're investigating a case."

"How exciting. Just like on the telly." Her whole face lit up. "Is it something juicy? Murder or spies maybe?"

"No, we're checking on establishments that are trying to evade paying their VAT," Watkins said and grinned to Evan as she suddenly remembered something she had left cooking on the stove and beat a very hasty retreat.

The next morning the full English breakfast was rather on the meagre side, with two strips of very thin bacon, a fried egg and one grilled tomato slice.

"At least the wife can't complain I'm getting too much cholesterol," Watkins said as they left the dining room.

"Of course, she didn't see that steak you had last night," Evan pointed out.

Watkins grinned. "Bloody good, wasn't it? You can keep your French food. Just give me a good piece of red meat any day."

They had checked the yellow pages to see if Madame Yvette's French restaurant still existed under new ownership, but there were no establishments listed which sounded promising. The only one that described itself as French was called the Oasis, and it was in a new shopping centre.

In the end they had eaten at a nearby pub. The food had been cheap and well prepared, the waitress friendly. They had asked her if she remembered a French couple who had run a restaurant just outside of the town, but she shook her head. "We never eat in places like that. And Eastbourne's a big town, you know. There are always new restaurants opening up and closing again."

After breakfast they tried the borough council offices, but the clerk couldn't come up with anything that sounded remotely like the place they were looking for.

"She said it was just outside of the town," Evan pointed out. "Would those records be kept somewhere else?"

"If it wasn't actually in Eastbourne proper, they'd be kept in the county offices at Lewes, wouldn't they?" the girl said.

They drove half an hour to the old town of Lewes, nestled in the South Downs.

"Nice place," Evan commented, looking with approval at the green hills that ringed the town.

"Can't do without your bloody mountains, can you?" Watkins chuckled.

At county hall a young girl in the records office eyed Evan with interest and became instantly helpful. She helped them check through ledgers until finally Evan pointed at an entry halfway down a page. "Here it is. Chez Yvette in Alfriston. Licence granted . . . let's see . . . six years ago."

"We're not much the wiser, are we? It just gives the owners' names as Jean-Jacques and Yvette Bouchard. Residence address at the restaurant." He beckoned the young clerk over. "Do you have any details on when this place closed?"

She shrugged. "Sorry, that's all we have. All we can tell is that the licence wasn't renewed. Restaurants come and go all the time, I'm afraid."

"So where exactly is this place?" Watkins asked.

"Alfriston?" the girl asked. "It's not far from Newhaven. Sort of between Eastbourne and Newhaven. It's a little village on the Downs — very pretty, actually."

"Between Eastbourne and Newhaven, eh?" Watkins asked as they left the building. "Is that where the ferries go from to France?"

"Right. Newhaven—Dieppe. I went that way once."

"Very convenient, I'd say — near a major port if you wanted to smuggle drugs into the country."

"Maybe they needed to pop across to France to get supplies they couldn't get in England," Evan suggested. "Or they liked to visit the family."

"Okay, I won't say any more until we know some details," Watkins said with a smile. "I'll drive and you navigate or we'll take all day to get there."

Alfriston was a pretty village with old-world charm. Some of the cottages were thatched and it looked as if it might appear on a calendar of *Beautiful Britain.*

"Nice spot," Watkins said. "But I don't see any restaurants. A couple of tea rooms and the pub. Let's ask in the Copper Kettle over there. They look as if they've been around since the year one, and I could do with a coffee."

They crossed the street and took a table by the wall. Watkins waited until the girl had brought two coffees before he asked, "Do you happen to remember a French restaurant that used to be in this village?"

"Chez Yvette, you mean?" She had a pleasing country burr to her voice and a fresh-scrubbed, red-cheeked face. "It's been gone about two years now."

"Where was it? We couldn't find where it might have been."

"Well, you wouldn't, would you?" She looked puzzled. "The new bank's on the site now. The Westminster on the corner over there."

"Oh, I see. Did they pull it down?"

A shocked look came over her face. "Oh no, sir. It burned down, didn't it? Burned to the ground."

CHAPTER 16

"Two restaurants burning down!" Sergeant Watkins stood in the village street, staring at the modern glass-and-concrete structure of the Westminster Bank. It looked completely out of place next to an old-world whitewashed antique shop and a solid Georgian redbrick house with a brass plate outside, announcing it as a doctor's surgery. "Now that's too much of a coincidence, wouldn't you say?"

Evan nodded. "I'd say there were pretty high odds against it happening twice, unless she was a very careless cook who was always leaving pans of hot fat on the stove unattended."

"And you don't think she was a careless cook?"

"The kitchen was spotless when I saw it," Evan said. "She strikes me as the sort of person who always knows exactly what she's doing."

"I reckon now's a good time to go and talk to the local police," Watkins said. "I'll be very interested to hear what conclusions they reached about the fire."

They returned to their car and drove slowly down the village street until they were back among the green hills again.

"Oh, and Evans, let me do the talking, okay?" Watkins said. "You know how touchy some people can be if they think you're treading on their turf. They'll want to know why we didn't call them and ask them to take over this investigation."

"And why didn't we?" Evan asked.

"Because we don't know what we're bloody well looking for yet," Watkins growled.

* * *

The closest police station turned out to be in Seaford, a small town on the coast, about five miles away. The desk sergeant shook hands as Watkins introduced himself and Evan. "North Wales Police, eh? You're a long way from home. What brings you down to this part of the world?"

"We're following up on a restaurant fire that happened earlier this week," Watkins said. "The restaurant owner was a Madame Yvette Bouchard. We've just discovered that she was involved in a restaurant fire down here, in the village of Alfriston."

The sergeant's face suddenly showed interest. "A couple of years ago in Alfriston? Yes, I remember it."

"Would you happen to have the incident report lying around? We'd appreciate it if we could take a look at it."

The sergeant got up. "I'll just go and check," he said, "but it's my recollection that we don't have anything on that fire."

"Wasn't it your station that would have handled it?"

"Oh yes. It was our CID man that was sent out right enough, but if I recall correctly, the fire was deemed to be accidental in nature, so there were no criminal charges to follow up on."

"The fire was an accident? Were they sure?" Evan asked, forgetting that Watkins had warned him to keep quiet.

"As far as they could tell," the sergeant said. "It was a listed building, dating from the sixteenth century. Thatched roof, half timbered, very quaint but a real tinderbox. God knows what rubbish was stuffed into those walls. Of course it went up like a torch. There was nothing left by the time they put it out — burned right to the ground. I saw it myself. The fire had been so hot that the stove and the fridge looked like melted lumps of metal. Horrible it was. But they couldn't find any evidence of an outside agent being used to start it, and they couldn't come up with any kind of motive either."

"Madame Yvette hadn't received any kind of threatening letters?" Evan asked, making Watkins look sharply in his direction. "She hadn't come to you for protection?"

"Threatening letters? Nothing like that, as far as I can remember." The sergeant looked a little baffled. "Hold on and I'll go and check. I think the inspector's in his office. He'd know more than I would."

He returned a few minutes later with a hollow, tired-looking man with greying hair and a bristly moustache. "This is Detective Inspector Morris. He was in charge at the time of the incident."

Inspector Morris shook hands. "I don't know if I can be of much help," he said in an accent that betrayed a long-ago stint at a public school. "We all took it to be a simple accident — the kind of thing that tends to happen to old buildings. Are you saying it wasn't?"

"We don't know yet," Watkins said. "But Madame Bouchard's restaurant in North Wales has just burned down — which is a coincidence, don't you think?"

The inspector was now clearly interested. "I'd say so," he agreed.

"Of course, it could have been the latest in a string of arson fires," Watkins continued. "The others appear to be the work of an extremist group — you know, Wales for the Welsh, that kind of thing. But this one doesn't seem to fit the pattern." He paused, glanced at Evan and then said, "And there was another element involved. A body was found in this fire."

"A body? So it's a murder investigation, then?"

"It looks that way," Watkins said.

The inspector looked at them with new respect. "I see. Well, there was no suspicion of anything like that down here.

We had our arson boys check it over and they came to the conclusion that it was probably faulty wiring. The owners had been told to replace the wiring when they first took over the building. Apparently they didn't do so. And they didn't have a working sprinkler system in place, which was a violation of code, but we didn't cite them, considering the circumstances."

"Circumstances? Was there any loss of life involved in your fire?" Evan asked.

"Luckily no. There could well have been if the firemen hadn't responded so quickly. They found the owner just inside the door. She'd collapsed, overcome with smoke, trying to get out. Another couple of minutes and she'd have been a goner. As it was she was pretty badly burned. I remember seeing her — God she was a mess. Hair all burned off . . . I think she spent a long time in the burn trauma unit at the Brighton infirmary and she had to have a lot of plastic surgery."

An image swam into Evan's head — Yvette's luxuriant hair piled on her head and no sign of burns. She'd apparently made a remarkable recovery.

"Was she the only person in there?" Watkins asked. "Nobody else was trapped inside?"

The inspector shook his head. "It was the middle of the night, luckily. She ran the place alone after her husband died. A lot of work, if you ask me. I think she got a local girl in to help wait on tables at weekends, but she did all the cooking and clearing up herself." He paused, then asked, "Look, do you want to come into my office and sit down? I don't know what else I can tell you. As I say, the report stated that there were no signs of the fire being deliberately set, so that was pretty much that. We sent the report on to her insurance company and they paid out as far as I know."

"And Madame Yvette never came to you before the fire? She never mentioned that she'd been threatened?"

"No. She never came to us. Are you saying that she received threats where she is currently?"

"She got two threatening letters and she felt she was being watched," Evan said.

"Was she the one killed in the fire?"

"No, she's alive and well. She got out in time," Watkins said. "Our body is an unidentified male, probably French. And he was dead before the fire started — stabbed."

"Fascinating," the inspector said. "What does she have to say about it?"

"She claims to have no knowledge of anyone else being in the place. She'd already locked up for the night. She has no idea who he was." Watkins said. "Essentially she's given us her name, rank, and serial number, nothing more. If she knows anything, she's not talking. That's why we decided to come down here and see if we could unearth any skeletons in her closet."

"I'm afraid not," Inspector Morris said. "Not with us, at least. Of course, we're just the local chaps. The highlight of our week is usually a breaking and entering, or a drunk and disorderly."

"So if we were dealing with something on a bigger scale," Watkins said cautiously, "importation of drugs from across the Channel, for instance . . . you wouldn't have any ideas on that score?"

"I think you'd have to ask HQ about that," Inspector Morris said. "But we'd have received a directive to be on the lookout if they'd had any suspicions about this area. Of course drugs are probably coming in all the time in dribs and drabs, but it's so easy these days, who can check? You can go across on the morning ferry, do your shopping and come back on the afternoon boat and half the time they don't even check your passport."

"But if it was a large-scale operation — an international group of organized crime?" Evan asked.

"Then it would be HQ, with Scotland Yard providing assistance in all probability. You're not saying that these restaurant fires had anything to do with that kind of thing, are you?"

"We're just trying to examine all possibilities," Watkins said. "We need to find out how a man she apparently didn't know was found dead inside her locked, burned-out restaurant."

"I'd check with our HQ if I were you," Inspector Morris said. "They have a drug task force. All I can tell you is that we never received any hint that there was anything suspect about that place." He reached for the nearest phone. "Look, do you want me to call Lewes and see who's around to answer questions today?"

"Uh — no thanks. Maybe we'd better wait until we've cleared this with the DI at home," Watkins said quickly. "He might want to have a chat with your drug squad himself. We don't want to overstep our directive."

"No, you certainly don't want to do that." The inspector gave a tired smile.

Watkins extended his hand. "Thanks for the offer, and for your help."

"I'm afraid I haven't been of much help to you, but we had no reason to suspect we were dealing with anything other than faulty wiring in an old building. Let me know what the outcome is, will you? I'd like to find out if I'd had a hotbed of drugs under my nose and never knew it."

"We'll keep you posted if we find anything," Watkins said.

They came out to a stiff sea breeze from the Channel. The water was dotted with whitecaps. A ferry was just leaving Newhaven bound for Dieppe. They stood for a moment watching it before Evan said, "I notice you got cold feet suddenly."

Watkins nodded, still not taking his eyes off the ferry. "It occurred to me that we have no directive to look into anything more than a murder and an arson fire. I don't want to put my foot into anything that might spoil the DI's big roundup — his Operation Armada. It's amazing how word gets around, isn't it?"

"And if the drug route into Wales is part of an organized crime ring, they'll probably have tipsters all over the place." He shook his head. "Funny, but I don't picture her as a cog in the wheel of organized crime somehow."

"People can find themselves trapped in these things, can't they? Maybe she owed protection money or she was a small-time user and next thing you know, they're leaning on her to do them a favour." The ferry was now just a dark blob in an angry sea. Watkins turned away and started to walk back to the car. "Or it might turn out that this has nothing whatever to do with drugs. I just wish we had one solid lead. I feel like I'm floundering in the dark."

"So are you going to call the DI and then go back to the local headquarters in Lewes?"

Watkins stared out to sea again. "I don't fancy facing the DI at the moment. He thought this jaunt was a waste of time to start with."

"Maybe we should try the local paper," Evan suggested. "They would have reported the fire, and who knows — they might have come up with some interesting titbits the police didn't know about."

Watkins sighed. "It's worth a try, I suppose. It can't do any harm — although we're not exactly dealing with the *Sun* down here, are we? I mean they're not likely to be digging down for deep dark secrets."

Evan grinned. "More like who won the baking contest at the townswomen's guild?"

They checked at the nearest telephone booth for the newspaper offices and then drove back into Eastbourne.

"Nice country, this," Evan commented as he drove between hills covered in smooth green grass on which sheep were grazing. "Sort of clean and fresh, if you know what I mean."

"You make it sound like a deodorant ad," Watkins said. "And don't go breaking into song, either. I'm not feeling ultra-cheerful at the moment."

"Have last night's steak and wine come back to haunt you?"

Watkins shook his head. "No, I'm just trying to decide what we should do now. We know the restaurant burned down but everyone here thinks it was an accident and they had no suspicions about Madame Yvette or anything illegal going on. It doesn't look as if we'll get much further on our own."

"We've only been here half a day, sarge. Give it time."

Watkins sighed again. "I'm afraid we're barking up the wrong tree. The body in the restaurant might have had nothing at all to do with Madame Yvette or her restaurant. It could turn out to be a botched robbery or even Welsh extremists having a falling out . . ."

"Come on, sarge," Evan said. "Two restaurant fires in two years? There's something going on here and Madame Yvette's mixed up in it somehow."

The offices of the Eastbourne *Herald and Evening Argos* were in a modern glass building on the outskirts of the town.

"You'll want the archives centre." The girl at the reception desk had startlingly red lips, long red nails, and a curtain of hair that covered one eye, but she looked impossibly young underneath the veneer. "It's down the hall on the right. It's all interactive now. The back issues are on our website."

"Bloody 'ell," Watkins muttered as they opened the door and found themselves facing a table with a computer on it. He looked around hopefully. "So what do we do now?"

"Do you need help?" A large, motherly woman appeared outside the half-open door.

Watkin's face lit up. "We're actually not very good with these things," he said. "Do you think you could find us someone who could trace a back issue for us?"

The woman smiled, crossed the room and hit a key on the keyboard. "It's loading now," she said. "Just click on the date that you want. Would you like a cup of tea?"

"Just click?" Watkins looked at her dubiously. "Are you sure I can't blow up anything?"

She laughed. "It's ever so easy. It only took me a two-day course." She patted his shoulder reassuringly. "So where are you gentlemen from? Wales?"

"That's right," Evan said.

"I thought so. I could hear the accent." She looked pleased. "You're a long way from home then, aren't you? I'll go and get you that tea."

"Humiliating, that's what it is," Watkins muttered as the woman walked away. "First our Tiffany and now a woman old enough to be my mother. I feel like a proper charlie. I'm going to take a course as soon as I get home."

"Maybe PC Davies will give you private lessons," Evan teased.

Watkins grinned. "I wouldn't say no to that, but I got the impression she'd rather be working one-on-one with you than with me." The program finished loading, leaving them with a screen full of choices. "You could do worse," he added.

"Oh, come on, sarge," Evan felt himself blushing. "She was just being friendly."

"Friendly, my foot. She fancies you, boyo."

Evan nudged Watkins. "Go on, then. Click on the button of the year that you want."

Watkins pushed the mouse in Evan's direction. "You do it. I'll probably wipe the whole thing."

Evan leaned across and clicked. "We don't know what month it was, do we? So we'd better start with January and work forward."

"I'm glad it's only a weekly and not a daily," Watkins said. "We could be here all night."

Items of local news flashed to the screen and vanished again. Borough council grants for improving the swimming pool. Hooliganism on the pier. The tennis tournament at Devonshire Park . . ."

"Surely it would have made the front page?" Watkins said in frustration.

"Unless it was a big week for news — it's not likely to shove out Martina Hingis winning the tennis tournament or the Eastbourne Show."

They got as far as September. "Wait." Evan put his hand on Watkins's arm. "Page three. There it is."

A somewhat fuzzy black-and-white picture of the devastated site came onto the screen under the headline LOCAL RESTAURANT BURNS DOWN.

Evan skimmed the article. There was nothing that the police hadn't already told them. Fire started in the middle of the night . . . quick response of local fire brigade saved owner's life . . . She was rushed to the East Sussex medical centre burn unit.

Then the article concluded, "This is the second tragedy to strike the vivacious Frenchwoman, whose husband died in a yachting accident three years ago. Since that time she had valiantly tried to keep the restaurant going single-handedly and was gaining a reputation for her haute cuisine."

"Nothing much there," Watkins said.

"Except for one thing," Evan pointed out. "Her husband didn't just die. He was killed — in yet another accident."

"So either this woman is a walking Jonah," Watkins began, "or she's good at making things look like accidents. We should check on how much the insurance policy was for — and whether there was a big policy on her husband's life."

Evan nodded. "Of course there is another option. It's just possible that someone's out to get her in a big way."

CHAPTER 17

Watkins looked up sharply. "You think that could be it? A hate crime? A vendetta?"

Evan shrugged. "We've no way of knowing at the moment, have we, but you have to admit it's just as good a possibility as anything else. Her husband falls off his boat, her first restaurant burns down, and then her second restaurant burns down. Someone could be after her."

Watkins shook his head. "If you're right, you'd have thought she'd have got the hint by now and mentioned something of this to the police. She must at least suspect who's behind it."

"And may be too afraid to tell the truth. She was pretty upset the first night she came to me with a threatening letter."

Watkins started to get up. "I'm going to call home and see if they've made any progress on the fingerprints on those notes. I bet they haven't checked them against French lists. And I'd dearly like to know if this really was the beginning of the trail. What made her come to England in the first place? Had someone been threatening them back in France? Had they owned yet another restaurant which burned down over there?"

"Maybe we should just pop over and see for ourselves," Evan suggested, half joking.

"Go to France? You're not serious, are you?"

"I wasn't, but it's not so far-fetched. You can drive through the Chunnel in half an hour these days."

"Not that we'd have any idea where to begin in France."

"We know she went to cooking school in Paris, and we know where Philippe du Bois is."

"Hardly enough to warrant charging across the Channel."

They broke off as the woman came back with two cups of tea and shortbread biscuits sitting in their saucers. "Here you go," she said. "How have you been getting along?"

"We found the article we were looking for," Evan said.

The woman peered at the screen. "Oh, that restaurant fire. I remember it. It was so sad — she'd lost her husband and then she nearly lost her own life. I remember because I'd just lost my husband around that time, so I felt for her."

"This man drowned, did he?" Evan asked.

She nodded. "He was a very keen sailor, apparently. Anyway, he went out in bad weather and they never found him. Fishermen found a mast floating in the area where his boat had been, but they never discovered either the boat or his body. Of course, that's not unusual around here. The tides can whisk a body through the Channel and dump it in France or out in the Atlantic."

"So the husband was never found." Watkins stared at the screen. "It gets more complicated by the minute, doesn't it?" He looked up at the woman. "Do you happen to remember when this accident happened?"

She chewed on her lip. "Not off the top of my head. I know it was at least a couple of years before the restaurant burned down and I know it was late in the year to be sailing — around this time of year, maybe."

"It said in the article that her husband died three years previously," Evan pointed out. "Go back and try September three years earlier."

"Go back and . . . who do you think I am, Bill bloody Gates?"

The woman chuckled. "It's not hard, really it's not. Here, move over. I'm not supposed to do this for visitors but I've got a few minutes to spare. Watch. You just go back a screen, select the year here, and there you are. A five-year-old could do it."

"A five year-old does do it," Watkins said bitterly. "That's just the problem."

The woman slid out of the seat and Evan took her place. "Of course, there might not have been a whole article on an accidental drowning. It could just have been an obituary."

They worked their way through several issues and then finally there it was. "*Jean-Jacques Bouchard, Restaurateur.*" It was only a few lines in the obituary column, with a photo above it. Evan stared hard at it.

"I wish the photo was better," he said.

"Why — do you think you know him?"

Evan took a deep breath. "He looks like a younger version of the man who came into the restaurant that evening."

"Are you sure?" Watkins peered at the grainy snapshot. The man was squinting into bright sunshine and his curly hair was windswept. He looked like a sailor.

"I wouldn't swear to it and the photograph's not very good, but it looks like him, right enough."

"Well, I'll be . . ." Watkins began. He looked up at the woman. "Is there a way of printing this out?"

"You just click on Print." She started to explain, then thought better and did it for them. A sheet of paper emerged from a printer in the corner. Evan took it. "This is wonderful. Thank you. You've been a big help."

She gave him a very non-motherly smile.

* * *

"Finally we're getting somewhere," Watkins said as they left the newspaper offices.

"Yes, but where?" Evan asked. "Frankly I'm more confused than when we started."

"How about this — what if her husband didn't really die in the boating accident?"

"You mean he faked his death?"

"People do, don't they? Maybe he just wanted to get away from her and start a new life."

"Or maybe someone really was after him, so he decided to vanish conveniently," Evan suggested.

"But then, according to you, he shows up at the restaurant again. She wasn't pleased to see him and she stabbed him."

"There's only one thing against that. I saw him come in. I'd swear she didn't recognize him."

"She might be a good actress."

"Not that good." Evan shook his head. "That had to be an Oscar-winning performance. She was at our table at the time. There was no feeling of tension, no flicker of reaction. If you were Yvette and your husband who had been missing for five years, showed up, you'd react, wouldn't you?"

"Unless this was something they had planned between them. She might have been in contact with him, so she was expecting him that evening." Watkins put the key in the car door. "Five years. That's significant, don't you think?"

"You mean he can now be declared legally dead?"

"Exactly. So if there's a large insurance policy to collect on, this would be a good time to reappear."

"But then why would she stab him?"

"Because she wanted the insurance money for herself." Watkins slapped his hand against the car door as he opened it. "It's all fitting together nicely now. All we need to do is get some proof that our body is really her missing husband — dental records would do nicely — and I think we've got ourselves a case." They got into the car and Watkins started the engine. "I think this deserves a celebration, don't you? That pub we ate at last night wasn't bad. Let's go and see if they do a good lunch."

Half an hour later they were sitting over ploughman's platters, with crusty rolls, four kinds of cheese, and pickled onions, as well as pints of Whitbread Pale Ale.

"Ah, that's better." Watkins put down his glass. "I'm beginning to feel human again. I think I could even face talking to the DI Now what did we need to ask him?"

He got out a notebook.

"About the insurance policies, for one thing."

Watkins nodded and scribbled. "And the fingerprints."

"And if there's been any news from France yet — about Philippe du Bois and who might have decided to apply for a passport in his name."

"Right." Watkins got up. "I think the DI will have to be impressed with the amount we've ferreted out in one morning, don't you? Maybe it will prompt him to have another chat with Madame and see if she's more forthcoming."

"As long as he doesn't scare her off with his usual heavy-handedness."

He went to the phone on the pub wall. Evan finished his roll and double Gloucester and washed them down with the last of his pint.

Watkins was on the phone for a long while. Evan noticed him smiling and glancing in his direction. He was still smiling when he came back.

"That was young Glynis," he said. "She sends her regards, by the way. I've asked her to send the fingerprints from the two threatening notes to the Sûreté in France to see if they can find a match. There's nothing from the mental hospital yet. The DI is out working on Operation Armada — bloody silly name if you ask me. Still he always did fancy himself as Lord Nelson . . ."

"The Armada was Drake," Evan pointed out.

Watkins grinned again. "Bloody know-it-all. Anyway, I spoke to Constable Perkins. I gather they've removed various kitchen implements from the scene of the fire and they're trying to determine the murder weapon and come up with prints. I asked him to check on the insurance policies and see who benefits."

"So they're no further along, really," Evan said. "They haven't identified the body or found the murder weapon."

"I wouldn't mind betting my pay cheque that the body is her vanished husband," Watkins said.

"And you think she killed him?"

"It's pretty obvious, isn't it? She thought she'd got rid of him five years earlier and was annoyed to find him turning up again, still alive."

A memory was beginning to stir in Evan's mind. He had been so preoccupied with making a graceful escape from her sofa that he'd forgotten until now. "She did say that he was a bastard and a monster and it was her happiest day when she escaped from him."

"Well, there you are, then. Perfect motive. We'll get this case sewn up in no time at all. Now all we need is positive identification of the body."

"Got any thoughts on how we're going to do that?" Evan asked.

"A wedding photo of the happy couple? That might shake her composure, wouldn't you say?"

"So we prove she was married to him. That doesn't prove that she killed him. And if they really were on the run and hiding from someone, maybe this proves they were found."

Watkins nodded. "Okay, so what do you think we should do?"

Evan stared out of the pub's bay window to the seafront beyond. The wind had sprung up, making flags stand out stiffly and awnings flap wildly. "I think we have to find out more about their life in France. We need to know what happened to them and why they came to England."

"And how do you propose doing that?"

Evan pointed to the copy of the obituary. "This mentions the town where he was born and we know she went to the Cordon Bleu school in Paris. Two known facts. We can work from there."

"Go to France, you mean?" Watkins laughed.

"Why not? I told you it's only half an hour through the Chunnel these days. We could go over there for the day."

Watkins grinned uneasily. "I'm not too hot at driving on the proper side of the road. And I don't speak Froggy."

"We'll manage," Evan said. "I don't mind driving. I think we should do this if we want to solve this case, sarge. We're not going to get too much help in a hurry from the French police — that's pretty obvious, isn't it? Let's find a map of France and see where his birthplace is."

There was a W. H. Smith's on the corner and they found a map of France. "Port St. Valery — how do you spell it?" Watkins asked, looking at the index.

"Here it is on the coast, not far from Calais." Evan pointed at the entry. "The sort of place where you'd expect a man to be interested in boats."

He studied the map, his finger on St. Valery, tracing the line from the Channel crossing. Then he tapped the page excitedly. "And look here, sarge. It's only a few miles from Abbeville, where Philippe du Bois is in the mental hospital. Another coincidence, do you think?"

Watkins grabbed the book. "All right. Let's buy the map. But we can't just go jaunting off to France without permission, you know. They weren't even too keen about letting us come to Eastbourne. And DI Hughes is out playing at drug wars."

"So call the old man."

"Call the DCI.?" Watkins's eyebrow twitched. "Oh, I don't know about that, boyo. He'd say I was overstepping the bounds of my authority and getting too big for my boots."

"It's only a day trip we're talking about — it's not as if we're going on our holidays at their expense!" Evan paused. Watkins stood clutching the Michelin guide, still undecided.

"Tell him we're in the middle of a murder investigation and if we wait for the French authorities to come through, it might be too late. It's possible that Madame Yvette's life is still in danger, you know."

"You could be right there," Watkins agreed. "I'll ask the DCI, to put surveillance on her. That would be a good way to start the conversation, wouldn't it? Make him realize this is important." Evan nodded. Watkins swallowed hard. "All right. I'll call him."

They paid for the map and then found the nearest phone booth. Evan waited outside on the busy pavement. He saw Watkins's face twitch as he started speaking. Evan heard him say, "I'm only talking about going over there for a day trip, sir, not for my summer holidays." Then, "No sir. I wasn't trying to be funny. I was just pointing out that it's only half an hour through the Chunnel."

Finally he hung up and came out of the booth.

"Well?" Evan asked. "Did he chew you out?"

A smile spread across Watkins's face. "He said go ahead, but if he gets expenses for Paris hotels and the Folies Bergères, he's going to veto them."

* * *

"It doesn't make sense to go until the morning," Watkins said. "By the time we got over there everything would be closed. And we've already paid for our hotel here. I bet that old dragon wouldn't refund us our money."

"So what shall we do for the rest of the afternoon?" Evan asked. "We could always go and talk to the ex-neighbours in the village. One of them might have been friendly with her or might have seen something useful."

"It's worth a try," Watkins said. "It's either that or an hour's kip in a deck chair — and the wind's a little cold for that."

They drove back along the windy Downs Road to the village of Alfriston. A coach was parked outside the Packhorse pub and tourists were cluttering the high street, taking pictures and looking into antique shop windows.

They went into the pub first and chatted to the landlord. Yes, he remembered the restaurant. It hadn't done too well, although people said the cooking was very good. Still, most folks didn't go in for fancy French muck, did they? he asked genially. And most trippers came out for an afternoon drive, had a cup of tea and went home.

"Tell me about the couple who owned it — the Bouchards," Watkins asked. "Did you know them?"

"I said good morning when we passed in the street," the publican said, "but I can't say that I knew them. They kept themselves pretty much to themselves. Always together, they were. And after he died, you hardly ever saw her. Of course, she was trying to run that place alone. I don't know how she did it. I'm run off my feet here and I've got the two girls to help me."

"But what did you think of them?" Evan interrupted.

The man shrugged. "I don't know what to say to that. They didn't cause no trouble, if that's what you're getting at. Quiet. Good-looking couple, in a foreign kind of way. She was more friendly than him. He was a bit on the surly side, but maybe his English wasn't as good as hers. I know he did all the heavy work and she did all the cooking. She told me that. She said she was a trained chef — very proud of it, she was."

"Did she have any friends here in the village?" Evan asked.

"I think she was quite chummy with Brenda in the greengrocer's. She used to buy a lot of her fresh produce from them."

"The greengrocer's?"

"Just down the street. You can't miss it. There's five shops and that's one of them. Now if you'll excuse me, I've got customers waiting."

He turned away, wiping his hands on his apron as he went. "Now then, ladies, what will it be?"

Watkins and Evan walked around the trippers and continued along the high street until they came to the greengrocer's. A large-boned woman was carrying out a box of cabbages as they approached. She put it down and smiled as she saw them standing there.

"What can I get for you gentlemen?" Her voice had a pleasant country softness, and her face had the rosy cheeks of a life spent in the open air. It was hard to judge her age, but Evan thought she was possibly younger than she looked.

This was borne out by a toddler on a trike appearing from inside the shop.

"Get that thing back inside, Jimmy. Not near the street. I've told you a thousand times," she said and gave him a little shove to redirect him. "Sorry. He's at that age," she said. "A right terror like his big brother was."

"Are you Brenda? We're from the North Wales Police," Sergeant Watkins said. "We understand that you used to know the French couple who owned the restaurant that burned down."

"The police?" A wary look came over her face.

"We're investigating another restaurant fire and we think they might be linked," Evan explained.

She nodded. "What a terrible thing to happen. I looked out of my window and I saw those flames. There was nothing anyone could do. It went up like a torch — well, it would do with the thatched roof, wouldn't it? Regular firetraps, those old buildings are. I'm only glad they got her out alive, although I hear she was badly burned. I often wandered how she was doing."

"She's fine," Evan said. "She moved to North Wales and opened another restaurant."

"Did she? Fancy that. North Wales, eh?"

"Did you know her well?" Watkins asked.

"I wouldn't say well. We didn't go out together socially or anything — not that either of us had time for socializing, especially after her husband died. She was running herself ragged trying to keep that place going. Hire someone to help you, I told her, but she said she couldn't afford it at the moment."

"Did she ever talk to you about her husband's death? Did she seem very upset by it?"

"Oh yes. Very upset — well, you'd expect it, wouldn't you? She thought the world of him. She said she didn't see how she was going to manage without him. And it was worrying for her, too, not knowing. They never found the body, see."

"Did she ever seem afraid to you? Did she ever hint that her husband's death might not have been an accident?" Evan asked.

Brenda looked shocked. "Oh no. Nothing like that. She was surprised, I think, because he was such a good sailor. She said it wasn't like Jean to go taking risks. He knew the sea too well. His family had been fishermen, so I understand. He used to go to Hastings and buy fresh fish from the boats for their restaurant. I never ate there personally. I wanted to go but my hubby flat refused. He's very finicky about his food."

"So you don't know if she'd had any threatening letters? You never saw any strange visitors?"

Brenda shook her head. "I don't know anything about that. But like I said, we didn't know each other well — not well enough to tell me that kind of personal thing. Are you saying that someone burned down that restaurant on purpose?"

"It's possible," Evan said. "We're trying to find out if anyone might have had a grudge against her. Did she ever talk to you about her life in France before she came here?"

"She told me about the cooking school," the woman said. "And about meeting her husband in Paris."

"Did she come from Paris?" Watkins asked.

A puzzled look crossed her face. "She wasn't really French, was she? I always thought she was English."

CHAPTER 18

"Well, that's a turn-up for the books," Sergeant Watkins muttered as they drove back to Eastbourne. "Not really French, eh?"

Evan stared out of the windscreen at the rolling hills. "I can't believe that, sarge. I've spoken to her several times. There was no hint that she wasn't French."

"Like I said before, she might be a bloody good actress."

Evan shook his head. "But even the best actress would slip up. You know when they're doing dialects on telly. Every now and then you hear a word that's wrong and you think, She's not really Scottish or Yorkshire. Madame Yvette never slipped up. She even put in French words when she couldn't think of English ones. I'd swear that she was really French."

"Then what made Brenda think she was really English? Certainly not if she spoke with an accent like that."

Evan shook his head. "I've no idea, but this whole thing is getting more and more confusing. Brenda said she idolized her husband and Yvette told me that he was a bastard. That doesn't make sense either. Get onto HQ and see if they can get her date and place of birth verified. Then we can check that out as well when we're in France tomorrow."

"I'd say we have a busy day ahead," Watkins said. "I just hope we come up with enough useful information to justify the Chunnel crossing, or else the chief's going to blow his top."

* * *

A heavy sea fog draped the south coast as they arrived at the Channel Tunnel early on Thursday morning. The terminal building loomed ominously from the swirling whiteness and added to the surreal quality as they drove their car onto a train.

Half an hour later they emerged into a similar sea fog on the French side.

"Phew, I'm glad I'm not claustrophobic," Watkins said as Evan drove out of the terminal and onto a French motorway. "It doesn't bear thinking about — all that water over our heads. I wouldn't like to think what a breakdown would be like in that tunnel." He glanced at Evan, then looked at him critically. "You're sweating like a pig," he said. "Don't tell me that you—"

"I'm a mountain man, aren't I?" Evan demanded, taking out a handkerchief and wiping his forehead. "I'm not designed to go burrowing into the earth like a bloody Rhondda Valley coal miner." He smiled sheepishly. "I never could stand being shut in. When I was a little lad the teacher shut me in the cupboard as a punishment for fighting and I got so hysterical that they had to get my mother. I thought I'd grown out of it, but obviously I haven't."

"I can see we'll have to make sure you have a couple of brandies before we make the return trip," Watkins said, "or maybe champagne. Let's hope it's a victory celebration, eh?"

Evan nodded. The clammy nausea was retreating as good fresh air blew into his face from the open window. He felt ashamed of himself for betraying a weakness. He was glad it was Watkins who had seen and not Bronwen — or PC Glynis.

"Now I really wish we'd brought young Glynis along," Watkins said, making Evan wonder if he had been reading his thoughts. "Look at these signs — they're all in bloody French!"

"Don't worry about it, sarge." Evan felt fully recovered and ready for anything. "You're dealing with an expert here. I did the navigating when I came over here with the rugby team."

"Hmm." Watkins nodded, impressed.

"Actually I was the only one who wasn't pissed out of his mind and who could still focus on the road signs," Evan admitted. "We had an awful lot of victory celebrations during that trip. Ah, here we are." A bank of road signs appeared from the mist. "We need the Dieppe road, I think."

Fields of stubble lined the road with the dark shapes of hay rolls looking like large reclining beasts. A distant line of poplar trees appeared like eerie sentinels. Now and then they passed a few sorry sunflowers, left to die at the edge of what must have been an impressive field of gold. They saw no sign of houses until they left the main road and followed the signs to St. Valery. They began to pass isolated farmhouses, then cottages with slatted shutters over their windows — the first indication that they were in France.

By the time they drove through the narrow cobbled streets of St. Valery and came out to the sea front, the mist was rising, giving glimpses of a blue sky above.

"It doesn't look very foreign, does it?" Watkins commented. And indeed it could have been a replica of one of the towns on the English side of the Channel, except for the shutters on the windows, the striped umbrellas at the corner café, and a peeling advertisement for Dubonnet painted on a building wall.

"Hôtel de Ville," Watkins commented, pointing at a red brick building set back from the street. "That looks quite posh if we have to stay here the night."

Evan smiled. "That's the town hall, sarge."

"Bloody silly name. Why call it a hotel then? Why don't you park over there and we'll start at the hôtel de ville. That's where we'd expect to find records, wouldn't we?"

Between Evan's rusty French and a young male clerk with a smattering of English they established that there were no Bouchards currently living in the town. Back records indicated that an elder Monsieur Bouchard had died eight years previously. His wife had followed him the next year.

"His occupation is listed as fisherman, monsieur," the clerk said. "You could ask down at the harbour. Someone there might know what has become of their children."

"There was a son," Evan said. "His name was Jean. He was lost at sea five years ago. Have you no record of that?"

"*Hélas*, no, monsieur. If he was no longer living in the community, how should we know of this?" the man demanded with a sad shrug of the shoulders. "I show no Jean Bouchard registered here. I can only conclude he did not live here. I am sorry."

"Oh well, down to the docks," Watkins said. "How do you think your French will stand up to talking to fisherman?"

"We'll have to see, won't we?" Evan said.

They left the car in the central Place de la République and walked down a narrow cobbled alleyway back to the seafront. The town might have looked like its English counterpart, but now that they were out of the car, their nostrils were assailed by distinctly non-British smells. Newly baking bread competed with roasting coffee. From an open kitchen window came the heady smell of garlic. And as they came out of the alley the salty, seaweedy tang of the Channel came to greet them, tinged with a slight fishiness.

A distinctly French voice was singing on somebody's radio. The barrow at the waterfront was selling crêpes instead of candy floss.

At one end of the promenade, brightly painted fishing boats were bobbing behind a sturdy concrete harbour wall. Several old men were sitting up on the wall with faded blue fisherman's caps on their heads. One was mending a net.

"I'll leave you to do the talking," Watkins muttered to Evan as they approached the old men.

"You'll have to, won't you?" Evan shot him a quick grin. "Unless you're really good at hand signals."

"Cheeky monkey," Watkins muttered. "Go on, then. Dazzle me with your French."

Evan took a deep breath. *"Bonjour,"* he said. Then he tried to explain that they were inquiring about the family Bouchard. Blank faces met him. The old men looked at each other and shrugged in the way that makes the speaker feel that what he said probably wasn't worth saying.

The old men exchanged a few words with each other. Then one of them got up and shuffled off.

"Oh, you really seem to have got through to them," Watkins muttered sarcastically. "Now they're all bloody escaping. They must think we're lunatics."

Evan shrugged and started to walk away. One of the old men grabbed his arm.

"Attendez, monsieur," he said, and gestured toward the promenade.

"He wants us to wait," Evan said.

"What for?"

"I'm not sure."

A few minutes passed. Gulls screamed overhead. A boat chugged out of the harbour.

At last the old man could be seen returning with a young girl at his side.

"Ma petite fille," he announced.

The girl looked at them shyly. "My grandfazzer," she said, pointing at him. "I learn English in zee school. Please tell me what ees you want?"

Evan told her. She listened solemnly, nodded, then let out an explosion of rapid French.

"Aah!" The old men looked at each other, nodding and smiling.

Evan heard the word *Bouchard* repeated many times. Then torrents of rapid French came flying back at the child.

"Monsieur Bouchard ees dead — many years now," she said. "His wife, she ees also dead, five or six years ago. Zere was one son, but he is gone away."

"Can they tell us about the son?" Evan asked.

Another quick exchange.

"He went away. He worked on the ferry boats from Calais. Nobody has seen him for many years now."

"Do they remember his wife?" Evan asked.

The old men couldn't seem to agree on this one. There was a lot of gesturing and shrugs.

"Zey sink he marry zee local girl but zey do not know her name. Zis man say he meet her once . . . she was very pretty, but zee ozzer men say at ees age he sink zat all young girls are very pretty, no?" She smiled shyly at Evan.

The old man who was mending the net said something else.

"He sinks zat she come from zee *orphelinat* . . . orphanage in Abbeville, but maybe no."

"Would they have heard if Jean Bouchard had died?" Watkins asked.

More shrugs greeted this question.

"They have not seen him for several years. Not since his mozzer die. He not come 'ere no more."

"So he had no friends in the town who might know about him?"

"Zey do not know. Perhaps he 'ave zee friend. They can only say zat they do not see him 'ere no more."

"Do they know if any members of the family are still alive in this area?" Evan asked.

They debated this with animation until Evan caught the word *imbécile.*

"What was that about an imbecile?" he asked.

She shrugged, a perfect imitation of the elders' gesture. "Zere ees nobody alive now but possibly zee imbecile ees still living. Zee brozzer of Madame Bouchard. He went — how you say — crazy?"

"Was his name du Bois?"

No reaction from the old men. They had never met him personally. They could only repeat what they had heard. But if he was crazy, they said, he would surely be in the hospital in Abbeville because that was where all the crazy people went.

* * *

"At least we've established one thing." Watkins looked pleased as they drove out of St. Valery. "Philippe du Bois could have been his uncle. His mother might have had guardianship over him."

"Which meant she would have opened his mail, signed his checks . . ." Evan continued the train of thought.

"Applied for a passport in his name?" Watkins finished.

The two men exchanged a grin. It felt good to be getting somewhere at last. It was a small fact, but it was the first sliver of proof of what had been all conjecture until now.

"And if Jean's wife came from the orphanage in the same town, we can kill two birds with one stone and find out more about her background," Watkins went on, sounding really animated now.

"He could have married more than once," Evan pointed out. "Yvette could be his second wife."

"Do we know her maiden name?" Watkins asked.

"She put something like Hétreau on the form she filled in for us."

"Yvette Hétreau." Watkins repeated the words. "We'll see if that rings a bell with anyone at the orphanage, but let's start with the hospital first. We know where to find that."

The Hôpital St. Bernard was a square brick building at the edge of the town. It was surrounded by neat, leafless plane trees and wide sandy paths, newly raked. They went inside and were met by a nun in full habit, who understood a little English and listened politely.

"Philippe du Bois? We have had other inquiries about him."

"Yes, that was us. North Wales Police. Somebody rented a car using Philippe du Bois's name. We're still trying to find out who might have done that."

"You had better talk to Mozzer," she said and swept down a wide corridor to an office at the far end. The elderly mother superior welcomed them graciously. Yes, she had received their inquiries but she regretted she could tell them nothing. "Poor Monsieur du Bois. He was in his own world. Such a shame. A clever man once — a mathematics teacher. But then the illness struck, and now he doesn't know where he is or who he is." She shrugged. "And to see him — he still looks healthy — handsome, big, lots of dark curls . . ."

"Does he ever get letters or visitors from the outside?" Watkins asked.

"Not anymore. What point would there be?" She smiled sadly. "And now his family is all gone, I believe. His sister used to come, but she died years ago now."

"So who would his guardian be?"

"The state is his guardian, monsieur."

"And he never goes out, ever?" Evan asked. "Would he be able to get out if he wanted to?"

The mother superior looked surprised. "He does not wish to leave, monsieur . . . but to answer your question, it would be possible to get out, if he desired. Of course, we would soon notice he was missing and bring him back, but he has never wanted to wander. Some of our patients — we have to keep a very close eye on them, but not Philippe. He is happy in his room."

"Would it be possible to visit him?" Evan asked suddenly.

Watkins looked surprised. So did the mother superior.

"I suppose, yes. But I do not think he will speak with you, monsieur."

"All the same, I'd appreciate it," Evan insisted.

"Very well." She put her hands together, then rose from her seat. "Zis way, please. Follow me. And I must warn you that you may hear sounds zat are not very pleasant. Not all of our patients are docile."

She swept ahead of them down the hallway and unlocked a door at the far end. The odour was the first thing that assailed them — a strong smell of disinfectant that didn't entirely mask other, more unpleasant, smells. Someone screamed. There were distant moans. The nun kept walking until she came to a door at the far end of the hall. She took out a large key and put it in the lock.

"We may go in. He is of no danger."

She opened the door and went into the room ahead of them. "Bonjour Monsieur Philippe. How are you today? I bring you some visitors."

The man was sitting on a chair, staring out the window. He turned around briefly at the sound of her voice but his eyes registered no interest in the two men and he turned back to the window.

"He does that all day, messieurs," the nun said. "He likes to watch the birds. It is the only thing that gives him pleasure now."

Evan watched the man carefully. The nun was right. He did still look strong and healthy with his black curly hair and his dark complexion.

"Ask him if he remembers Jean Bouchard, his nephew," Evan suggested.

She put the question but this time he didn't even turn around. After a few minutes they left again.

"Just what were you getting at?" Watkins asked as they left the mother superior and made their way back to the front door. "And why did you want to see him so much?"

"It was just a thought," Evan said. "There's a young kid in Llanfair, young Terry. He's a proper tearaway, always in trouble, out on his bike until all hours. He claims a foreigner asked for directions to the restaurant right before it burned down. He said the man had dark curly hair and looked sinister. I assumed he'd seen the same man I saw, the one we now think is the victim. But what if someone else had been on his trail, or trying to find Madame Yvette?"

"Philippe du Bois?" Watkins shook his head incredulously. "He's lost all contact with the real world. She said so."

"Crazy people can be very cunning when they want to."

"You've seen him now. You want me to believe that he slipped out of this place, went over to England, then found his way to Wales, killed someone and got back again?"

Evan sighed. "I suppose it is a little far-fetched. If he's checked as often as they say, someone would have noticed him missing. And he would have needed money and a passport — which he might have had, of course. I just wanted to see whether he could have possibly rented the car, not our victim. But you're right. Now I've seen him I think it's highly unlikely that it was him. We'll have to put Terry's sinister stranger down to too much television."

"And he didn't react at all to the mention of Jean Bouchard's name," Watkins said. "So where now? To the orphanage to check on Yvette?"

"I wouldn't say no to a bite of something to eat," Evan said. "It's been hours since we had breakfast."

"Sounds good," Watkins said. "Let's find out where this orphanage is first, shall we?"

They found the young nun at the reception desk and asked her the question. She looked puzzled. "Zere is no orphanage 'ere, monsieur."

"But we were told it was in Abbeville." Evan managed the words in French.

"Once I sink zere were zee orphans who live in our convent," she said. "Wait 'ere. I bring one of zee sisters who perhaps remember zis."

She bustled off and a few minutes later returned with a round-faced nun who smiled shyly at them.

"Zis is Sister Angélique," the young nun said. "She once 'elped wiz zee *orphalines*."

The nun nodded. "*Les petites filles*," she said, holding out her hand to indicate the height of the children.

"Ask her if she remembers Yvette Hétreau."

The older nun's face became animated. She spoke rapidly to the younger woman, nodding and smiling as she talked.

"She remember 'er," the young nun said at last. "She was very clever — no? She leave 'ere when she is maybe sixteen and she go as *au pair* to work in England and zen later Sister Angélique 'ear zat she become zee famous chef. Sister Angélique say she is very proud of 'er."

"Does Sister Angélique know anything about her marriage or where she lived more recently?"

The older nun shook her head when asked the question.

"She 'eard no more from Yvette after she write to say she will study at zee Cordon Bleu school in Paris. She wish Yvette would write to her or come to visit."

"We'll tell her to write," Evan said and the old nun's face lit up again.

* * *

"All right, let's go over what we know so far," Watkins said. They were sitting in an outdoor café on an old square and working their way through a basket of croissants and brioches.

"We've established that Jean Bouchard could have got his hands on Philippe du Bois's identity. We've learned that Yvette went to England as a young girl and then to the cooking school, but we've no proof of her marriage or what she did when she came out of cooking school. I'd like to know what the Bouchards did before they came to England. Did they own any previous restaurants that burned down, or did they get themselves mixed up in undesirable company?"

"And how do you think we're going to find that out?" Watkins reached for another croissant and helped himself to another spoonful of apricot jam to go with it.

"I think it will be easy enough to come up with the marriage certificate," Evan said, "but I think that maybe we should go to Paris and check on her time at the cooking school."

Watkins grinned. "Any excuse to get to Gay Paree, eh?"

"Not me, sarge," Evan said. "I can't say I like big cities, not even Paris. And I certainly don't want to drive there. I don't harbour a death wish at the moment. When we get to the outskirts I suggest that we find a place to park the car and then take the metro."

* * *

Delicious smells wafted through the hallways of the Cordon Bleu school, reminding Evan it must be lunchtime, even though they had had a late breakfast at Abbeville. He felt exhausted and his nerves were frazzled from driving into Paris. They had left the car at a suburban metro station, but even getting that far had necessitated driving the wrong way around several roundabouts and negotiating some giant French lorries on narrow streets. Then they had had to navigate through a couple of changes of train to bring them to Rue Léon-Delhomme and the cooking school.

"I wonder if they have samples of their work for tasting?" Watkins echoed his thoughts. "A bifsteak and pommes frites would fill the spot nicely."

"I don't think people pay to go to a school like this to learn to cook steak and chips," Evan retorted.

The young woman at the reception desk was probably Dutch but certainly multilingual. Her English had only the slightest trace of accent.

"Yes, we can check on a former student for you," she said after she had examined their police credentials. "What year was she here?"

"We don't know that," Watkins said. "It must have been at least seven or eight years ago." He looked at Evan for confirmation of this.

"Do you know if she did le Grand Diplôme or did she just take one of our intensive courses?"

Watkins looked at Evan. "I'd imagine it was the whole thing," Evan said. "She says she's a qualified chef."

"Then it would be le Grand Diplôme," the girl said. "That will be easier to trace for you. Okay. What name was it?"

"Her name is Yvette Bouchard," Evan said, "but we have no way of knowing if she was already married when she was here. Her maiden name was Hétreau."

The girl frowned. "It would be easier to look up if you knew the year," she said. Then her face lit up. "I know — we have class pictures on the walls of students graduating from our diploma program. Please look at them and see if you can find her. I'm awfully busy and that would save us all time."

Watkins nodded. "Good idea. At least we know what she looks like. That's one thing we do know."

They followed the girl to the front corridor. Solemn groups of young people in chef's hats stared at them from black frames, dating back to the turn of the century when the groups were mostly composed of males with droopy moustaches.

"How old would you say she is now?" Watkins asked. "Late thirties? That means the earliest she could have done this course was about sixteen, seventeen years ago. Okay, let's start over here."

They scanned photos from the early eighties, moving slowly down the hall. At last Evan pointed at a face. "Look, that's her."

"Finally!" Watkins nodded. "All right. We've got the class number. Let's see what we can find out."

The young woman looked up and tried to manage a friendly smile as they came back. "Have you found her? Brilliant. Okay, let's go and see what we can turn up in the records."

She led them down stone stairs into a gloomy basement. "I'm afraid our filing system was still terribly primitive ten years ago. Now of course we've got it all on the computer." She pulled open a drawer in a big filing cabinet and took out a folder.

"Yvette Hétreau, did you say? Yes, here she is." She pulled out a single typed sheet with a passport-size photo clipped to the top and handed it to them.

Evan looked over Sergeant Watkins's shoulder.

"Wait a second," he said. "That's not her."

"Didn't I give you the right one?" the Dutch girl asked. "You said Yvette Hétreau, didn't you?"

"Someone must have mixed up the photos," Evan said. "This isn't Madame Yvette."

"Are you sure?" Watkins peered more closely at the photo. "It was taken a long time ago, remember."

"It's not unlike her," Evan said, trying to bring a picture of Madame Yvette into his mind. "Same kind of hairstyle, same Roman nose but . . ."

"People change and put on weight," Watkins pointed out. "And she was burned in a fire, remember."

Evan shook his head. "There's something about the shape of the face — this one is more heart shaped. Madame Yvette has a longer face. And look at the way she's smiling. You can't change your smile, sarge."

"This isn't the person you're looking for?" The Dutch girl looked confused.

"It's not the person whose photo we saw in the entrance hall," Evan said. "We recognized her there easily enough."

"Is it possible the photos got mixed up?" Watkins asked.

"I suppose it's possible, although I can't see how or why," the girl said. "Student chefs have to submit a photo with their application and it stays attached to it. No one would have any reason to remove it." She put the folder on top of the filing cabinet. "Please, look through these applications and see if you can find the person whose photo you saw in the hallway."

They went through the applications one by one. Then there she was — a younger, prettier version of Madame Yvette smiling at them. "This is her," Watkins and Evan said at the same time.

The name on the form was Janine Laroque.

"Yes, they do look a little alike," the Dutch girl said. "They both do their hair in the same way. So you say this is really Yvette Bouchard? I should put the pictures back where they belong." She unclipped the photo, then stopped with the photo lying in the palm of her hand.

"I think you gentlemen are mixed up," she said. "Look at this."

On the back of the photo a spidery French hand had written, "Janine Laroque, Paris, 17 Feb. 1988."

"I don't understand," Watkins said.

"Unless . . ." Evan began.

"Unless what?"

"There's only one explanation," Evan said. "That the person up in Wales right now isn't really Yvette Bouchard."

CHAPTER 19

"Who the hell is she?" Watkins demanded, as soon as they were back on the crowded Paris street "And what has happened to the real Madame Yvette?"

Evan was wrestling with probabilities and he didn't like any of them. In his heart he had wanted to find that the woman he knew as Madame Yvette was an innocent victim. Part of his eagerness to come with Watkins and solve the mystery had been the desire to clear Yvette's name. He realized he had cast himself as the knight in shining armour again, ready to rescue the damsel in distress, or what Bronwen would call his boy scout syndrome.

And now it appeared that he had been duped — taken in by a pretty, helpless woman. Sweet, gentle, abandoned Madame Yvette, appealing for his help, had been using him — hoping to keep the police from delving deeper into a shady past. She had identified him correctly as the soft-hearted village constable. Had she also added "not too bright" to that description? Now Evan saw that she had probably planned the whole thing — the threatening notes, the phoney seduction, too.

"No wonder she didn't recognize her husband when he came into the restaurant," Watkins said, chuckling. He was beginning to enjoy himself, clearly looking forward to going home with the riddle solved and the criminal apprehended. "Boy, what a shock that must have been for her."

"He must have told her who he was," Evan continued the scenario, "which was why she was so upset when she came to our table and nearly set fire to us when she tried to cook the crêpes Suzette."

"What are they? Pardon my ignorance but I don't go eating at posh places like you."

"Crêpes Suzette, you mean? They're little pancakes. You flambé them in liqueur — you set them on fire."

"I know flambé. I'm not that much of an ignoramus. I've flambéed in my time."

Evan grinned. "I remember. Hamburgers on that new barbecue last year, wasn't it?"

Watkins gave him a withering glare. "Okay, so the husband showed up at the restaurant and found out she wasn't his wife . . . She panicked when she realized she'd been found out, lured him into her flat, stabbed him and then set fire to the place to cover up the crime."

"It certainly looks that way."

"What other explanation could there be?" Watkins asked.

Evan thought, then shook his head. "I don't know. It all seems to tie in, doesn't it?"

"There are still a lot of things we don't know and we'll have to find out. Why did he decide to show up then, after having been missing all that time?"

"I thought he'd already decided that — he's been missing long enough to be declared legally dead. If they had taken out an insurance policy, his wife could now legally collect. They probably planned this whole thing between them, either for the money or because it was prudent for him to vanish."

"But if the wife was no longer around — if she'd died in the meantime, after that fire maybe, and Janine Whatshername was her friend . . ." Watkins continued, looking to Evan to take this one step further.

"Janine knew about the insurance policy and decided to impersonate Yvette and collect the money. She opened a restaurant where nobody would remember the real Yvette — who spoke English as well as a native, remember — and worked on establishing her credibility."

"So you think the real Yvette died?"

"She was badly burned in that fire, wasn't she?" Evan said. "Maybe she's too disfigured to go out in public again."

"Either way, it doesn't look good for our friend Janine," Watkins said. "It's a premeditated crime, even if the murder was spur-of-the moment panic."

Evan nodded. "She couldn't have known that the husband was still alive, could she? She didn't know him when he came in and she certainly wasn't expecting him to show up again . . ."

They had reached the metro station. Evan looked up and glimpsed the shape of the Eiffel Tower in the distance. "Eiffel Tower, sarge," he said.

"So it is. Oh well, so much for the grand tour of Paris," Watkins sighed. "I don't think we've even got time for a quick lunch at Maxim's, have we? It will have to be a sandwich on the autoroute if we want to get home tonight."

He headed down the steps into the gusty darkness. Evan gave the Eiffel Tower one more glance before he followed. "The first thing to do is to find out if the real Yvette is still in any kind of hospital. That should be easy enough . . ."

"Oh no, boyo," Watkins said, his voice echoing from the tiled walls. "The first thing to do is to have the phoney Yvette brought into custody before she decides to do a bunk on us."

"Do you think we should visit the police here in Paris before we go?" Evan asked. "We should find out if Janine Laroque has a criminal record."

Watkins looked uncomfortable. "I don't think I want to go that far. Contacting the French police would be something for the DI, wouldn't it? Especially as we're not officially over here. We'll phone HQ as soon as we get back to England. I'm not messing with French phones. I did that once. Never again. We'll suggest they bring in Janine Whatsit and let Glynis find out about her record. With any luck we'll know everything we need to when we get home. And I think they'll have to say we did a bloody good job over here, don't you?"

* * *

They took the Chunnel back to England at five that evening. Evan had hoped the crossing would be easier the second time, now that he knew what to expect, but he still found himself drenched in a cold sweat and wished he'd taken Watkins's advice.

"I told you to have a couple of brandies before we started," Watkins said as they came out into twilight near Folkstone. "You look green around the gills."

"I'll be all right," Evan said. "And I could hardly risk being pulled over and breathalyzed, could I? It wouldn't look good for the North Wales Police."

"I could drive," Watkins said.

"Yes, and we'd spend the night going around the ring road trying to get away from London." Evan managed a grin. He was recovering quickly now that they were on the open road.

"What time do you reckon we'll be home?"

"In the middle of the night if we drive nonstop," Evan said. "But we should pull off at the first place we see and make our phone call to HQ before they all go home for the night."

"Good idea," Watkins said, "and it would be a good excuse to stop for a pint and a bite of good English food at the same time." He chuckled. "I never thought I'd hear myself saying the words good English food — but I'd kill for a plate of bangers and mash or even a warmed-over meat pie."

They pulled off at the first pub that they saw. Watkins conveyed his message to headquarters and they had a satisfying plaice and chips before heading back to Wales. It was two-fifteen in the morning when Evan drove up Llanfair High Street. The floodlights outside the pub and the Everest

Inn had been turned off and the street was in almost total darkness. Llanfair felt like an abandoned, gloomy sort of place, and Evan shivered. He let himself in silently and took off his shoes before he tiptoed up the stairs. His eyes were prickling with tiredness.

Suddenly he gasped as an apparition in white loomed in front of him. At the same moment the apparition gave a scream. Evan recognized the powerful lungs.

"It's only me, Mrs Williams," he said.

"'Deed to goodness, Mr Evans!" Mrs Williams gasped, leaning against the banister and clutching at her ample bosom. "You nearly scared the daylights out of me."

"Sorry I scared you, Mrs Williams, but I just got back from France," Evan said. His own heart had been racing, too.

"From France? Whatever next. And I don't suppose you've had a decent meal in days if you've been in France. I've got some veal and ham pie downstairs . . ."

Evan put out a hand to stop her from going downstairs.

"No thanks. I don't need anything except a good night's sleep, Mrs Williams. Go on back to bed. I'll see you in the morning."

"You're sure you don't want a nice cup of cocoa?"

"Nothing, thanks. I've been driving for twelve hours straight. All I need is sleep."

"Well, I hope it was worth it," she said. "I hope you found out who set fire to poor Madame Yvette's restaurant and killed that man."

"I think we might have done, Mrs Williams. We'll just have to see in the morning if we were right," Evan said.

He continued down the hallway and collapsed onto his bed, falling asleep before he had time to undress.

* * *

In his dream he was in a dark place — he wasn't sure if it was a coffin or a tunnel, but he could sense the roof pressing down on him and feel the sweat trickling down his back.

Whatever it was, there was no way out. Then a bell started to ring. "My funeral bell," he said to himself. But funeral bells were usually slower and more sombre.

He opened his eyes and realized that it was the telephone. The morning sun was painting stripes of light on his wall. Heart still pounding, he ran downstairs and got to the phone before Mrs Williams could emerge from the kitchen.

"Did I wake you?" Watkins demanded.

"Of course you bloody woke me." He glanced at his watch. "It's only just seven, isn't it, and I didn't get to bed until after two."

"Well, the DI woke me and I saw no reason why you shouldn't share the news."

"What is it?"

"Madame Yvette has vanished. She left the pub two days ago without telling anyone where she was going."

"Damn," Evan muttered. "So we were right. She did get the wind up."

"The DI's got an all-points bulletin out for her but she could have slipped across the Channel, or taken the ferry to Ireland. She could be anywhere by now. I blame myself. We should have taken her into custody before we left."

"On what grounds, sarge? You know very well we had no good reason to bring her in before we went to France. She could just as easily have been the victim as the criminal."

"Well, I suppose it's not up to us any longer," Watkins said. "There's nothing more we can do until they catch her — which I don't think is very likely, if you want my opinion. You can go back to working on your serial arsonist and I can see if they'll let me come aboard onto Operation Armada again. But thanks for all your help, boyo. You win some and you lose some, I suppose."

Evan put the phone down and stood there in the dark, narrow front hall, staring at the flowery wallpaper.

"Damn," he muttered again.

"Mr Evans! Such language! It's not like you." Mrs Williams's head poked disapprovingly from the kitchen.

Evan grinned sheepishly. "Sorry, Mrs Williams."

"You're obviously overtired. A nice cup of tea will set you right."

He followed her into the kitchen, where warm, inviting smells were coming from the stove. He sat musing, with the cup cradled in his hands. What Watkins said was probably true. There was little likelihood of catching Madame Yvette. She had probably fled back to France — in which case it was out of their hands. It was frustrating not to be able to see it through. Maybe he'd never know whether she killed Jean Bouchard and maybe even started the fire that killed the real Yvette, too. Funny — but she still hadn't seemed like a murderer to him.

Well, he was up and awake now, so he'd better get on with his day, back to the old routine and probably a pile of complaints from Mrs Powell-Jones about the van. He showered and put on his uniform, then decided he might have time to see Bronwen before school started.

As he walked up the village street, Llanfair was coming to life. Evans-the-Milk was heading toward a doorstep, milk bottles rattling in his hands. "'ello, Evan *bach*," he called. "Back from your jaunt to the South then, are you?"

Evans-the-Post came out of the post office, extracted a postcard from his mail bag and stood in the middle of the street, studying it. He jumped guiltily when he saw Evan.

"It's from Mrs Jones, Number 24's sister," he said, waving the postcard in Evan's face. "She's on holiday in Bournemouth. Look, see the picture? That's the pier. They say you went down south, too. Did you go on the pier when you were down there, Mr Evans?"

"Your snooping is going to get you in trouble one day," Evan said. "That's personal stuff you're reading there."

"I don't do no harm," Evans-the-Post protested. "I don't read letters from the income tax or the pensions, do I?"

"Only because you can't open them," Evan said with a grin. Evans-the-Post grinned too and loped off down the street.

Evan moved on. Even Evans-the-Post, with his limited brainpower, knew of his secret mission. No wonder Madame Yvette had heard about it and fled.

He was deep in thought as he continued up the street. Maybe Madame Yvette had even heard somehow that he'd gone to France. Nothing seemed to escape the Llanfair spies. Suddenly he looked up and found himself confronted with a large green bus. It was parked outside Chapel Beulah and painted on its side were the words

CELESTIAL OMNIBUS. CHAPEL BEULAH. LLANFAIR.

And in smaller letters underneath, *We pray in Welsh, we sing in Welsh, we preach in Welsh!*

It completely dwarfed the plain grey van parked across the street outside Chapel Bethel.

Evan started to laugh. What next? Would Rev. Parry Davies have to indulge in a helicopter? A fleet of limousines? He looked forward to having a good chuckle with Bronwen about it. He felt a sudden thrill of anticipation about seeing her again. He had only been away three days, but he had missed her. That was a sign that he must be serious about her, wasn't it?

But as he put his hand on the playground gate and looked across at the schoolhouse with the smoke curling from its chimney, he felt suddenly hesitant. She'd obviously be busy preparing for the school day and probably wouldn't have time to talk to him. And it was absurd to be missing her when he'd only been gone such a short time. He'd come back when school was over this afternoon.

He turned and began to walk away, half hoping that he'd hear his name called and see her standing there. But he reached the police station door without being stopped.

Inside, the green light was blinking on his answering machine and a pile of letters lay on the mat. He picked up the letters and noted the top one. It was on good stationery paper, headed *Grantley, Straughan and Grantley, Solicitors* in Buxton, Derbyshire. He couldn't make a connection until he began to read. The letter was written on behalf of Mr and Mrs Paxton-Smith, owners of cottage Ty Bryn. Evan nodded to himself. The English couple — so that was their name. He'd bet it wasn't really hyphenated, but just plain Smith. Obnoxious prigs! Mr and Mrs Paxton-Smith were not satisfied with the original police report . . . possible negligence . . . understood he was the officer on duty . . . wanted his first-hand account of the handling of the fire . . .

Evan put it down in disgust. They'd collect on the insurance but it sounded as if they were preparing to sue somebody as well. He'd pass it on to HQ and let them handle it. He put on the electric kettle for tea, then sat at his desk and punched Replay on the answering machine.

"Constable Evans?" The voice was soft and Welsh. "This is Mrs Parry Davies at Chapel Bethel. There is a large bus blocking the entire street. It's creating quite a traffic hazard. Please have it moved immediately."

Evan grinned.

The next message made his pulse quicken. "Constable Evans, this is PC Glynis Davies from headquarters. I just thought you'd like to know that Forensics have found the murder weapon and they're attempting to get a good set of prints from it. Oh, and there's no answer from the French police yet to any of our inquiries so we're not much the wiser — bye."

Evan smiled to himself as an image of Glynis's stylish, elfin face swam into his mind. Would finding out about the prints on the murder weapon give him a good excuse to go down to HQ and maybe see her again? Wait a second, he reminded himself severely. A few minutes ago you were pining for Bronwen. What's wrong with you, boyo?

"Evans!" Sergeant Potter's voice barked from the speaker, instantly banishing any thoughts of Bronwen or Glynis from his mind. "I want to see you in my office right away. I think we may have the answer to our serial arsonist. I need you to make the identification."

Short, sweet, and to the point, Evan thought. At least now he had his excuse to drive down to HQ. It was strange, but he'd pushed the whole arson aspect of the case aside the moment they started to focus on Madame Yvette and the murder. Obviously there was still a serial arsonist out there, even if he might not have torched the restaurant. Evan wondered if it would turn out to be the Meibion Gwynedd extremists who were responsible for the fires after all. It would be nice to solve at least one aspect of this case.

CHAPTER 20

As luck would have it, Evan literally bumped into PC Davies as he came through the swing doors.

Oh, I'm sorry," he exclaimed as she staggered backward, then realized whom he was steadying and felt doubly stupid.

"Oh, Constable Evans, it's you," she said, not looking at all flustered. "Welcome back. How was Paris?"

"All I saw was one street, one metro station, and a glimpse of the Eiffel Tower," Evan answered.

"Too bad. And too bad that the Frenchwoman got away after all your efforts. I bet you were amazed when you found out she wasn't the real Madame Yvette, weren't you? The DI couldn't believe it when he heard."

"I still haven't got the whole thing straight," Evan said. "It got more complicated by the minute. And now that Janine's disappeared I wonder if we'll ever know the truth. By the way, thanks for keeping me updated on the murder weapon."

"I thought you'd like to know and I didn't imagine anyone else here would remember to tell you," she said, glancing around with a guilty smile. "I'm escaping to get my coffee fix again. I don't suppose you've got time to join me?"

"I've been summoned to the presence of Sergeant Potter," Evan said.

"That awful Englishman? Talk about God's gift to the world of forensics!" She grinned. "Good luck."

"Thanks, I'll need it," Evan said.

"I'll bring you back an espresso if you like. I think strong coffee is in order after you've been in with him."

"Thanks, Glynis," he said. She really was very nice, as well as being pretty and clever. Close to perfect, actually. He still couldn't tell whether she really did fancy him, or if she was just friendly to everyone. Better to keep it strictly on a professional level, just in case, he reminded himself. No more calling her by her first name . . .

"Only don't let on to Sergeant Potter that I'm bringing you back a coffee," she murmured, leaning close enough to him that he got a whiff of a very nice spicy perfume. "He asked me to get him a cup of tea the other day and I told him not to expect maid service just because I was a woman."

Evan laughed. "I'll remember. So what's the latest on the murder weapon — did they find any prints?"

"Yes, two sets. One belonging to Madame Yvette, or whatever her real name is — which makes sense because it was her biggest kitchen knife, but a thumbprint that doesn't belong to her. And it doesn't match any print that we've looked at so far.

"Man's or woman's? Can they tell?"

"It was bigger than hers but not necessarily a man's. I'll keep you posted if I hear any more, okay?"

He nodded. "Brilliant."

"Although her sudden disappearance must point to her guilt, don't you think?" Glynis asked. "You don't run away if you've got nothing to hide." She looked up at him. "Do you think they'll ever catch her?"

"I hope so, but I wouldn't bet on it."

"I wonder who tipped her off that you'd gone to France and were checking into her background?"

Evan smiled. "You don't know how the local bush telegraph works in places like Llanfair. It would have been around the whole district in seconds."

"Doesn't it drive you mad, trying to work in a little village like that?" she asked. "Why don't you ask for a transfer to headquarters?"

"I'm sort of used to it now," Evan said. "It's my own little niche up there."

"You're too young to get stuck in a rut, Constable Evans," she said. "It's about time you thought about getting ahead." Then she realized what she had said and blushed. "I'll bring you back that coffee."

Evan went in search of Sergeant Watkins but couldn't find him. The DI was out, too. He was met with blank faces when he inquired where everyone might be, which must mean that Operation Armada was in full swing and they were out on the coast somewhere. The whole building had an empty, deserted feel to it and more than ever he felt like an outsider.

All right. He'd get the interview with Potter over as quickly as possible. He knocked on the office door and went in.

"Ah Evans, you finally got here. Took your time, didn't you?" Sergeant Potter looked up from his desk.

"Sorry. I was with Sergeant Watkins over in France — didn't they tell you?"

"No, they didn't bloody tell me," Potter growled. "Bloody half-arsed operation here. The right hand doesn't know what the effing left hand is doing. No wonder nothing gets solved. But they've got Peter Potter now. Things will change. At least I'll show them how I solve my cases."

"So you think you've found the serial arsonist?" Evan asked.

"I know we have, son." Potter looked smug. "It's all a question of profiling. I took a look at your lists of names and I talked to the fire brigade and only one person fits the bill. He was there in the thick of it, all three times. Classic serial arsonist — does it because he likes fires and he likes to help putting them out, too. I took photos at the restaurant fire. Here, take a look at this." He handed Evan a blown-up photo. "See that young chap?"

"That's Terry Jenkins," Evan said. "He's only a little kid."

"You'd be amazed what an eleven-year-old boy can do if he sets his mind to it." Potter was still looking smug. "He's the perfect candidate for my profile — wild kid, not much supervision, loner so they say, and the fire captain said he was always there in the thick of it, trying to help — at all three fires. You know him, do you?"

"Yes, he lives in our village."

"See? I knew it had to be a local. Okay, go and bring him in, Evans. I'm looking forward to a chat with him. I'll make the little bugger confess."

"Hold on a minute, sarge." There was a sinking feeling in his stomach at the thought of bringing Terry to meet Sergeant Potter. "What about the note? Would a little kid get it into his head to write a note like the one we found?"

"They watch the news on the telly, don't they?" Potter said with scorn. "He probably saw a report on Welsh extremists burning cottages and that gave him the idea in the first place. Like I said, kids are sharp. They don't miss much."

"I got a sample of his handwriting," Evan said. "Shouldn't we run that through a check before we pick him up?"

"Match it to the note, you mean? Yes, we can do that. And I'll get his medical records checked, too — ten to one he's seeing a shrink. He's probably talked about arson fantasies — they do, you know — but the stupid doctors never think of getting in touch with us, do they? But I still want to see the little bugger. He won't put anything past me."

"I'll bring him in after school, then, shall I?" Evan asked, hoping to forestall Potter from bursting into Bronwen's classroom, probably waving a weapon or an arrest warrant into the bargain. "We don't want to upset the rest of the children, do we?"

"If you ask me, everyone panders to kids too much these days," Potter said. "But I can wait until school's over, I suppose. Just bring him in. I'll be waiting."

Evan still felt slightly sick as he drove back up the pass. The strong espresso hadn't agreed with his lack of sleep and gnawed at his stomach. He wasn't used to drinking it like that, without milk, but he wasn't going to admit such a failing to Glynis. Maybe the sour feeling in his stomach had to do with bringing in Terry. He hadn't told Potter that he'd also suspected the boy. Poor kid. Unfortunately Terry did fit the profile . . .

On impulse he stopped at Roberts-the-Pump's petrol station.

"Off jaunting again?" The garage owner, asked. "Where is it this time — the Monte Carlo pally?"

"I don't need petrol. I just want to ask you something," Evan said, beckoning the man closer. "Have you sold any petrol to young Terry Jenkins recently?"

Roberts frowned as he thought. Then he nodded. "Yes, I have, as a matter of fact. He came in here about a week or so ago with a can. He said his mother wanted it for the lawn mower." Realization dawned as he picked up Evan's train of thought. "Wait a minute — they only have a pocket handkerchief square of lawn, don't they? Why would they need a motor mower?"

"Exactly," Evan agreed. "Oh dear. It looks like young Terry's in for it."

"Only a matter of time, wasn't it? I thought as much when we caught the boy busting into my chocolate machines. Sometimes they're born with criminal tendencies, aren't they?"

Yes, but not Terry, Evan wanted to say. Terry was just a bright, angry boy who needed a father. With a heavy heart he waited at the police station until it was time to walk over to the school. A group of boys pushed through the gate but Terry wasn't among them. Then Evan saw him climbing the fence and leaping nimbly down — a typically Terry thing to do. Evan intercepted him as he landed. The boy's face lit up.

"Constable Evans! You're back? Did you catch the killer yet? Was it that creepy guy with the gun that I saw? I bet he was a mafia bloke, wasn't he? International crime and all that."

Evan put a hand on the boy's thin shoulder. "Terry, you and I have to go and talk."

"What about?" The boy's face was still alight with anticipation. "You want my report on what went on while you were away?"

"It's a little more serious than that, Terry," Evan said. "Sergeant Potter in Caernarfon wants to talk to you about the fires."

"He does?" Terry still looked excited. "You're going to take me down to Caernarfon?"

"We should tell your mother first," Evan said.

Terry shook his head. "She's out at work, isn't she? We'll be back before her."

"We have to call her, Terry," Evan said. "She has to know."

Terry opened his mouth to protest.

"You don't want her to worry, do you?" Evan asked.

Terry shrugged and followed Evan down to the station to make the call.

"Does Sergeant Potter want me to be a witness?" Terry asked as he climbed into Evan's car. "I didn't see anybody light the fires, you know."

"Didn't you?" Evan asked. He started the engine and moved away from the curb.

"What do you mean?" For the first time the young face looked troubled.

"What did you buy petrol for, Terry?" Evan asked. "You don't need a motor mower for your little lawn."

Terry's face flushed. "No, I know," he said. "I thought I might get a job, see — mowing lawns. We've got a motor mower in the shed. But nobody around here has a big enough lawn, do they?"

Evan looked at him, wishing he could see inside the boy's head. "Petrol was used to start two of those fires, Terry.

You were the first person to spot the fire at the Everest Inn, weren't you?"

"I was out on my bike," Terry said.

"You must be feeling pretty angry that your dad walked out," Evan said.

"Yeah, I suppose so. What's that got to do with anything?"

"Angry enough to start some fires?" Evan asked.

Terry looked shocked. "I didn't start those fires — why would I want to start fires? I told you — I want to be a fire-man like Bryn and put them out." He turned to stare out of the car window. Evan tried to think what to say next. When Terry looked back at him, his face was a blank mask, and Evan felt a terrible sense of having betrayed the boy.

"I can prove I didn't start the first fire, anyway, because Dai Mathias saw me climbing out of my window and he said, 'You're going to get it, Terry Jenkins,' and I told him I'd beat him up if he told on me."

Evan digested this piece of information. It had the ring of truth to it — not the kind of thing a child would make up on the spur of the moment.

"All right. We'll talk to Dai," he said. He reached out and touched the boy's arm. "Look, Terry, I'm only doing my job," he said. "I was told to bring you in and I'm bringing you in. Just tell the truth and nothing bad can happen to you."

Terry managed a weak smile. "All right, Mr Evans."

As they passed the burned-out shell of the restaurant, Terry's face became animated again. "Guess what, Mr Evans? I saw that man again."

"What man?"

"You know, the one I told you about — the foreign-looking bloke with the gun . . . driving the red sports car."

"Wait a minute, Terry . . ." Evan was confused. "You're saying you saw him again? Recently?"

"While you were away. He stopped me again and he asked me about the fire. He spoke really funny. I could hardly understand him. He wanted to know if anyone was killed in the fire and I told him they'd found a body."

"While I was away, you say?"

Terry nodded. "He a creepy-looking guy, Mr Evans. Real scary-looking and he had a scar and everything — just like a gangster."

Evan glanced at the boy. Was this a diversionary tactic to take the heat off the boy himself? Evan wondered.

"He asked about the French lady, too," Terry went on. "I said I didn't know where she was, in case he was the killer, even though he gave me a pound."

He grinned at his own cleverness.

"Even though I do really know, but I promised Miss Price I wouldn't tell."

"Miss Price?" Evan stopped the car and stared at him.

"Yeah. Miss Price said she wanted it kept quiet that the French lady was staying with her."

Evan's jaw dropped open. "Are you saying that the French lady is staying with Miss Price — right now?"

"I think she's still there," Terry said. "Hey, aren't we going down to Caernarfon?"

"Later, Terry," Evan said as he swung the car around with tires screeching. "We've got more important things to do first. Sergeant Potter will just have to wait."

* * *

Bronwen was out in the playground with a large broom, sweeping up the leaves that had blown across the netball court. She was wearing her red cape and her hair was unbraided, blowing out behind her in the wind. She looked like a character from an old fairy tale. As he opened the school playground gate it squeaked. She looked up and her face broke into a smile.

"When did you get back? How was the south coast?"

"The south coast was only the beginning. I went to France yesterday," Evan said.

"France?"

"There and back in a day, thanks to the wonders of modern transportation."

"A good thing, too," Bronwen commented as the last leaf was whisked into the pile. "No time to get too acquainted with Gay Paree and Frenchwomen."

"The closest I got to the high life was a cup of disgusting coffee and a thin ham sandwich that cost me five pounds on the autoroute," Evan said. "No, I lie. I did have a cup of coffee and a croissant, too."

"Living the high life, eh?" Bronwen smiled. "Hold the sack for me, please, so that I can get these leaves in before they blow away." Bronwen handed him the sack that lay beside the leaves. He took it, caught off guard and wondering how she could be acting so normally — wondering how to ask her and why she hadn't told him before. "They're wonderful as compost. They'll help with next year's vegetable garden and nothing tastes as good as home-grown food, as I'm sure Madame Yvette can tell you."

"Ah yes, about Madame Yvette . . ." Evan began.

"So what happened?" she asked. "Did you find out anything about her in France?"

Evan nodded. "Oh, yes, we found out plenty — the major fact being that she's not really Madame Yvette."

"What do you mean? Who is she?"

"Her real name is Janine Laroque. She was a classmate of Yvette's at the Cordon Bleu school."

"So why is she claiming to be Madame Yvette? Is there a real Madame Yvette?"

"The real Yvette was badly burned in a restaurant fire in the South of England."

"And died?"

He shrugged. "We don't know yet. We've no idea what happened to her, whether this woman started that fire . . . but we suspect that the body we found in the restaurant is the real Yvette's husband."

"Evan, that's terrible," Bronwen put her hand to her mouth. "Are you saying that she — killed him?"

Evan shrugged. "It looks that way, doesn't it? We tried to bring her in for questioning, but she's disappeared — you wouldn't know anything about that, would you, because I heard the strangest rumour from young Terry . . ."

"Do you think she's dangerous?" Bronwen still had the stunned look on her face. "Oh dear." She bit her lip. "I think I might have done something rather silly."

"What have you done, Bronwen?" He stepped closer to her.

She turned to stare at her front door. "I've got Madame Yvette in there," she said in a low voice.

"Then Terry was right. What were you thinking of, Bronwen? You could be up for harbouring a fugitive from justice."

Her cheeks flushed. "I had no idea! I did what I thought was best. I was only trying to be kind, look you. How was I to know?"

"Why on earth did she come to your house?" Evan fought to remain calm. He couldn't dismiss the thought that Bronwen had been sheltering a possible killer and might have been in danger herself.

"I invited her," Bronwen said simply. "Remember I told you I felt sorry for her having to stay at the pub and not knowing what was going to happen next? It's a miserable place, that pub, and she had no clothes, no toiletries . . . I had the spare room, so I invited her to come and stay with me until she was free to leave. She was very grateful, Evan."

"Bronwen Price — one of these days . . ." Evan put his hands on her shoulders. "I've got enough to worry about without having to worry about you doing stupid things!"

"Stupid things indeed," she said, tossing her mane of hair. "You should be thanking me that I've kept her on the spot, just where you want her. Now you don't have to go chasing after her, do you? Although I must say I can't believe that she's as wicked as you say. She seems so nice and polite and grateful."

"There are plenty of serial killers who seemed nice and normal to those around them," Evan said. "But you're right — I do have to be grateful to you. When she hears what we've discovered, maybe she'll finally tell us the truth."

CHAPTER 21

The woman he had known as Madame Yvette was sitting beside the Aga stove in Bronwen's kitchen, wrapped in one of Bronwen's fringed shawls, and looking remarkably like a witch, her hook nose more pronounced and her eyes hollower than he remembered.

She looked up when she saw him and smiled warily. "Ah — it is Monsieur Evans. You went down to Sussex, I 'ear. But you did not see zee remains of my poor restaurant, I sink — zey tell me zere ees now a new building where it used to be and zere ees nossing to show zat I was zere anymore."

He looked at her. She was still relaxed, confident that they had found nothing that could incriminate her.

"We didn't just go to Sussex," he said, watching her face. "We went to France as well."

There was another flash of wariness, then she shrugged. "A wasted journey, I should sink. Nobody ees alive now in France who remember me."

"On the contrary," Evan said. "It was most informative."

The wariness returned to her face.

"We learned, for example," Evan went on, "that the body in your restaurant was that of Jean Bouchard — your husband who died five years ago, Madame Yvette. It seems he returned from the grave to die again. And you know the strangest thing? He came into the restaurant and you didn't recognize him. I don't think a person changes that much in five years, do they?"

Madame Yvette drew the shawl around her. "I don't know what you talk about," she said. "I had nevair seen zat man before in my life."

"What man?" Evan asked.

"The man who came into zee restaurant while you were 'aving dinner," she said, then flushed when she realized he had tricked her. "You saw 'im come in. He was a stranger, monsieur. I swear zis on my honour."

"Of course you do," Evan said, "and I know you're telling the truth — why would you recognize Yvette Bouchard's husband when you aren't Yvette Bouchard?"

He heard a sharp intake of breath and the dark eyes flashed at him defiantly. "Can you prove zis, monsieur?"

"Of course," Evan said. "We went to your cooking school. I've got your photo with your name written across the back in your own handwriting — the same handwriting in which you signed your police report — and Yvette's photo, too. So you were classmates, were you? Did you come over to console her when her husband was lost at sea? The next thing we know, her restaurant burns to the ground and poor Madame Yvette is dragged out, badly burned. Was that really an accident? I can't work out what would make you do it, unless it was spite and jealousy. Were you jealous of your friend, Madame? Did you begrudge her the good life she had in England?"

A look of scorn crossed her face. "Zee good life you say? Eet was a life of drudgery, monsieur. She struggle to keep zat place going. Wizout me she would have 'ad to close long ago. I kept her going—"

"And then burned her to the ground? Why?"

"As you say, why? Why should I want to burn down 'er restaurant? Let me tell you, monsieur. When zat restaurant burned, my own 'opes of freedom were destroyed."

"So you're saying that you didn't burn down the place? You were certainly quick enough to take advantage of the situation, weren't you? Madame Yvette was badly burned in the fire. Did you decide to take her place, knowing she's still lying in some hospital, burned and disfigured?"

Yvette got to her feet. "You policemen, you sink you are so clevair. You sink you know everysing. But you 'ave zee whole sing wrong," she said. "It was I who was badly burned. I who was disfigured — I who lay in zee 'ospital suffering for months—" With a dramatic gesture she grasped at her hair and whisked it from her head. The right half of her scalp was bald, covered with angry red-and-purple scars that ran down the back of her neck.

"Not very attractive, *eh?* Why do you sink I always wear zee high necks and long sleeves, monsieur? I wish to hide my burned body from the world."

"And yet you tried to seduce me," Evan said, conscious of Bronwen standing behind him. "Weren't you going to take your clothes off if I'd taken up your offer?"

The Frenchwoman laughed. "Zat was just a game — to prove to myself zat I was still a woman and I still 'ad zee — how you say — sex appeal. I didn't really sink you would take me up on it. But if you 'ad, I would have turned out zee light — and I sink you would have been too busy to notice!"

Evan cleared his throat. "So you're trying to tell me that you were the one in the restaurant fire, not Yvette Bouchard? Where the hell was she, then?"

"She died, monsieur," the Frenchwoman said simply. "She died in a fire so hot that nozzing remained. And zay didn't search for zee leetle pieces of bone zat might have been 'ers, because zay thought only one person was in zee building and zay rescue one person — me. You see, nobody but Yvette knew zat I was zere."

"Why?" Bronwen asked.

"Let's just say I got out of France in a 'urry."

"You were running from the law?" Evan asked.

The Frenchwoman laughed bitterly. "From zee law? From zee law zat would not protect me, monsieur."

Bronwen pulled a chair close to the stove and patted the cushion for Evan to sit. "I think we'd better hear the whole story," she said. "I'm still awfully confused."

Evan sat and Bronwen pulled a kitchen stool beside him.

"Very well, I tell you zee story." The Frenchwoman toyed with the wig in her hands. "And zen you can see zat I am not a criminal." She stared at the stove, turning away from them. "You are correct — my name is Janine Laroque. Yvette and I were classmates at zee Cordon Bleu. We become friends immediately. We came from zee same situations. We both had nobody in zee world: she was from an orphanage and zen she had worked as an au pair in England for many years. I was raised by an old aunt who died when I was sixteen. We both wanted to be zee world's greatest chefs . . ." She smiled at the memory and looked up with the smile still on her face. "I was better zan she was. She was — *pas mal.* I was good. I could have been a great chef, I sink, but I was stupid. I did what young girls do. I fell in love." The smile faded.

"When we finish at zee Cordon Bleu, I get a job in a famous restaurant in Paris. She goes back to work in England. She loved England. She spoke English very well — she 'ad zee gift of languages. I 'ad zee gift of cooking. I tell her she should be zee teacher or zee interpreter, but she want to be zee chef also.

"Yvette also fall in love wiz a young man she meet on zee Channel boats. She makes a good choice. I do not. I meet my husband when he came into zee restaurant. He was very 'andsome — bronze skin, dark curly hair — like a young god, monsieur. And he was rich. He spend lots of money on me. He sweep me off my feet, as you say. But what do I know of men? When I marry 'eem, I find he is zee bad man — jealous and violent. If I speak wiz a man in the market he goes crazy! I know I must get away, but where? I 'ave nobody." She turned to look at Bronwen, her eyes imploring her to understand. "Zen my friend Yvette write to me. She has saved up enough money to buy a little restaurant in England. And zen tragedy comes to 'er as well. Her husband falls from his boat and drown. She writes and says she ees all alone and she wish I could be wiz her.

"Zen a miracle happen. Zee police come and arrest my 'usband. Zat night I take zee boat to England. Yvette welcome me and say I can stay wiz her and we will tell no one zat I am zere. So I stay. I do zee cooking and she serve zee customers."

"Did Yvette know that her husband hadn't really drowned?" Evan asked.

Janine shook her head. "She nevair tell me. Sometimes I suspect zat Jean ees not really dead, but she does not want to tell me, so I do not ask again. Now I see zat zay plan zis whole sing . . . I get a letter, monsieur. It tell me zat Jean is now dead five years and I can now receive zee insurance money — one hundred sousand pounds, monsieur. *Pas mal.*"

"And would you have cashed that cheque?" Evan asked.

Yvette shrugged. "Who can say? I sink Jean is dead, *n'est-ce pas?* But now I see what zay have planned. Zay get zee life insurance money and zay live 'appily ever after." She sighed. "Zere is no 'appy ever after, monsieur. One night zee restaurant catch on fire. I do not know 'ow, but Yvette smoked cigarettes. She was sometimes so tired zat she fall asleep with zee cigarette in 'er hand. Maybe zat is 'ow it started. All I know is zat I wake wiz my room full of smoke. Zere was no window in my little room, no way out except zee door to zee kitchen. Zee kitchen is full of flame. I try to run through those flames but I don't get as far as zee door."

"Zee next sing I know, I wake in zee 'ospital bed. I am in zee great pain. My 'air is all burned away. Who would recognize me, zee way I look? Zay are calling me Madame Bouchard. I alone was saved from zee burning building. And zen I realize — zis is my chance. Now I can start a new life. I am Yvette Bouchard."

She put her wig back on her head. "For a while zay did not know if I would live or die. But I lived — I went on living as Yvette Bouchard. I thought zat I am safe because Yvette had nobody in zee world who know 'er. She was an orphan, you know. She 'ad no family. I come to a distant place and start again. At last, I am free."

"Until Jean Bouchard turned up," Evan said. "That must have been a nasty shock for you."

"A nasty shock you say? I almost die when he tell me who 'e ees. And 'e ees so angry. He say, 'What 'ave you done wiz my wife? You keel my wife!' He blame me, monsieur. He think I keel his wife."

"And so you had to kill him," Evan said.

She spun around to face him. "I did not keel him, monsieur. I swear to you by all zee saints, I did not keel him."

"Oh come on now," Evan said. "You were desperate. This man would ruin your life. You had no choice — you had to stop him somehow."

"I am very upset and confused when I see 'im. I tell 'im to go to my apartment and we will talk as soon as I get rid of zee patrons. You are zee last patrons to leave. I run up zee stairs and zen I see 'im. He is lying on zee floor — dead. My kitchen knife is sticking from 'is chest. Zere is blood everywhere . . . Mon dieu, eet is terrible! I don't know what to do." She spread her hands in a very French gesture. "Who would believe me if I tell zee truth? Zay will sink, like you, zat I keel 'im. So I remember 'ow zee fire in Sussex burn everysing so well that nossing is left. I pour cooking oil everywhere and I put a big pot of oil on zee stove and I set my beautiful restaurant on fire . . . and once again, my dreams go up in flames."

She sank down in her chair, looking frail and old. Bronwen came over to her and put an arm around her shoulders. "It's going to be all right, Janine."

"How?" Janine asked in a cracked voice. "I sink it will nevair be all right for me."

Evan didn't know how to answer that one. He thought it was all too possible that a jury wouldn't believe Janine's far-fetched tale. In fact, every instance pointed to her guilt — hiding out at a friend's restaurant so that nobody knew she was there, that restaurant burning to the ground with its owner inside, and now the owner's husband lying stabbed with Janine's own kitchen knife. It was all too possible that the thumbprint on the knife was the victim's own as he tried to grab it away from her, or pull it from his chest. People had been hanged in the past on less evidence when there was still a death penalty.

"We have to help her, Evan," Bronwen said. "She's already had enough rotten luck."

Evan looked at Bronwen. Her eyes were pleading.

"I'll come with you down to headquarters, Janine," he said. "We'll see what we can do." Then he picked up the phone to call the squad car.

CHAPTER 22

Evan hesitated in the vinyl-tiled hallway and stood staring at the door he had just closed behind him. Usually there was satisfaction in bringing a case to a close, and a criminal to justice. Never had he felt more ambivalent than now. He wanted to believe that Janine Laroque was innocent, but reason told him that she had to be guilty. Unfortunately he was sure that DI Hughes would come to the same conclusion — and so would a jury. There was little hope of Janine getting off, unless he could prove that someone else committed the murder.

He sighed. He had done his job and delivered the suspect to the proper authorities. Now he could go home and catch up on some well-earned sleep. He had to learn not to become so emotionally involved with his cases, he told himself. A good policeman stayed detached.

A door opened down the hall and Evan realized, a second too late, that he should not have dawdled.

"Evans, is that you?" Potter's voice echoed. "Where is he, then?"

"I . . . I had . . . I mean something else came up." Evan was caught off guard.

"Something else came up? I gave you an order, sonny. It was up to you to obey it."

"Look, I'm sorry." Evan felt the colour rise in his cheeks. "But when I say something else, I mean something more important. I found the Frenchwoman who's the murder suspect everyone's been looking for. I've just brought her in. She's with Sergeant Watkins, waiting for the DI to get back."

"And you got yourself a nice pat on the back for that, did you? Well, I've got a case to solve as well and I want that kid brought in here. Now do you think you can find him, or do I have to send squad cars out for him?"

"Oh, I found him all right," Evan said. "In fact he was the one who told me where Madame Yvette was hiding out. I had a long talk with him, and I think you're making a mistake, sarge. I don't think he set those fires."

Potter's face was a mask of stone. "Oh, and what makes you the expert suddenly?"

"For one thing he hero-worships a young fireman and he wants to be a fireman too when he grows up. For another he claims he has an alibi for the cottage burning. Another kid saw him climbing down the drainpipe after the fire had already started and they ran up to the fire together. That will be easy enough to check."

"Kids? They'll say anything not to snitch on each other, won't they?"

Evan wondered if Sergeant Potter had any children of his own. If so, he was sorry for them.

"So you still want me to bring him in?" Evan asked.

"Of course I bloody want you to bring him in. If it's not too much to ask, that is?"

"Right. I'll go and get him now," Evan said. "Please tell Sergeant Watkins where I am, in case he needs me for anything."

He turned and strode to the front door, his feet making a satisfying clatter on the bare floor before he slammed the door behind him.

This is what happens when you're a village constable, he told himself as he drove, somewhat too fast, back through Llanberis and up the pass. You get walked all over. People order you around. He allowed his mind to drift into a fantasy in which he went back to detective training and did so well that he jumped through the ranks to inspector in a few months. Then he pictured himself walking in and telling Peter Potter exactly what he thought of him. It was a childish daydream and he was already smiling at himself by the time he reached Llanfair.

Nobody came to the door when Evan knocked at Terry's cottage. He drove up and down the village street, then parked his car and checked out all the likely places — the sports field, the school playground, the sweets counter at the village shop. Nobody he asked had seen Terry Jenkins. So the boy was in hiding. Evan couldn't say he blamed him. He'd probably have done the same thing at Terry's age. Oh well, give him time. He'd show up when he was hungry.

Around five-thirty he checked the Jenkinses' cottage again. Terry's mother had just got home and had frozen lasagne on the table, ready for a microwaved supper.

"I don't know where he is, Constable Evans," she said apologetically. "You know Terry. He's never home if it's daylight and not raining. He could be anywhere on that bike of his. I worry that someday he's going to get run over, but he seems able to take care of himself. There's not much I can do, is there?"

"You could try setting some rules," Evan said and wished instantly that he hadn't.

A defensive look spread across her face. "What, and have him hate me as much as he does his father? I'm trying to make up for his dad, Mr Evans, and that's not easy."

"I'm sure it's not," Evan agreed. "Let me know when he gets home, will you?"

He went back to the police station and phoned HQ. Glynis answered. It seemed as if she was turning into the maid of all work down there.

"You want me to tell Sergeant Potter that you can't find the boy and you'll bring him in as soon as you do. Okay. I'll probably get my head bitten off, but I'll do it for you." She paused then went on in a lower voice, "It's a shame you left when you did. You weren't here for the excitement."

"Why, what happened?"

"We got a match on that thumbprint."

"The one on the knife?"

"That's right."

"Incredible. Whose was it?"

"Nobody you'd know. A drug dealer."

"A drug dealer — so there was a drug connection after all. Janine might have been telling the truth that she had nothing to do with it."

"Possibly. Although I suppose she could be in it as deeply as anyone. You have to admit her restaurant would make an ideal distribution point for drugs that were coming in from around the coast here. I shouldn't be surprised if we don't find out that she was set up here for that very purpose."

"I suppose so." Evan didn't want to believe it, but it was hard not to. "So how did you manage to match the prints? That was rather clever of you."

She laughed. "I found the match by sheer accident, actually. Scotland Yard sent us everything they'd got on the traffickers they suspect are behind the shipments. It's a multinational gang, mainly Algerian and French, with connections in Europe and North Africa. They sent us several sets of prints. Just out of curiosity I ran a computer match on them and I nearly died when one of them matched our thumbprint."

"What's his name?"

Glynis chuckled. "He's got a string of aliases as long as your arm but he likes to be called, get this, Le Tigre — the Tiger!"

"Sounds like something out of a bad film," Evan said. "Congratulations. That kind of thing will definitely get you noticed around here."

"Thanks. As I say, it was pure luck, just fooling around to see what the system can do, actually."

"Has the DI been told yet?"

"Yes. He came in only a few minutes ago. He's quite excited — well, as excited as a someone like him can get."

"Is he in with Madame Yvette — I mean Janine — now?"

"Not yet. In fact, I don't think he's going to have time to question her tonight, because of everything that's happening. We can't keep her here because our only cell has a couple of lager louts from the rugby match in it. So I understand he's planning to send her back to where she was staying with a WPC escort — which I suspect will end up being me, because I'm the only one still on duty. So I suppose I might be seeing you later. She's staying somewhere up near you, isn't she?"

Evan's brain stopped functioning rationally. All he could think was that Glynis would be arriving at Bronwen's house.

"Are you still there, Constable Evans?"

"Yes, I'm still here. Sorry. I was thinking."

"I know. It's all so complicated, isn't it. But you're off the hook, aren't you? Now they know who they're looking for, so I suppose it becomes part of Operation Armada."

"Right. I can go back to finding lost car keys."

Glynis laughed. Evan didn't think it was funny.

"See you later maybe, then," she said again as she rang off.

Evan hung up the phone and sat staring at his desk. So their first hunch had been correct after all. It was all tied in with the drug shipments. Of course. Why else would an outstanding chef open a French restaurant in such an out-of-the way place? The drugs would arrive in small boats, be whisked up from the coast to the restaurant and get picked up from there. A great setup. It probably could have gone undetected for years if they hadn't had the tip-off and there had been no fire.

Jean Bouchard had been the real Madame Yvette's husband, but he was also involved in the shady world of drug dealing. That was probably why he'd chosen to fake his death and disappear five years ago. And now he'd been sent here to help with the drug shipments. It was probably pure chance that he had happened on the restaurant and discovered the woman impersonating his wife. If Janine hadn't stabbed him, who had? Had he fallen out with fellow gang members, or crossed paths with a rival gang? Evan wondered if they'd ever know.

He felt both pleased and annoyed. He was pleased that his gut feeling was correct and Madame or Janine or whoever she was had probably not committed the murder, but annoyed that he was once again being left out just as things heated up. He thumped his fist onto the table in frustration. Then he reminded himself that he had work to do. He still had to find Terry Jenkins.

He checked the village once more, looking in all the sort of places an eleven-year-old boy might want to hide. Then he went back to his car. The sun had sunk behind the western mountains and the valley was bathed in twilight. Evan had to agree with Terry's mother for once — he didn't like the thought of the boy out on his bike in the dark. Cars drove up the winding road too fast to see a boy on a bike.

He drove first to the top of the pass and looked around the Everest Inn car park, then slowly back down the hill. Terry really must have gone into hiding — perhaps he was more scared of being taken to the police station than he wanted to admit. Perhaps he knew more than he was admitting, as well.

Evan had almost reached the village of Nant Peris when he spotted something shiny, almost hidden among the thick brambles beside the road. He stopped the car and jumped out. It was Terry's bike. Evan picked it up and stood there, his hand on the saddle. Why had Terry abandoned his bike? If he'd wanted to hide up on the mountain, there were plenty of tracks leading from Llanfair itself. He wouldn't have had to ride down to Nant Peris first. Was he possibly on his own quest, looking for something down here — something to do with the fire?

The ruined restaurant stood at the upper end of the village, its stone walls etched in the dying light like jagged teeth.

"Terry?" Evan called. "Are you there, Terry? Your mum's worried. She wants you home right now."

Silence, except for the wind sighing on the hillside and stirring the ashes of the fire. He stood looking around, not sure what to do next. The Vaynol Arms sign squeaked as it swung in the wind. A car door slammed and a couple got out of a car. Evan watched them go into the pub, arm in arm and laughing.

He pulled the bike out of the brambles, then scrambled over the dry-stone wall that bordered the road to the meadow beyond. As he began to climb, his nostrils picked up a smell, a little off to the left where a small track went up the mountain. Evan followed his nose until the smell became identifiable. He bent down to a large rock and sniffed. There was no visible sign, but then the smell always lingered long after it had evaporated. Petrol had recently been splashed on this rock. A little higher up another whiff . . . Someone had been carrying petrol up the mountain.

Idiot, he muttered to himself. He had wanted to believe that Terry was innocent, so he had refused to see the signs. Of course Potter was right. Terry was a classic case of someone who could become a serial arsonist. He'd even admitted to buying petrol. So what was his next target?

Evan climbed onto the wall and scanned the hillside. The meadow rose steeply until it met the dark line of fir trees — the spruce plantation the locals so disliked. Was that where Terry was heading? The peaks above, the Glyderau, were still bathed in rosy sunlight, making their rocks glow red, in contrast to the gloom of the fir trees at their base. Suddenly Evan's sharp eyes picked out a moving figure, not on the track, but further over to the right, going straight up the mountain and moving fast. But it wasn't Terry. It was a grown man and the impression was one of darkness — dark hair, dark jacket, swarthy skin. He was moving through the dry bracken with a kind of animal grace, furtively, as if he didn't want to be seen, and Evan could almost hear Glynis's voice echoing in his head: "He likes to be called the Tiger."

Wait a second — hadn't he just seen . . . ? He glanced back at the pub car park. Yes, he was right. He had noticed a red sports car there when he'd watched the young couple get out of their car. Now he heard Terry's voice like an instant replay in his brain. "I saw that man again, Mr Evans. The one who drove the red sports car and had the gun . . ."

Evan could feel the back of his neck prickle. The man who drove the sports car and carried the gun and who had spoken to Terry Jenkins, asking about the restaurant . . . His heart racing, Evan took this one step further — and Terry was the one person who could identify him and tie him to a place and time. Had Terry spotted the red car? Had the man seen Terry and caused him to hide his bike and flee up the mountain?

For a second he stood poised on the wall, undecided. Should he run back to the pub and call for help or go after the man? This is no time for heroics, he told himself. What could he do against a man who called himself the Tiger, trafficked in drugs and had already killed at least once? And yet he had to do something to save Terry if he could.

He jumped down from the wall, sprinted across the street and into the pub. The bar was empty except for the newly arrived couple and two old men sitting in a corner. "Call 999," Evan yelled to the barmaid. "Tell them to get units up here right away. Our suspect is up on the hill. I'm going after him."

He didn't wait for an answer. He began to climb the hill. It was getting dark now and Evan could no longer see the man moving among the dry bracken. Which meant he had to have reached the spruce plantation. The boy must have made for the trees, hoping to hide himself in the dark forest, not realizing that there was no place to hide among the slim, even rows of spruce.

Was the man carrying a gun? That made all the difference. Terry was a smart mountain-bred kid. Evan hoped he'd know the area well enough to slip through the forest and double back down to Llanfair — or at least find a good hiding place among the rocks until morning. Evan felt anger, as well as fear, welling up in his throat. He couldn't let that monster get to Terry. He couldn't wait for reinforcements to get there. He hurried on. Light was fading fast and sheep drifted like ghostly shapes, their mournful bleating echoing back from crags above. A bat skimmed low past him, making him jump.

Suddenly he stiffened as he heard a noise on the mountain above — a popping sound. His first reaction was gunfire, but then a motorbike appeared, bumping down the track ahead. Evan waved his arms. The bike swerved and for a moment it seemed to speed up.

"Stop!" Evan yelled and made a grab for the rider.

"Constable Evans!" the rider gasped.

"Oh, it's you, Bryn." Evan felt a great wave of relief. "You haven't seen young Terry, have you?"

"Terry Jenkins?" His eyes darted around warily. "I haven't seen anybody. I've just been for a ride."

"Up on the mountain? I shouldn't imagine it's very good for the bike. So you haven't seen anybody? Not a man with dark hair?"

"Nobody." His fingers twitched at the accelerator. "I have to get home, Mr Evans . . ."

"I need your help, Bryn," Evan put a hand on the handlebar. "Young Terry's up there somewhere and a man's trying to kill him."

Bryn swivelled to stare up at the hillside. "Terry's up there?"

"He probably went into the tree plantation."

"Oh no, Mr Evans, don't say that!" Bryn leaped off the bike and flung it down on the grass. "We've got to get up there, fast, before it's too late."

He started scrambling up the hill with Evan at his heels. "I hope we're not too late, Mr Evans." Evan could hear the boy sobbing. "I didn't mean any harm. Honest I didn't. It was a bit of fun really . . ."

"What are you talking about, Bryn?"

"We've only got a few minutes before the fuse burns through, then the whole forest will go up."

Evan grabbed his arm and spun him around. "What are you talking about, boy?"

Bryn was really crying now. Large tears were welling out of his eyes. "I set a fire up there, didn't I?"

CHAPTER 23

Evan grabbed the boy's arm. "You set a fire? Are you out of your mind?"

Bryn shook him off and staggered upward. The hillside had become steep. Bryn was scrambling up on all fours, like a dog.

Evan saw how blind he had been — how blind they had all been. Bryn had sounded the alarm both times. Bryn had been first on the scene. "It was you!" he yelled. "You set the fires, so that you could look like a hero and put them out again!"

"I didn't mean no harm," Bryn said again. "They said I'd never amount to much — my dad and granddad and the teachers at school . . ."

"So you decided to show them!"

"Yeah. I only set fire to things that nobody wanted anyway. Everyone was glad when that cottage burned down, weren't they? And everyone hates the Everest Inn and the plantation . . ."

"Do you know how dry it is?" Evan could hear himself screeching. "It won't stop with the plantation. The whole mountain will go up — sheep and Terry and all."

The dark line of trees loomed ahead of them.

"We might just be in time," Bryn gasped. As he ran toward the trees there was an explosion and a ball of flame shot up. The dry bracken crackled as the flames raced along the ground and the dry needles on the spruce trees spattered and sparkled like fireworks. Evan was yanking off his jacket as he ran. He reached the flames and began beating at them.

"It's no use, Mr Evans," Bryn yelled. "I set a line of petrol all the way up. We'll never put it all out before it takes hold."

"We've damn well got to try," Evan said.

They worked side by side, beating desperately as the flames rushed up the side of the plantation, feeding on the dry grass and bracken. Evan could feel the sweat running into his eyes. It was hopeless. They'd never do it. A dry twig caught on fire. He yanked it off the tree and stamped out the fire. He did the same with another and another, but it was only a matter of time before a whole tree went up like a torch and then they'd lose.

Out of the corner of his eye Evan saw Bryn flailing at the flames with his jacket, kicking up dirt over the flames. Then suddenly the wind swirled around, sending flame into Evan's face for a moment. He jumped back and crouched, shielding his face with his arms, feeling the heat envelop him. Then the fire passed them. It was gone, over to their left and racing up the mountain away from the trees. The wind had changed.

Evan grabbed Bryn's shoulder. "With any luck it will burn itself out when it gets to the rocks if the wind holds," he yelled over the roar and crackle. "Anyway, there's nothing more we can do about it. We have to find Terry."

He plunged into the forest. Dark smoke wreathed around the slim trunks and stung his eyes, making it nearly impossible to see where he was going. He wondered if the Frenchman had seen the fire and decided to abandon his quest and get out of harm's way. He scanned the hillside below but it was too dark to pick out a person among the scattered rocks and sheep. He could hear Bryn's laboured breath behind him, but their footfalls made no sound on the thick carpet of rotting needles. Nothing moved. Ahead he could see the sunlight on the rocks at the top of the plantation. There was no sign of Terry.

As he came out on the far side Bryn grabbed at his arm and pointed. "There's something up there!" he hissed.

Evan followed the direction he was pointing. Straight ahead of them the cliffs of Glyder Fawr rose sheer from the edge of the forest. Smoke from the fire curled around their base so that they seemed to hover, unlinked to reality. And just above the smoke there was a bright splash of red. It had to be Terry's anorak — he was on a narrow ledge that petered out just ahead of him. The boy had worked himself into a position where he was as vulnerable as a duck at a shooting gallery. Whoever was stalking him could take his time to pick him off.

Evan crouched frozen, trying to decide what to do. If he went up after the boy, he'd also be an easy target. If he called out, he'd alert the man to the boy's presence, on the off chance that the man hadn't spotted him yet. Evan stood there, looking and listening. His senses were fine-tuned as he heard the distant crackle of the fire and smelled the herby smell of burning heather. He strained his ears to listen for any movement. Then he heard something. Over to his right, among the tumble of rocks at the base of the cliff, a crisp metallic click. And he knew what it meant. A safety catch had been released from a weapon.

Evan felt his mouth go dry and his heart hammered in his throat. Had the man spotted them, and was the weapon pointed at them, or at the boy? Not for the first time did Evan wish that ordinary British bobbies could be armed. He, too, was completely vulnerable, standing in the open at the edge of pencil-thin trees. He turned to Bryn. "He's over there," he mouthed. "Behind those rocks. Get down and try to find cover. I'm going after him."

He moved forward as silently as he could, knowing that silence was useless if the man already had him in his sights. If he was a drug dealer, he surely packed plenty of firepower

— something semiautomatic at the very least. He dodged behind the first of the rocks, his face close to its rough, lichen-spotted surface. Cautiously he moved around it and dodged from rock to rock until suddenly he saw a dark shape rise up ahead of him. It was him all right — a dark-haired man in a dark leather jacket, and he was aiming up at the ledge.

Evan bent to pick up a rock. If he threw it at the man as he fired, at least he had a chance of diverting the path of the bullet. As Evan drew back his arm to throw, the man's finger began to close around the trigger and a shape hurtled past Evan.

"No, you bastard!" Bryn yelled as he flung himself at the man.

The gun swung around and exploded with a deafening boom that echoed back from the cliffs. The Frenchman staggered as the boy's weight knocked him backward. Then Bryn let out a little cry and slid to the ground. In that fraction of a second Evan smashed down the Frenchman's wrist, causing the weapon to fly out of his grasp and slide down the rock. The man let out a snarl of pain and lunged for the gun as Evan kicked it a further away. Again they both scrambled for it. The Frenchman was the swifter, but Evan came at him with a flying rugby tackle. They crashed together to the rocky ground. As the man wriggled to get free, Evan reached out and snatched up the weapon.

The Frenchman leaped to his feet, his face distorted, snarling like a wild beast. Evan pointed the weapon at him, afraid he'd go for the gun again. Instead he gave Evan a look of sheer contempt, almost as if he was daring him to shoot, then turned and ran off through the trees.

Evan was conscious of Bryn's body at his feet and Terry cowering up on the mountain. He longed to go after the fleeing man, to squeeze that trigger and to have the satisfaction of watching him sprawl to the ground. Instead he lowered the gun and let the man go, praying that the backup units would have arrived by now.

He dropped to his knees beside Bryn's body. A red stain was already running down the rock. Gently he turned the boy over. Bryn's face was ashen grey. Evan felt for a pulse, then struggled to open his shirt. As he did so, the boy's eyes fluttered open.

"I'm a hero, right, Mr Evans?" he asked.

"You certainly are, Bryn."

"Am I going to die?"

"I think you're going to be okay," Evan said, putting his hand gently on the boy's arm. "You were lucky. The bullet went clean through your shoulder. You won't be putting out any fires for a while, that's for sure — or starting any."

The boy managed a grin. "About that, Mr Evans . . . I'm really sorry. I really am. Will they put me in jail?"

Evan took a deep breath. "If it never happens again, I doubt they'll ever get to the bottom of it. What do you think, Bryn?"

The boy's lip quivered. "You mean you're not going to tell them?"

"As I said, if it never happens again, I don't reckon the case will ever be solved."

"It won't happen again. I promise." He tried to sit up and gasped in pain. "When I thought that the kid was in those trees . . . I swear, I'd have done anything . . ."

"You did, Bryn. You risked your life. And bloody silly it was, too, diving at an armed man. Lucky you're in the fire brigade and not the police, or they'd have your hide for that one."

Bryn grinned again. Evan took off his shirt and folded it over the wound. "Here, keep some pressure on that. I'm going down to get help. I won't be long."

"What about young Terry?"

"I'm going to get him down first."

A few minutes later he climbed up onto the ledge and was met by a frightened pair of eyes as the boy tried to make himself invisible against the rock wall.

"It's all right, Terry, it's me. You can come down now," he said.

Relief overwhelmed the boy's face. "I heard shooting," he said. "I didn't dare move."

"It's all right. Bryn and I got the gun away from him," Evan said.

"Bryn? He's up here with you? He came to rescue me?" A big smile lit up his face.

"Yes, and he got a bullet through his shoulder stopping the bloke from picking you off."

"He got shot?" Terry scrambled from the ledge and started to climb down the boulders. "Is he going to be okay?"

"Yes, I think he'll be fine. Why don't you stay with him until I bring help?"

"All right, Mr Evans." Terry was still beaming. Evan saw him run to Bryn. "I'll stay with you," he heard the boy say. "Here, let me put my jacket over you."

Evan smiled as he left them and ran down through the trees. The land around the forest was blackened and still smoking. He hadn't gone far when he saw the fire crew hosing down the hillside.

"We've got our arsonist, Constable Evans," one of the firemen yelled as he approached them. "Foreign-looking bloke came running down here as if the hounds of hell were after him. A couple of our men nabbed him and they're taking him down to your chaps. Fought like a tiger, he did, when we got him. Who'd have thought it was a foreigner, eh? And I don't mean an Englishman, either." He paused and took a good look at Evan. "Are you all right, Constable Evans?"

"Yes, I'm fine." It only just occurred to him that he must look rather the worse for wear — blackened from fighting the fire and probably bruised and cut from wrestling with the Frenchman. But he had won. He had the gun in his hand. Not bad for a village bobby!

"I've got a wounded boy up there," he said. "Gunshot wound. I'm calling for an ambulance as soon as I get down, but if you've got anyone who is a trained paramedic . . ."

"Elwyn is. Hey, Elwyn," the fireman yelled. "Get over here."

* * *

Two squad cars were parked at the bottom of the hill. Two officers were just putting handcuffs on Le Tigre as Evan arrived, out of breath and aching from his exertion.

"What the . . . Evans?" Sergeant Watkins ran to meet him.

"Here's his gun, sarge." Evan handed over the weapon. "There's a wounded boy up the mountain. Call the ambulance, please."

"Are you okay?" Watkins put a hand on his shoulder. "Come and sit down. Nice work, by the way. Trust you to have found him!"

"All luck, sarge, and a lot of help," Evan said.

At that moment another police car pulled up and Glynis Davies jumped out. "What on earth's happening?" she asked.

"It looks as if we've just nabbed our suspect," Watkins said. "Thanks to Constable Evans."

The other car door opened and Janine Laroque got out. She stood there with a look of horror on her face as two policemen led the handcuffed prisoner past her to the squad car. The man spotted her and unleashed a torrent of abuse.

Suddenly Evan realized the truth. This man was the "monster" she had had to run away from — the rich, handsome man she had married and who had made her life hell. It made sense after all.

CHAPTER 24

Later that evening Evan sat in Bronwen's warm kitchen as Janine busied herself at the stove, preparing them what she called "a simple meal." After a long soak in Mrs Williams's bath he felt almost human again, although his hair had been singed and he had some impressive bruises.

"This must be like a huge weight lifted from you, Janine," Bronwen said. "How awful to have lived in such fear."

Janine nodded. "It was unbearable, mademoiselle. As soon as I marry zis handsome, charming man I find out 'e ees a monster. A bad man. A crazy man. I nevair know where 'is money come from, and 'e nevair tell me, but I know it ees somesing bad. He tell me if I leave 'im, I die. When I became Yvette Bouchard I sink I am finally safe. 'E will nevair find me now. But 'e did find me. I am stupid and vain, no? I let zem take my picture and put eet in zee paper."

"And your husband was here, scouting out the territory in preparation for the drug shipments," Evan said. "Pure bad luck that he saw your picture and came to see you."

"But I nevair see 'im, monsieur. Ozzerwise I would 'ave told you. Believe me, if I suspected zat Gaston 'ad found me again, I would 'ave come straight to you."

"So you never saw him," Evan said. "He must have sneaked into your living quarters to surprise you alone — but Jean Bouchard was up there. Who knows what they said to each other — but if Jean said he was Yvette's husband, and Gaston thought you were using the name Yvette . . ."

"Zat would have been enough to make Gaston fly into a rage. He was crazy wiz jealousy."

"Well, it's all over now," Bronwen said. "You're finally free."

"Not exactly free," Evan said. "She still has charges to face — impersonating another person to collect the insurance; trying to destroy evidence. Those are serious offenses. But I suspect the jury will be lenient when they hear what you've already gone through."

"Eet does not worry me anymore," Janine said. "Now zee police 'ave Gaston, I am safe. Maybe I'll open a new restaurant someday."

"Why not rebuild here?" Bronwen said. "Who knows, the locals might eventually develop a taste for good food."

* * *

A few days later Evan was sitting at his desk, working on an application for detective training, when Sergeant Watkins came in.

"Hello, boyo, hard at work are we, then?" he asked as Evan shoved the application form hastily under the incident book. "What are you looking so guilty about — fiddling the travel expenses?"

"No, nothing like that, sarge. I leave that to you."

Watkins chuckled. "So it's back to business as usual after all the excitement, is it?"

"It seems that way," Evan said. "What brings you up here?"

"Just thought I'd stop by and say hello," he said, "and thank you for what you did. It seems you might be in for a citation — catching that Gaston bloke single-handed."

"I didn't do it single-handed," Evan said. "And I couldn't have done it without young Bryn. And even then I let the bastard walk away . . ."

Watkins put a hand on his shoulder. "Don't think they're not grateful. Your catching that Gaston bloke was the big break we needed. Apparently the rest of the gang didn't put too much faith in his silence. It seems they've given up on the idea of coming into local ports, at least for the time being."

"They'll show up again, somewhere else," Evan said.

"Yes, but it won't be on our turf, will it?" Watkins beamed. "And it looks as though Gaston will be returned to France to face prior charges there. Between us we've got enough on him to put him away for life."

"Janine will be pleased," Evan said.

"Is she still staying with your schoolteacher friend?"

"No, she's gone," Evan said. "She was given bail and she's left to sort things out."

"She's got some pretty unpleasant times ahead of her, I'd say. She's not out of the woods by a long way."

"It's still probably nothing to her compared to knowing she's finally safe from her husband. And when the jury hears what she's been through, I think she'll get off lightly."

"Too bad she's gone. The wife had been badgering me to take her to the French restaurant. Now I've blown it, haven't I? She won't let me forget it in a hurry, either."

Evan returned his smile, then became serious again. "I don't suppose Gaston has ever said exactly what happened in Madame's flat that night — why he killed Jean Bouchard, I mean? Do you think there was a drug connection and he'd traced down someone who double-crossed him?"

"I don't think so," Watkins said. "I got the impression that he found another bloke in his wife's bedroom. That was all the incentive he needed to kill."

"If he'd asked him who he was, Jean Bouchard might have said he was Yvette's husband — which wouldn't have been a good answer, considering."

"Well, now they're gone — the lot of them," Watkins said, walking past Evan's desk to stare out the window at the hills. "I don't suppose that Englishman is going to rebuild that cottage up there, is he?"

"I doubt it very much." Evan got up to look as well.

"So your butcher friend will be happy — Llanfair has been ethnically cleansed and is now purely Welsh again. The boy's doing okay, is he — the one who got shot?"

Evan started, uneasy that Watkins had linked Bryn's name subconsciously to the fires. "Yes, he's making a good recovery. He was bloody lucky the bullet went through where it did. A couple of inches further down and he would have been a goner."

"So we never really found out who was behind the fires, did we?" Watkins asked.

"Maybe Sergeant Potter is still working on it," Evan said.

Watkins chuckled. "No, didn't you hear? He's got a transfer to Chester. He couldn't get the hang of Welsh, you see, so he had to give up and look for a job in England. Can't say I'm too heartbroken, are you?"

"The man was a pain," Evan agreed.

Watkins went to perch on the corner of Evan's desk. "I'd still like to know who wrote those notes. If there are extremists at work, I'd like to know it."

"So would I, but I wonder if we ever will."

Watkins slid off the desk again. "All right. Well, I'd better be getting along. I've got a burglary down in Beddgelert to look into. Same old routine stuff after all the excitement. That's the problem with this job. When it's all routine, you wish for excitement and when it's all go, you long for regular hours. Ah well, there are worse ways of learning a living."

"I'm thinking of asking for a transfer myself," Evan said. "I'm finally going to send in my application for detective training."

Watkins didn't smile, as Evan had expected. Instead he looked uncomfortable.

"What?" Evan demanded. "You don't think I'd be good enough for the job."

"I know you would, boyo," Watkins said. "You'd be bloody good. It's just that it won't be for a while, that's all. We're in hot water with the commissioner, so it seems, because North Wales Police has the lowest percentage of female detectives. So the next recruits have to be female — starting with our Glynis Davies. She's been accepted for the next training class. She'll make a good detective, don't you think? Very ingenious. Very thorough."

"Oh yes, great," Evan said half-heartedly.

"It was matching those prints that got her transfer through in a hurry," Watkins said. "That and the fact that her boyfriend happens to be the commissioner's nephew." He grinned at Evan, then slapped him on the back. "Be seeing you then, boyo. Take care of yourself."

* * *

As soon as Sergeant Watkins had gone, Evan took out the application and tore it up. He tried not to feel angry or disappointed, but he couldn't help it. It looked as if he was destined to be stuck in Llanfair, at least for the immediate future.

He glanced at his watch. Almost five o'clock. He'd put in enough overtime to leave early for once. He closed up for the day and came out into the soft glow of late afternoon. Without any clear idea of where he was heading, he started up the street. It wasn't Glynis's fault that she'd been chosen over him. And she was bright, too. She'd do well as a detective.

He strode past the school without looking to see if Bronwen was there. He needed to walk, to feel the wind in his face. He realized that he not only felt disappointed, he felt stupid. So Glynis was only being friendly to him after all. He'd read far too much into her overtures. Lucky he hadn't encouraged her — his career certainly wouldn't have been helped if the commissioner's nephew had found that Evan had been flirting with his girl.

"Stupid!" Evan said out loud to the empty street. Stupid to allow himself to be flattered by a good-looking girl. He was too gullible where women were concerned. Well, from now on it would be different.

He passed the chapels, with their respective vehicles parked beside them, and continued up past the Everest Inn until he stood at the top of the pass. Here the wind was blowing strongly with the tang of salt in it, and dark clouds raced across the sky. Out at sea the horizon was a hard line. It would rain before long. The Indian summer was finally over.

It's not a bad place to be, he told himself. His gaze scanned the green hillsides. The burned-out cottage stood like a dark wound amid the green. Watkins was right. Those English people would never be back . . . which started him thinking. What would happen to a ruin like that? Would it be too hard to rebuild? It already had water and electricity and a good solid foundation, and the walls were still standing . . . The wheels in his head started to turn and his gaze wandered involuntarily down to the schoolhouse.

At that moment the rain began, falling as isolated drops that spattered on the asphalt to begin with; then came more and more of them until the heavens opened. The rich creosote smell of wet macadam rose up to his nostrils. He turned to walk back.

As he passed the schoolhouse the front door opened and Bronwen ran out, holding a large umbrella over her. "Evan, you're soaked to the skin. What were you doing up on the pass? Is something the matter?"

"No," he said, looking down at her anxious face. "Everything's just fine. I went for a little walk."

"Come inside. I'll make you a cup of tea," she said, "and if you're very good, you can try a slice of the baguette I've just made."

She led him across the playground and in through the open door. The kitchen smelled of freshly baked bread. Bronwen pointed proudly at the table. "I learned a lot while Janine was with me. I think I've turned into a pretty good cook." She poured a cup of tea from the brown earthenware pot. "What were you doing up on the pass?"

"Just thinking," Evan said. "Trying to clear my head."

She nodded. "We're lucky where we live. You can't get too upset by little problems when you're surrounded by mountains. They keep everything in perspective."

Evan took the cup and drank. "Bronwen," he said after a sip. "Do you think this is such a bad job for a man? Stuck up here, I mean. Not applying for promotion?"

Her eyes flashed. "A bad job? You're needed up here, aren't you? If you hadn't been here, Bryn would likely be in jail by now and his whole future would have been wrecked."

Evan looked surprised. "You know about Bryn?"

"Terry told me. Bryn told him." She saw the alarm on his face. "Oh, don't worry. They won't tell anyone else. Those two are as thick as thieves — sorry, bad metaphor." She smiled then put her hands on his shoulders. "You've done some good things while you've been here," she said. "You've touched lives."

She leaned over to kiss him on the forehead. His hands closed over hers and she rested her cheek against his.

"You'd better get out of those wet clothes," she said, "before you catch pneumonia."

"You're sending me home?" Evan got to his feet.

"Not if you don't want to go. I could always run you a nice hot bath and I've got big fluffy towels and a bottle of wine in the fridge which we could drink after—"

"After what, Bron?" His eyes were teasing.

"I was going to say after you've dried off, but I'm open to suggestions." She shot him a challenging look over her shoulder as she walked ahead of him down the hall.

* * *

There was quite a crowd in the Red Dragon on Friday night.

"Here he is now, the man himself," Charlie Hopkins announced. "What are you drinking, Evan *bach?*"

"Guinness tonight, thanks, Charlie." Evan squeezed in beside the bar.

"Guinness for Evans-the-Law, Betsy *cariad*," Charlie said. "He's getting his strength up tonight, for some reason!" He winked at Evan as he chuckled.

Betsy gave Evan a quick glance. "It better not be for a visit down to Caernarfon," she said.

"Caernarfon?" Evan looked puzzled.

"I heard there's a young policewoman down there," Betsy said smoothly. "It seems she's been asking questions about you."

"Only doing her job, Betsy love," Evan said. "She's familiarizing herself with the personnel. She's about to be promoted."

Betsy drew the pint and put it down none too gently in front of Evan. "You tell her not to familiarize herself too much with this personnel," she said. "In fact you tell her if Bronwen Price ever falls off a cliff while she's birdwatching, I'm next in line."

Evan grinned as he heard the chuckles around him. Charlie put a hand on his shoulder. "How about our Bryn, eh, Evan *bach?* A hero — that's what the newspaper called him. His grandma's sent copies of the article to everyone she knows. Who'd have thought it, eh? Frankly we never thought the boy would amount to much, but he's gone and surprised us all."

"You never know what a person's capable of until you give them a chance, do you, Charlie?" Evan said.

"Too true," Charlie said. "And talking of that, I had a word with Owen Gruffudd — you know, he runs the Gegin Fawr café down the hill. He was asking me about the French lady — upset something dreadful, he was. Then it all came out. He wrote her that note, telling her to get out and all. He thought she'd take away his trade, you see. But it had been preying on his mind ever since."

"So he wrote the note." Evan chuckled. "It looks as if there was no extremist group at work after all."

"Of course there wasn't," Charlie said. "We're all live and let live up here in Llanfair, aren't we?"

At that moment there was a deafening crash outside — the sound of metal hitting metal and glass splintering. The bar emptied instantly as the men poured out into the street. The road ahead was completely blocked by the collision of two vehicles. As Evan hurried toward the scene, he could see that one of the vehicles was a grey van, the other a green bus. Apparently they had just backed into each other and the drivers were climbing out, rolling up their sleeves and ready to fight.

THE END

ACKNOWLEDGEMENTS

I would like to thank my editor, Reagan Arthur, and my publicist, Elizabeth Shipley, for making my life at St. Martin's run so smoothly. Thanks also to Tom Novara for his arson advice. And I dedicate this book to my fellow mystery authors, mystery booksellers, librarians, and readers who make me feel that I am part of a wonderful extended family.

ALSO BY RHYS BOWEN

CONSTABLE EVAN EVANS SERIES

Book 1: EVAN ABOVE
Book 2: EVAN HELP US
Book 3: EVANLY CHOIRS
Book 4: EVAN AND ELLE

Thank you for reading this book.

If you enjoyed it please leave feedback on Amazon or Goodreads, and if there is anything we missed or you have a question about, then please get in touch. We appreciate you choosing our book.

Founded in 2014 in Shoreditch, London, we at Joffe Books pride ourselves on our history of innovative publishing. We were thrilled to be shortlisted for Independent Publisher of the Year at the British Book Awards.

www.joffebooks.com

We're very grateful to eagle-eyed readers who take the time to contact us. Please send any errors you find to corrections@joffebooks.com. We'll get them fixed ASAP.

Printed in Dunstable, United Kingdom

69192591R10133